DONE AND DUSTED

DONE AND DUSTED

A Novel

LYLA SAGE

The Dial Press
New York

2023 Dial Press Trade Paperback Edition

Published in the United States by The Dial Press, an imprint of Random House, a division of Penguin Random House LLC, New York. Originally self-published by the author in 2023.

The Dial Press is a registered trademark and the colophon is a trademark of Penguin Random House LLC.

Dial Delights and colophon are trademarks of Penguin Random House LLC.

This book contains an excerpt from the forthcoming book *Swift and Saddled* by Lyla Sage. This excerpt has been set for this edition only and may not reflect the final content of the forthcoming edition.

ISBN 978-0-593-73242-7
Ebook ISBN 979-898-778130-2

Printed in the United States of America on acid-free paper

randomhousebooks.com

randomhousebookclub.com

68975

For Leo. My Highwayman, my sunshine, and my single drop of rain. I miss you every day.

AUTHOR'S NOTE

When I started writing *Done and Dusted,* I wanted to write a character who I, and other women like me, could relate to. I love to read, and like you, I've read a lot of books. There are so many characters out there who I hold close to my heart, but who I couldn't relate to as deeply as I wanted to because living inside of their heads was so different than being in my own.

The main character in *Done and Dusted* is named Emmy. Emmy and I don't have that much in common, but like me, Emmy has ADHD. The differences in the way our brains work can be subtle, but it doesn't mean that they don't exist or make an impact on the way we live our lives.

I know being diagnosed with ADHD looks different for all of us, but if you've ever had a hard time explaining why you leave literally everything until the last minute, why you feel out of control, why your tongue feels like it doesn't belong in your mouth when the music is too loud, or any of the countless other things we feel that are a part of ADHD, you might see yourself in *Done and Dusted*.

Emmy and I are right there with you.

Happy reading,
Lyla

Additional content warnings are available on my website authorlylasage.com.

DUSTED /D - UHST - ED/ (WESTERN SLANG): VERB.

To be thrown from a horse.

EMMY

"Clementine Ryder, I swear to god, if you're going to mope all night, I'm taking you back home," Teddy said.

"I'm not moping!" I protested, even though I was definitely moping. Being home had that effect on me. So did Teddy's usage of my full name. Seriously, who named their only daughter after a fruit?

When it came to a night out, Teddy meant business, and when Teddy meant business, there was no arguing with her. Usually, I didn't mind. Teddy was my best friend. She knew me better than I knew myself and knew what I needed before I even did. When I made the decision this morning to pack up my apartment, break up with my boyfriend using a Post-it note on the fridge, and leave the barrel racing circuit, I drove 300 miles straight to her house in our small hometown.

I hadn't even unpacked my truck yet—it was sitting in Teddy's driveway.

I recognized the dirt road Teddy was driving us down and immediately wished I was back with my truck.

"The Devil's Boot? Really?" I asked. I knew we didn't have a lot of options in Meadowlark, but The Devil's Boot was one place I would like to avoid. The chances that I knew every single one of its current occupants was dangerously high.

My dad and brothers didn't know I was home yet, and I needed them to stay out of the loop for a little bit longer.

"Yes, The Devil's Boot. It's fun and mindless," she explained. "And you need fun and mindless, Emmy." Honestly, I probably did need that, but Teddy's definition of fun had historically been a little different than mine.

"You know what's fun?" I asked. "Wine and—"

Teddy interrupted me and finished my sentence. "Wine and *Sweet Home Alabama is* fun. You're right," she said. "But, Emmy. You've been sitting in your apartment in Denver doing wine and *Sweet Home Alabama* for a month. Literally, every time I FaceTimed you, I could hear Patrick Dempsey getting dumped at the altar, and then I could see his teary blue eyes in my mind—there's only so much of that I can take."

"That's the best scene in the whole movie," I

argued. "It breaks your heart *and* puts it back together."

Teddy placed her hand over her heart. "I am not undermining the merits of *Sweet Home Alabama*," she said. "I would never. I'm just saying, there's a reason you came home instead of watching it for a thirty-second time."

Damn. I hated it when she had a point.

"Fine," I conceded. "But you're getting every round."

Teddy laughed. "You're thinking too small. Why should I pay for your drinks—or my own—when I know there are at least a dozen men in The Devil's Boot who would love to buy them for us?"

"You're overestimating my powers of male persuasion," I said.

"And you're underestimating mine," Teddy said with a wink. "Plus," she added, "you're Clementine Ryder, champion barrel racer and member of Meadowlark's most beloved family. People will probably be fighting over who gets to buy you, and me by association, a drink."

I huffed in annoyance.

Teddy gave me one of her winning smiles. "Between college and racing, you've been gone almost a decade, and when you do come back, you only see your family and me," she continued. "You went from Meadowlark's sweetheart to Meadowlark's mystery. People will be happy to see you."

Teddy's truck rolled to a stop. I looked out the passenger side window at the familiar dirt parking lot. It was full. Of course it was—it was a Friday night in Meadowlark, Wyoming.

Why couldn't the episode that led me to pack up my life in Denver and hightail it back home have waited until Monday?

The Devil's Boot was one of Wyoming's oldest bars, and it sat almost directly on the Meadowlark county line. It was far enough out of the way that its occupants were almost always exclusively local. From the outside, it didn't look like much. Hell, it didn't look like much on the inside, either. It was an old wood built in a classic saloon style. There were patches of faded paint, an excess of neon signs, and a piece of plywood that hung above the front door that had a spray-painted cowboy boot with a devil's trident inside it. It didn't actually say "Devil's Boot" anywhere in the place—not on the door, not on the pint glasses, not on anything. It was always just the lonely boot and the trident.

Even though we were still in the truck, I could hear the band. They were playing a Hank Williams cover. It was only nine o'clock, so the country classics would continue until the crowd demanded some newer hits they could dance and sing to. I had my fingers crossed Teddy and I would be out of here by then.

But I wasn't holding my breath.

"Hey." Teddy's voice was soft from the driver's side.

"If you really don't want to be here, then we can go, but I can't think of anything I would rather do than spend my best friend's first night home at a place we both secretly love." I did love this place, albeit begrudgingly. "We always have a good time here. It's low risk, high reward."

I sighed. There was a small part of me that was... excited to be at The Devil's Boot. To be home.

And an even smaller part that knew Teddy was right. We would have fun, people would be kind, and we probably wouldn't have to pay for our own drinks. That was the thing about Meadowlark–it was predictable. Comfortable, even. Two things I needed right now.

"What do you want to do, Emmy?" Teddy asked.

I looked over at her. "I want to stay," I said. And I meant it.

The megawatt smile on Teddy's face could've powered Meadowlark and all the surrounding counties. Teddy reached for my hand and squeezed.

"That's my girl. Let's do this."

Deep breaths, Emmy. I pulled on the handle to open Teddy's passenger side door and gave it a heavy shove. Her 1984 Ford Ranger had some quirks—barely functioning doors were one of them.

As soon as my boots hit the dirt, the knot in my stomach started to untie itself. There was something comforting about that sound. The way the rocks felt under the soles of my boots reminded me that I was okay. It was familiar. Everything was so unfamiliar lately, but not this. Not home.

After I spent so much time plotting my escape from Meadowlark, I didn't know how I would feel coming back. I came back for holidays, birthdays, and some weekends, but this felt more permanent. I thought I would feel trapped like I did years ago.

But I didn't. I felt blissfully normal.

I took a deep breath of the cool night air. It felt like the air entering my lungs was starting to push off the weight sitting on my chest.

I heard Teddy's boots coming around to my side of the truck as I pushed my door shut. "Damn, Ryder," she said. "I almost forgot how hot you are."

I smiled. A real one.

Compliments from Teddy were the best because I knew she meant them. Teddy was earnest, fierce, and loving. She never said anything she didn't mean.

"I'm already going home with you tonight, Andersen. No need to shower me with compliments," I said as I looped my arm through hers. "We make a good pair."

And we did.

Teddy and I had been inseparable since her dad started working on my family's ranch over twenty years ago. Even though we spent the last four years after college in different cities, we'd talked almost every day, and Teddy had made the eight-hour drive to Denver at least four times a year. I was lucky to have a friend like her, the type of friend most people could only dream about.

When I showed up in her driveway earlier today, I had my entire life in my truck. She didn't even bat an eye. She didn't ask about the apartment, the boyfriend, or the career I had left behind. She just fed me cheese and Diet Coke and let me sulk on her couch for a few hours. Then, she clapped her hands together, her signal that we were moving on, and told me to go find something in her closet to wear because we were going out.

I ended up in a simple white tank top, currently covered by my beloved shearling-lined denim jacket, and a black satin skirt from Teddy's closet. The slit went a little higher than I was used to—right above mid-thigh—but I loved the way it made me feel. Sultry. I was wearing black cowboy boots that should never be within a ten-foot radius of a horse, but they were perfect for a night at the bar.

Teddy was wearing a black, short-sleeved crop top and light-wash blue jeans that looked like they were literally molded to her body. Her copper hair was pulled into a high ponytail that bounced with her every move.

"You ready, babe?" she asked.

Another deep breath of cool Wyoming air. *You're okay, Emmy,* I thought to myself. *Your boots aren't in the stirrups anymore. You're on solid ground.*

"I'm ready."

2

EMMY

Crossing the threshold of The Devil's Boot felt like putting on your favorite pair of jeans. Everything about it just...fit. It was dark, dingy, and smelled like old cigarette smoke. Smoking inside became illegal in Wyoming in 2005, but no one said anything if someone lit up in The Devil's Boot every once in a while.

It was a complete and total dive bar, after all, lit only by a soft yellow light behind the bar, the stage lights, and a multitude of neon signs.

There was just something about a neon sign cutting through the dark.

My favorite sign was a cowboy riding a beer bottle like a bull, and it sat right above my favorite high-top table in the corner. I don't think I'd ever seen The Devil's Boot in daylight, and I don't think I wanted to. Everything felt more mystifying bathed in neon.

And everyone looked better, too. That's what got everyone inside The Devil's Boot in trouble.

After a few steps, I felt my boots start sticking to the floor—probably getting a delightful taste of spilled whiskey from thirty years ago—as Teddy and I made our way to my neon-cowboy corner.

"Alright, are we doing clear or dark liquor tonight?" Teddy asked me.

"Clear," I said, knowing that meant we had two options at DB: vodka or tequila. And there was no doubt in my mind that Teddy was going to pick Tequila.

"Tequila it is, then," she said. Some things never change.

There was nothing like the feeling of familiarity that only being around people you love can provide, and I loved Teddy in spades.

"You just stay here and continue to look hot and mysterious, and I'll go grab our first round," Teddy called over the band.

"Tequila soda, okay?" Knowing if I didn't clarify, she'd come back with two shots. Each. "Let me ease into it."

Teddy rolled her eyes and started to walk away. "Fine. Tequila sodas. For now."

"With an extra lime, please!" I called after her. She waved her hand back at me without turning around to let me know she heard me.

I shrugged my denim jacket off and hung it on the

back of my chair before taking a seat and taking in my surroundings.

I recognized some regulars at the bar—George, Fred, Edgar, and Harvey. I think they had been coming here every night since at least the beginning of time. There used to be a fifth member of their little cabal, but Jimmy Brooks passed away a few years ago. No one ever took their seats at the far end of the bar–even Jimmy's was still vacant. I wondered if anyone would ever have enough balls or stupidity to sit in it. The men were old, but that didn't mean they didn't scare the shit out of everyone.

Teddy made her way to the bar and was currently swinging her ponytail at Edgar, no doubt trying to con the old man into paying for our drinks.

The band moved on to a cover of Waylon Jennings's "I've Always Been Crazy." There was a crowd of people at the front of the stage scream-singing the chorus. I watched them, their unreserved joy bringing a big smile to my face.

"Emmy?" I brought my gaze away from the group of singing cowboys to the owner of the deep voice.

"Kenny, hi." I couldn't remember the last time I saw Kenny Wyatt—high school graduation?—but I recognized him immediately as he stood in front of me. His dirty-blond hair was cut short and he was sporting a neatly trimmed beard that I never could've imagined him with. Kenny was better known for being a former Meadowlark High School quarterback, but he was also a former Emmy Ryder Home-coming date.

"It's so good to see you," I said as I stood from my chair to give him a quick hug. He wrapped his arms around me tight and gave me a squeeze. When I pulled away, he kept one of his hands on my waist, so I kept one of mine on his shoulder. When in Meadowlark, I guess.

"Holy shit, Em. It's been a long time. I thought you would've been on the WRPA tour right now." The Women's Professional Rodeo Association probably thought that, too.

"I'm taking a break," I said. Starting in on the rehearsed speech I'd practice the entire drive from Denver to Meadowlark. "I've been racing a long time, so I figured I'd spend some time with my family for a minute. Plus, I really miss the ranch."

He gave my waist a small squeeze. I didn't hate it.

"Your dad and brothers are running quite the operation up there. I'm sure they're happy to have you back." Yeah, I'm sure they would be. Once they found out I was back. "How long are you going to be around for?" *Forever, probably,* I thought to myself, considering I couldn't even bring myself to get on a horse at this point.

For someone who had spent her entire life riding horses, not being able to get past the mental block of an injury that happened on horseback was a night-mare. I knew that if I wanted to get back on a horse, even if it wasn't to race, Meadowlark and Rebel Blue were the places to start.

"For a few months, at least," I said, trying to keep my voice enthusiastic, but not enough that it would sound forced. "It's good to be home."

Kenny smiled at me. A big, warm, genuine smile. "It really is good to see you, Emmy. You look good, too. Real good." I felt my cheeks start to turn a deep shade of crimson. Kenny had always been a smooth-talker. The way he was looking at me, like he'd been waiting for me all this time, in addition to the sincerity behind his words, made me want to run and hide.

Instead, I responded with a smile of my own, and said, "It's good to see you, too, Kenny."

"While you're here, we should see more—" Kenny's words were cut off by the band sloppily halting their performance of "Good Hearted Woman." A confused silence fell over the bar as everyone waited for their next move.

After a few seconds, the steel guitar player played the opening bars of—oh god, no—"Oh My Darlin' Clementine."

There were only two people who thought it was funny to torture me with that song every time I came into a room. One of them was my oldest brother, Gus, but I knew he currently wasn't even within Wyoming's state lines. That could only mean one thing. *He* was here.

I angrily scanned the bar, looking for him. *That*

fucker. The Devil's Boot patrons started to sing and sway, a lot of them throwing goofy smiles in my direction. This song was basically a town-wide inside joke at this point, and right now, I was laser-focused on finding the joker.

I didn't see him, but he had to be here somewhere. Why was he even at The Devil's Boot? Didn't he have beer can towers to make in his living room? Whiskey bottles to shoot at?

If he was able to convince the band to stop playing their set, he was probably near the stage. Without thinking, I started in that direction. I continued scanning the bar as I walked. Bad idea for a girl who is only coordinated when she's on the back of a horse.

I tripped over my boots and ran into something hard.

A chest.

A man's chest.

The man chest.

I looked up at its owner, who had a shit-eating smirk on his face.

It was *him*.

Luke Brooks.

3

LUKE

I saw her the second her black cowboy boots crossed the threshold of my bar. She was Meadowlark's sweetheart, a giant pain in the ass, and my best friend's little sister.

Clementine Ryder.

The last time I saw her was during the holiday season before last, but she had been leaving Rebel Blue Ranch as I was arriving. Because, as usual, I'd been late.

Gus had told me Emmy's schedule had been pretty intense over the last few years. Considering she was damn good at racing, I'm sure that was true. Considering the Ryders were the only real family I'd ever had, Emmy was a constant presence in my life, even though I rarely saw her these days. Occasionally, I was with Gus when she called, or I saw in the paper that she'd won another title, but that was different from her walking into my bar on a Friday night.

Looking like *that*.

Holy hell. Had she always looked like that?

Or was it just the way she looked in the neon glow?

Her hair was reckless and messy. It looked even longer than when I last saw her, hitting the middle of her back. She was wearing a skirt made out of some sort of shiny material; satin or silk, I think. It moved over her body like water. It made me wonder how she'd look wrapped up in bedsheets. But not just any bedsheets–*my* bedsheets.

Shit. Where the hell had that come from? What was wrong with me? It had obviously been too long since I'd gotten laid. I didn't want to think about how long.

That's your best friend's little sister, dipshit.

Two words rang in my head like alarm bells: off limits.

But damn. She did look good. It was okay for me to acknowledge she looked good, right? She was a grown woman. I was a grown man who generally enjoyed looking at beautiful women. I just hadn't seen one in a while.

At least, not one *this* beautiful. It wasn't like anything was going to happen between us, anyway. She couldn't stand me.

Joe, who was tending bar tonight, flagged me down,

jostling me from my inappropriate thoughts about Emmy Ryder. What the hell was she even doing here?

Usually, I heard about her visits because Gus wouldn't shut up for a few days leading up to her arrival, but I hadn't heard a peep out of him since he'd left for Idaho yesterday. Plus, when she did come home, she didn't leave the ranch. It was no secret that Emmy had always wanted to get out of Meadowlark. The only thing stronger than her desire to leave was her love for her family, and that's what dragged her back a couple of times a year.

"Brooks! We need change at the bar, man," Joe called over the music. Right, that's what I was doing before a certain brunette walked through the door and stopped me dead in my tracks. Since when did the youngest Ryder have any sort of effect on me?

Since now, apparently.

That was fucking annoying.

I looked back and gave Joe a quick nod, letting him know I'd heard him. That's when I noticed a redhead flirting with one of my horsemen at the bar. I recognized her bouncy-ass ponytail before I saw her face: Teddy Andersen.

If I would've seen Teddy first, maybe I could've prepared myself for Emmy's arrival. When it came to those two, one thing was certain: where one went, the other was sure to follow. It drove Gus bat-shit crazy.

He always thought Teddy was too much—too loud, too vulgar, and too much trouble.

I liked her. She'd always been a good friend to Emmy and was one of the few people who didn't shy away from Gus's general asshole-ness.

Plus, I could always count on my patrons to spend a little more money, and give my bartenders slightly bigger tips, when she was around. Teddy was good for business, but Gus didn't think she was a good example for his little sister. I thought Emmy deserved a little more credit. She was quiet, but she was scrappy. It's what made her and Teddy a good pair. Not that I'd ever tell Gus that.

Emmy was none of my business.

Teddy caught my eye, and her stare bore into me.

I couldn't place the look on her face, but then I saw her gaze shift to Emmy and then back to me. *Fuck*. I'd been caught staring where I shouldn't be staring. I turned quickly and made my way through the bar to my office. It was right behind the stage where my house band, Fiddleback, was working through a lot of Waylon, as usual.

The Devil's Boot had had a live band for as long as I could remember, but usually only on Fridays. Since I'd taken over, the house band played on Fridays, and other local bands covered Tuesdays, Thursdays, and Saturdays. They could play a few originals as long as they supplemented the set with the classics.

My patrons loved to sing. Loudly.

On the other days of the week, we went old-school on the jukebox.

I tried, and failed, to keep my eyes off Emmy as I made my way to my office. Catching a glimpse of her just as she slid her denim jacket off, revealing a low-cut white top that showed off her toned arms. *Christ.*

Between that and the fucking skirt, I wanted to scream.

Change, Brooks. Joe needs change. Just get the change.

I would get Joe his change, and then I would make myself the world's busiest bar owner. I just had to make it through the night, because in the morning, the neon glow would be gone, and Clementine Ryder would look like my best friend's little sister again.

Hopefully.

My office was small, but it had the essentials: a desk, a small couch, and a bottle of whiskey in one of the desk drawers. I didn't spend a ton of time in there. When it came to business, I usually did any work that had to get done out at the bar before we opened. I liked watching the place transform from day to night. It was like magic.

I never saw myself as a business owner. No one had. I wasn't exactly known in Meadowlark for being responsible, but this bar made me want to be more than other people's expectations of me.

I didn't know if I was getting there.

Because my office was right behind the stage, I could feel the kick drum. Its vibration shook the glass and whiskey I'd pulled out of my top drawer across my old oak desk. I poured myself a shot and threw it back, hoping it would dull the new effect Clementine Ryder was having on me.

Why was this happening to me?

I waited for the burn in my throat to go away before grabbing a wad of cash for the bar. I didn't count it, but based on the size, it should be more than enough to get them through the night. I, however, would probably need a few more office shots if I was going to have to look at Emmy all night.

I didn't even want to know what Gus would do to me if he knew what I was thinking about his little sister.

Maim me, at the very least. Murder me, probably.

I walked out of my office, cash in my back pocket, and locked the door. When I looked up, I had a perfect view of Emmy flirting with none other than Kenny fucking Wyatt.

That slimy little bastard. Sure, Kenny was the town golden boy, but Emmy's older brothers and I had not forgotten how he'd left Emmy for another girl at their senior Homecoming.

Describing Emmy's oldest brother as protective was the understatement of the century, and her other brother, Wes, was the same, but in a less intense way. Gus would be the one to beat the shit out of someone who hurt Emmy, and Wes would be the one to make sure she was okay.

I didn't have much of a family, but I had the Ryders, so I usually got dragged along when it was time to defend Emmy's honor, which happened more than one might think.

To this day, I don't think Kenny knew how his precious Mustang ended up on the other side of town with four flat tires.

And now, that piece of shit had one of his hands on Emmy, and she was *smiling* at him, so I did what Gus and Wes would've wanted me to do: I got his grimy little hands off of her. That's the only reason I did it. For Gus and Wes. Not for me.

Not because I was jealous.

I wasn't fucking jealous.

The look on her face as soon as she heard the steel guitar kick in was priceless. As a bonus, her hand immediately dropped from dickwad's arm. *Good*. But his hand stayed on her waist as she started to look around the bar—looking for me, probably. She had to know Gus was at that rancher's thing in Idaho, and I was the only other person who enjoyed pressing this button of hers.

I did my best to ignore the way Kenny kept his hand on her–like she was his–or else I would walk over there and break it. I watched her look around the bar. She was laser-focused, and I could tell she was madder than a hornet. There was something in her eyes I hadn't realized was missing when I'd looked at her before: fire. I started walking toward her, unable to help myself, ready to get burned.

· · ·

EMMY

I felt Brooks's hands grip the tops of my arms to steady me after running square into his chest, which felt like hitting a brick wall. It was *hard*. Was he benching cars or something?

His hands felt rough against my skin, and I hated the small thrill that went through me at his touch.

It didn't matter how old I was–when Brooks was involved, I was thirteen years old again, watching an eighteen-year-old him bale hay without a shirt. He'd been nice to look at then, and he was nice to look at now. Even though my adolescent crush on him dissolved as soon as I got smart enough to realize how annoying he was, there was just something about him that got under my skin.

I shrugged his hands off me, frustrated that he still had any sort of effect on me. I was tall, standing some- where around five-nine, but I still had to crane my neck to shoot daggers from my eyes at Brooks. He hadn't changed much over the past few years.

If anything, he'd just gotten more handsome, which irritated me more than I already was.

Brooks wasn't just tall; he was broad. His dark brown hair, which was always long, hit the middle of his neck. It had a slight wave to it that a lot of women would die for, including me.

Just like his stupid eyelashes that framed his stupid chocolate eyes. His hair was long enough that he could tuck it behind his ears, which meant I could see his stupid sharp jawline with its stupid five o'clock shadow.

I'm sure there were a lot of girls out there who would love for their brothers to have a best friend as good-looking as Luke Brooks. I was one of them. That is until he opened his stupid mouth and talked with his stupid low voice.

I really should have been more creative with my descriptive insults by now, but Luke Brooks had a habit of frustrating me enough that all coherent thoughts basically raced out of my head.

It was annoying.

He was annoying.

"Hey there, Clementine," he drawled. My harsh stare was doing nothing to quell the arrogance that was literally oozing from his every pore. It was palpable. He was always like this. If his ego were a physical thing, it would be bigger than the entire state of Wyoming. Probably Colorado and Utah, too.

"Fuck off, Brooks." He let out a low whistle that ended in a chuckle. I hated when he did that.

"Glad to see your tongue is still sharp as ever, sugar." The way he said "sugar" was almost demeaning.

"Don't. Call. Me. That." I paused after every word, letting my annoyance with Brooks punctuate every syllable.

"Don't let Kenny Wyatt put his hands all over you,"

Brooks fired back. "Then I wouldn't have to rescue you."

Was this guy for real? He was waging psychological warfare with that stupid song because a boy from *high school* put a hand on my waist?

A hand on the waist was probably the most innocent gesture in this bar's entire history. Seriously—I didn't even want to know how much of Meadowlark's population had been conceived in The Devil's Boot bathrooms.

"*Rescue me?*" I questioned. My voice was getting louder, but luckily not louder than the music...yet. "Get a grip, Brooks."

The band made it to the line about soft and fine bubbles—thank god. It was almost over. Almost everyone in the bar was singing, but most people had forgotten I was there after the first chorus, so Brooks's stupid joke hadn't lasted long.

"Yeah, Clementine. Rescue you. Your brothers would flip their shit if they saw you in here flirting with Wyatt."

"I wasn't flirting with Kenny. I was just saying hi. And even if I was, it's none of your business. You aren't my keeper, Brooks. And neither are Gus or Wes. I can take care of myself."

"Actually, what *my* patrons do in *my* bar is *my* business." His bar? Since when? "And your family is my family, Emmy, so even if you weren't in my bar, you would be my business. You've always been my business, and you'll always be my business." The level of authority in his voice told me he didn't want to be questioned.

I didn't care.

He had to be kidding. He didn't own The Devil's Boot. I didn't know who did, but there's no way it could be Luke Brooks. He was reckless and irresponsible. I was pretty sure the only things he'd ever owned in his life were a black Chevy C/K pickup truck that could barely be classified as a vehicle and a bunch of muscle tees that used to be t-shirts until he mutilated them with a pair of scissors.

"This isn't your bar," I said defiantly.

"This *is* my bar, sugar. And right now, my bartenders need change, so move your ass out of my way." He started to push past me but then turned to me one more time. "And tell Kenny Wyatt to keep his hands to himself, or I'll kick you both out."

4

LUKE

I woke up to the sun streaming through my window. It was probably a little after six. Shit, that meant I was already running late. If I were being honest, I probably wouldn't have made it through my morning run anyway. It took about three seconds of my eyes being open to regret the shots I did with Joe behind the bar.

I never did that.

Why the hell had I done that?

Oh yeah, because Emmy, with her messy hair and fucking bedsheet skirt, left my bar last night with Kenny Wyatt. Images of her throwing her head back and laughing at his jokes ran through my mind like a highlight reel.

Wyatt was not that fucking funny.

But he kept his nasty little fingers off of her, mostly thanks to Teddy pulling Emmy to the dance floor in front of the stage for most of the night. But when they were walking toward the door to leave, Wyatt snaked his skinny arm around her waist, and his hand was a little too fucking low on her back for my liking. I'd taken another shot before they even made it all the way out of my bar.

I gritted my teeth at the memory.

God, my head hurt. I never took more than one shot at work, and even then, I didn't do it very often. Last night, I let Emmy get to me, and I had no idea why.

It took ten more minutes and a lot of groaning for me to get out of bed and into a cold shower, where I tried to wash away every thought about her. It's also where I remembered I liked all of my appendages, and I didn't want to give Gus a reason to remove any of them.

After I slid on a pair of worn-out jeans, my phone went off. I looked at the screen. *Speak of the devil.* Gus.

Be cool, Brooks. You didn't do anything. You just eye-fucked his sister. That's fine.

Everything's fine.

I picked up the phone.

"Brooks, here." Did my voice just squeak? Yeah, my voice just fucking squeaked.

"Why are you answering the phone like it's a job interview?" What the hell was I supposed to say to that? It was either that greeting or accidentally telling Gus I thought his little sister was hot as hell.

"I'm a business owner. Gotta keep it professional."
Yeah, because that's what I was: a professional. Gus
stayed silent for a second.

"Are you drunk?" he asked.

"What? No. It's six-thirty in the morning, and you
know I'm teaching today."

"Just making sure," he said. "Can you pick up Riley
from her mom's on your way to the ranch this
morning?

"I thought Cam was dropping her off since you're
out of town?" Camille was a one-night stand from five
years ago that resulted in Gus's daughter, Riley. After
Riley was born, Camille and Gus messed around a
little bit, but they were never officially a couple.

Camille and Gus were on good terms, splitting
custody of Riley fifty-fifty. Gus even liked Camille's new
fiancé–as much as Gus could like a city boy, anyway.

Riley was the most important thing in the world to
Gus. When she came along, things changed for him,
and they'd changed for me, too.

I'd always been kind of a screwup, but to be fair, I
came from a long line of screwups. I was the result of
an affair my mom had with my dad. My dad wasn't like
Gus. He couldn't handle the responsibility. He couldn't
step up, so I'd ended up in a house with my mom, her
husband, and their sons.

Safe to say, I wasn't much liked around there.

My mom was still around, but I hadn't seen or
talked to her in years. Her husband didn't like her

having contact with me. Not talking to her didn't exactly feel great, but I would rather not talk to her at all than have to deal with my stepdad. John was a piece of fucking work.

She lived on the other side of town with him, and my brothers lived near them. If I had to guess, she was probably still on a diet of menthol cigarettes and Coca-Cola.

I spent the first seven years of my life wondering what was wrong with me. I still wonder about that, but everything changed when I met Gus.

Gus wasn't just protective of Emmy—he was protective in general. He'd always been that way, even back when we met in elementary school. Before I grew into my height, I was basically a walking telephone pole, and taller than everyone my age. My mom didn't have the money to buy me new clothes every time I had a growth spurt, so I ended up in clothes that fit really poorly. That, and being the kid from the trailer park, didn't really impress my peers.

Kids could be brutal.

But when Gus saw me getting tossed around by some fifth graders one day, he stepped in and basically told them to shove it–in the best way a fourth grader could. Afterward, I ate lunch with him. Well, he had to give me some of his lunch because I didn't have any, and after school, he told Wes I was their new friend.

That was it.

When I found the Ryder boys, they treated me like

I was worth something. Before I met them, I didn't even know what a friend was. I'd never had one, but that day, I ended up with two.

So, when I watched Gus step up to the plate to be a father to his baby girl, I wanted to step up to the plate, too.

I was still a screwup, but at least I was a screwup with a job, a savings account, and a few goals for my bar.

"Her fiancé is trying to close some big deal or something," Gus explained. "She tried to explain it to me, but she might as well have been speaking another language. All I know is that whatever it is apparently requires him to schmooze some people at the country club all day."

"Got it. Why don't you have Emmy pick her up?"

"Because Emmy is in Denver, dipshit," he said. "Are you sure you're not drunk?"

"*I'm* not drunk, but Emmy might be, considering how many Tequila shots she housed at my bar last night."

There was nothing but silence on the other end of the phone. I had a bad feeling I just threw Emmy under the bus. Why wouldn't she tell her family she was coming home?

I thought about it more. Why would she come home when her dad and brother were out of town? Not that Wes wouldn't be excited to see her, but he was covering Amos and Gus's ranch duties. It wasn't an

ideal time for her to show up, now that I thought
about it.

"Emmy is in Meadowlark?" Gus's tone was tight.

Shit. I definitely threw Emmy under the bus.

"Yeah, she left my bar with Kenny Wyatt last night."
Again, shit. Probably could've left out that little detail. I
hoped Gus hadn't heard the annoyance in my voice
when I mentioned his little sister and her ex-Home-
coming date.

"She went home with that asshole? And you didn't
stop her?" No. I wish I would've, but not for the reason
he was thinking.

"You know your sister is a full-ass adult woman,
right?" I said. Even though I wished Emmy hadn't left
with Wyatt, every once in a while, Gus still needed a
reminder that she could take care of herself. "Plus, she
was with Teddy. I'm sure her best friend can look out
for her."

"You know damn well that Teddy is trouble," Gus
said. He was getting angrier now. I probably shouldn't
have mentioned Teddy. Those two *really* did not get
along. I was on a roll this morning. "I can't believe
Emmy didn't tell us she was coming home."

"I'm sure she was planning to," I said, annoyed that
I felt the need to justify Emmy's actions. Since when
did I care? "She probably just didn't want to bother you
and your dad while you're in Idaho."

"I bet Teddy had something to do with it."

"You can't blame everything on Teddy."

"I can, I have, and I will."

"What are you going to do when Emmy makes a decision you don't like, and Teddy is nowhere around?"

"That's never going to happen." Gus was matter-of-fact, as usual. "Anyway, you're good to grab Riley? Now that I know Emmy is home, I'll ask her to come get her at the end of the lesson and take her to the Big House."

"Sure thing." There was no way I could avoid Emmy if she was coming to get Riley after the lesson. I could almost guarantee she would unleash her best verbal assault on me after finding out I was the one who ratted her out to Gus.

"Thanks, man,"

"No problem. I'll talk to you later."

"One more thing," Gus said. "Keep an eye on Emmy until I get home, okay?"

EMMY

Whatever that incessant buzzing was needed to stop. *Now*.

My head was pounding, and the buzzing—good god, the buzzing. *Make. It. Stop.*

I must've said that out loud because Teddy's voice came from her en suite bathroom, "Emmy, that buzzing is your phone ringing like it has been for ten minutes. It's not the sound of the apocalypse."

Oh. Whoops. I fumbled around, looking for my

phone. By the time I found it face down on the floor next to Teddy's bed, it had stopped buzzing.

When I flipped it around, I saw seven missed calls from Gus.

Shit.

Was Dad okay? Was Wes okay? Was Riley okay?

I went to call him back, but he called again before I could do so. I picked up immediately.

"Hey, everything okay?"

"You tell me, Clementine." Ugh, I hated it when Gus used his dad voice on me, but at least the annoyance and lack of urgency in his tone told me everyone in our family was safe and accounted for.

Which begged the question: why had Gus called me eight times at seven thirty in the morning on a Saturday? "Everything's fine. Why?"

"Where are you right now?" Gus asked. *Fuck.* He knew. He had to know. That's the only reason he would ask me that. "You better not be with Kenny Wyatt," he said.

I stifled a laugh. Was he kidding?

"I'm serious, Emmy." Oh, I knew he was serious. That's what made it so damn funny.

"First of all, whose bed I'm in is truly none of your business, and it's honestly creepy that you want to know that information."

"I don't want to know that information. I'm just saying that I hope you're not anywhere near that asshole."

"Relax, big brother. I'm in Teddy's bed." I heard Gus sigh on the other side of the phone. But it wasn't a sigh of relief—it was a sigh of annoyance, probably at Teddy.

"Kenny was nice enough to give us a ride home from The Devil's Boot last night since he didn't have anything to drink," I told him. "What an asshole, huh?"

"You know as well as I do that one good deed doesn't cover everything."

"Why do you hate him so much?"

"I just don't like him, okay?"

"Is this about Homecoming? Because you need to get over that," I said. "That was almost ten years ago, and I'm ninety-nine percent sure that you're the reason Kenny's car ended up in a ditch the morning after, so I think you got your revenge."

"You're my baby sister, Emmy. If someone fucks with you, they fuck with me," Gus said. He took his protector role very seriously. "You're like Mom. You're very forgiving, and people will take advantage of you."

Oh god. It was too early in the morning, and I was too hungover for Gus to bring up our dead mother. "And you can forgive people all you want, but it's my job not to forget," he concluded.

"Jesus Christ, August. It's not even 8:00 AM yet. Chill out."

"Why are you home, Emmy?" Gus asked. Not allowing the conversation to stray from the point for too long. Typical.

"I just needed a break," I said. Which was technically true. "I had an opportunity to take one, so I did. And I thought I'd spend it at home."

"How long are you around for?" My answer seemed to satisfy Gus. At least for now.

"TBD, but at least a few weeks." At the very, *very* least.

"Fine. I'll call Wes and tell him you're home."

"Okay." In less than twenty-four hours, my cover was blown, thanks to Luke Brooks and his big mouth.

"Riley has her group riding lesson at the ranch this morning. She'll be done around ten, and she would love to see her auntie, so can you pick her up and take her back to the Big House?"

"Anything for my girl," I said truthfully. I loved my niece. "But why isn't Cam picking her up? Isn't it her weekend?"

"Yeah, she had something come up. Listen, I just need you to get her after the lesson. Wes can take her, or Brooks can take her back home with him until her mom can pick her back up tomorrow."

"You actually leave your child alone with Brooks?" I asked. *Baffling.*

When we were growing up, Brooks was always around when Gus was stuck babysitting me. When they weren't totally ignoring me, I was their source of entertainment.

Turns out, being sent down the stairs to a very dark and very spooky basement in a laundry basket wasn't actually fun, no matter how hard your brother and his best friend tried to convince you otherwise.

Oh, and a pile of throw pillows wasn't enough to break your fall.

They also left me on the roof once. For two hours.

"He's a damn good uncle, Emmy. He helps all of us out whenever he can. He'll keep an eye on her. And you, until Dad and I get home." I rolled my eyes. I did not need Luke Brooks to keep an eye on me.

Someday, my brother would treat me like an adult. I hoped.

Hearing Brooks's name made me think of something he said to me last night. I had forgotten about it in my drunken haze.

"Speaking of the t-shirt mutilator, does he really own The Devil's Boot?"

"Why are you so adamantly against his love for the muscle tee?" Gus asked.

"It's not the muscle tee itself, but the man in the muscle tee who cuts them so aggressively." I didn't want to see Luke Brooks's nipples. "Answer the question."

"Yeah, he does," he answered.

"Since when?"

"You'll have to ask him about it. It's a weird-ass story. I gotta go, Emmy. I'll talk to you later." I guess I would never know how the poster boy for Coors got his hands on Meadowlark's most beloved, dirty landmark.

I didn't plan on seeing much—if any—of Brooks while I was here.

"Bye, big brother."

"Bye, Gussy!" Teddy shouted from her bathroom.

He didn't respond.

When I got off the phone with Gus, I had two texts: one from Kenny that said how good it was to see me last night, and one from my dad.

Happy you're home, Spud. I love you.

5

EMMY

Rebel Blue Ranch sat on nearly 8,000 acres of prime Wyoming land. This made it the biggest ranch in Meadowlark and the surrounding counties, as well as one of the largest ranches in the state.

My family's history with Rebel Blue went all the way back to the 1800s when my family made their way to the Wild West. The ranch was smaller then. Most of Rebel Blue's original structures still stood, in some form or another.

As I drove my truck through its big iron gate and onto the main dirt road that led to the Big House, my throat tightened.

I was home, and Rebel Blue was just how I'd left it.

The ranch was primarily a cattle ranch, just like it was when it started, but we also raised sheep and leased space for horses.

It was Wes's dream to convert some of the structures we didn't use anymore into a small guest ranch, but that was a massive project, and Gus wasn't exactly on board. He hadn't told Wes no outright–he was just hesitant.

It could still happen, though. Gus did a lot, but he wasn't the captain of the ship yet.

When something changed on the ranch, we usually voted, and it had to be unanimous. If the guest ranch ever came to a vote, I would vote with Wes. I wasn't sure how my dad felt about it, but if there was one thing about him, it was that he was all about big dreams.

At the center of Rebel Blue was Amos Ryder.

Even though my dad was closer to seventy than sixty these days, Rebel Blue was still very much run by him and probably would be until he physically couldn't do it anymore.

Wyoming was my dad's heart and Rebel Blue was his heartbeat—it pumped life through him.

No matter how badly I'd wanted to escape Meadowlark, I couldn't deny that Rebel Blue pumped life through me, too. It was hard to describe the way it made me feel. When I stood on the ranch and looked up at the blue skies or straight ahead at the mountains, it was like I was so small and insignificant. But not in a bad way; just in a way that reminded me that my problems were never as big as they seemed in the grand scheme of things.

About a mile down the dirt road, the Big House came into view.

It was built in a log cabin style and had six bedrooms: one for each of us, a guest room, and one that unofficially belonged to Brooks.

When we got older, Wes had decided to stay, probably to make sure someone was there with my dad, but Gus had moved to one of the cabins down the road.

My truck rolled to a stop next to a black Chevy K20 pickup I didn't recognize. I assumed it belonged to whoever was teaching the riding lessons this morning since Wes always parked his truck around back and the ranch hands had spaces outside their cabins.

I reached across my front seat to grab my phone and a pair of sunglasses. While I was looking down, someone banged a hand on the hood of my truck, pulling a jump so high out of me that I hit my head on the roof of my cab. God dammit. As if the hangover headache wasn't enough.

As I rubbed the top of my head, I saw my brother Wes out my front window. He was wearing a giant smile, and even though he had just caused me bodily harm, I couldn't help but return it.

Wes was the human equivalent of a golden retriever. Unlike Gus and I, he'd gotten my mom's features. Instead of dark hair, his was sandy. His green eyes were lighter than ours, and he also had two huge dimples that were often on display.

To be fair, Gus got the dimples, too, but he wasn't exactly known for smiling.

Wes walked to the driver's side of my truck, opened the door, and pulled me out into a fierce hug.

"Hey, baby sister," he said. His eyes were shining bright. I wished everyone was this happy to see me all the time.

"Hi, big brother," I responded. "What are you doing at the house this late in the morning? Shouldn't you be working?"

"Ha. Ha. Gus called me this morning and said you would be here by the end of Riley's lesson, so I needed to welcome you home and tell you two things."

"Go on."

"Dad has started doing yoga."

A shocked snort came out of me at the image of my sixty-five-year-old father doing downward dog. In my whole life, I could count on one hand the number of times I'd seen him wearing something other than jeans and a flannel.

"I know, I know," Wes said while shaking his head. "But he's getting really into joint health. He's eating vegetables and shit, too." Just when I thought nothing ever changed around here. "Anyway, the point is that your room is his most recent yoga studio. He moves them around based on where and when the sun comes in the window, and since it's summer, the sun is favoring your room."

"Okay..."

"So you have some choices: you can take Gus's old room, or the small cabin is open." The small cabin was set about 500 yards behind the Big House, surrounded by old aspen trees, and it was right next to the stream that ran through part of the ranch. It was also closer to the smaller stables that held most of my family's horses. Even though it was close to everything, it felt secluded.

Unlike the rest of the cabins, it didn't have a separate bedroom. It was basically a cabin studio apartment.

Private and cozy—it sounded perfect to me.

"Small cabin, please," I said.

"Good choice." Wes smiled. "I rode down there after Gus called this morning and cracked a few windows. It's been a while since anyone's been in there. Bedding and towels are in the wash for you, too."

While Gus was a fierce protector, Wes was a dedicated caretaker. I think that's why the idea of a guest ranch appealed to him.

Taking care of others was what made Weston Ryder happy, and he never expected anything in return. He didn't even think about it.

I gave him another squeeze. "I'll help you take your stuff down there after dinner, okay?" he said.

"Okay," I responded. " Also, there's room for Maple in the stables, right? Her transport should be here with her tomorrow." Considering how quick my Denver departure was, I hadn't had time to get my small horse trailer, and I didn't pick up Maple from her boarding stable—but I'd called them on my way here to arrange a transport for her.

"Of course, Emmy. There are, like, thirty stalls in the Ryder stable. You can put her by Moonshine. I'm sure they'll be happy to see each other." Moonshine was my horse, too. She was getting older at twenty-three and living out her golden years eating lots of carrots and apples.

"Sounds good. Is there a four-wheeler around that I can take to grab Riley?"

"Yeah, there's one in the garage. Keys are in the ignition," he said. "I've gotta go. The ranch hands will riot if they think I'm slacking off while the big dogs are out of town. Fences to mend, heifers to wrangle. You know the drill." I did. "I'll see you later, Emmy." He kissed me on the cheek and started to walk away.

"Wes?" I called.

"Yeah?"

"You didn't ask me why I came home."

"I don't care why you're here, only that you are." Those words went right to my heart. It took a lot of shitty things happening to me to finally force me back to Meadowlark, but I think I made the right choice coming home.

"Welcome home, Clementine," Wes said. He tipped

his hat, turned back around, and started walking toward the stables.

I CRUISED down the trail that led to the small corral the ranch used for lessons during the summer. My hair whipped behind me, and there was nothing but land and blue skies in front of me. God, this would never get old.

I had loved living in Colorado. I was happy anywhere there were mountains, but there was something about Wyoming.

As I approached the corral, I saw a few figures outside the fence, probably parents watching their kids, and five of our Shetlands with tiny humans on their backs.

The riding lessons were a new-old thing at Rebel Blue. My mom used to teach them, so they stopped when she died.

It wasn't until Riley was born that Gus decided he wanted to bring them back, not just for his kid, but for other kids in Meadowlark, citing my mom's philosophy that riding taught kids patience, empathy, and discipline.

I'd been too young to remember my mom teaching lessons, and by the time Gus started them up again, I had already left Meadowlark, so today was the first time I was seeing them.

I stopped the four-wheeler a good thirty feet away

from the corral. It didn't matter how calm and even-keeled the ponies were–you could never be too careful about spooking them when there were four-year-olds on their backs.

It was easy to spot Riley's curly black hair. It was a miracle that Camille's genes had stood up to Gus's, and it made for a damn cute kid—black hair, green eyes, and two massive dimples. She was riding her favorite pony: a chestnut-colored lady named Cheerio. As I approached the corral, I recognized a few of the parents and made my way over to stand near them.

One of the moms was whispering to another about someone's butt being "made for those jeans," and I stifled a laugh.

Gus must've picked a winner for a teacher. It took a second for me to spot the man they were talking about. His back was toward me, but it only took me half a second to identify his broad shoulders, the brown hair poking out of his worn baseball cap, and yes, his butt.

I could not believe Luke Brooks was an instructor of children.

And that all of them were still breathing.

Brooks hadn't seen me yet, so I did something I never let myself do—I watched him. He was helping another little girl adjust her hands on the reins and gave her hair a ruffle when she got it right. From the smile that little girl flashed up at him, you would've thought she'd just won a trip to Disneyland.

"Emmy, is that you?" The mom who was whis-

pering about Brooks's butt pulled me out of my state of
observation. I knew her. I recognized her face, but I
couldn't remember her name for the life of me. I think
she had a brother my age.

"The one and only," I said. I gave her a smile, trying
to channel my inner Teddy Andersen. She opened her
mouth to say something else, but was interrupted by a
kid yelling, "Auntie!"

I turned back to the corral to see Riley, Cheerio,
and now Brooks, facing my direction. The look Riley
gave me could've melted an iceberg. God, I missed
this kid.

Brooks smiled at me, too, but...it wasn't his normal
cocky smile. From the way he was looking at me, I
would've thought he was actually happy to see me.

That was new.

"Hey, Emmy," he called. I shot him some finger
guns.

I wish I were joking.

I internally berated myself, but Brooks seemed
unfazed as Riley asked him a question, and he bent
down to tell her she could dismount—*safely*, he speci-
fied—since it was almost time to untack. With one of
her hands under the pommel of her saddle and the
other holding the reins, Riley removed one of her feet
from the stirrups and carefully swung that same leg
over Cheerio's croup and down to the ground.

She was a natural.

Watching my niece with her pony made me drunk

with pride, but it also sent a baseball bat to my stomach. I hadn't been able to ride Maple in a month. I would get her tacked up and out to a ring, but when it was time for me to mount, I panicked.

Every time.

I'd been injured while riding before, but never like what happened in Denver last month. It wasn't the first time I'd ended up in the dirt because of a bucking horse, but it was the first time I'd ever completely lost control while riding, and I couldn't get any of it back. No matter how hard I fought.

From the beginning of that practice drill, I knew something was wrong. The horse I was training was agitated and skittish, but I ran him anyway.

I knew better, and I did it anyway.

I shuddered at the memory and felt my heartbeat making its way to my ears, but I kept my eyes on Riley, using my niece as a distraction from the onslaught of anxiety that flooded me every time I thought about that day.

Not now, Emmy. You can't do this now.

I took a deep breath, the same type of breath I'd taken outside The Devil's Boot last night, the morning air reminding me it was a new day.

And that I was home.

Riley handed her reins off to Brooks, who took them dutifully. She ran toward me—climbing through the gaps in the corral fence and throwing herself into my arms before I could take another breath. I stumbled back a step but managed to keep myself from falling on my ass despite the hangover.

"Auntie! You're here!" Riley put her little hands on my cheeks.

"I'm here, sunshine," I said, smiling at my favorite four-year-old.

"Did you see me riding?" she asked. "Did you see me and Cheerio?"

"I did—you might be a better rider than your dad," I said jokingly. Riley's smile grew.

"He says I should try to be like you because you're the best rider there is." The metaphorical baseball bat met my stomach again.

Yeah, I was a great rider. A great rider who couldn't even get on a horse. There had to be a joke in there somewhere, especially considering my last name was literally Ryder.

Riley leaned into me and took a healthy sniff. "Auntie," she said. "You smell smoky." Showing up to a riding lesson hungover and smelling like The Devil's Boot? Oh god, that sounded like something Brooks would do.

Shit.

"Riles!" Brooks called. "Time to untack. Unlatch yourself from Emmy, please."

I squeezed Riley tighter. She giggled. "Auntie won't let me go, Brooks!"

"Way to throw me under the bus, kid," I said as I set her down. She finagled her way through the corral bars and back to Cheerio. Brooks handed her back her reins and looked at me.

The smile he'd greeted me with was gone. Now, he looked annoyed.

Was he seriously annoyed that I interrupted the very end of his riding lesson–after the stunt he pulled at the bar last night?

Why was he even teaching riding lessons? This was the same guy who used to shoot clay pigeons from the bed of my brother's *moving* truck.

Brooks moved from the middle of the corral to open the gate. As he ushered the kids through and onto the path that led down to our stables, he looked at me again.

I hoped he couldn't see through my sunglasses that I was looking right back.

LUKE

God dammit. Emmy Ryder looked just as good in the daylight as she did in the neon. Which was damn good, by the way.

When I heard the four-wheeler stop near the corral, I knew it had to be her, and I hated how anxious I was to see her.

And here she was. In faded blue jeans and a ratty George Strait t-shirt that was cropped short, she was a walking wet dream for any cowboy.

It took effort to take my eyes off of her as she settled

in next to the group of moms, who for some reason thought I hadn't heard them talking about my ass for the last forty-five minutes.

There was another guy who taught lessons at the ranch every once in a while, but I'm pretty sure Gus purposely put him in the adult classes. I got the kids because Gus thought I was a "MILF Magnet."

But I wasn't interested in any of the women parked along the fence–until now. Emmy stood next to them, looking out of place. I watched her out of the corner of my eye. She politely said hello, but I knew she wasn't here to make small talk. She was here to see Riley.

Riley was obsessed with Emmy. She never shut up about her aunt, even when Emmy wasn't here. Normally, I'd wait until after the lesson was over, and the horses were untacked and back in their paddocks, to let the little hellion go over to her aunt.

Unfortunately, I was a fucking sucker for Riley, so as soon as she asked to go see Emmy, I gave in. Watching them reunite was honestly kind of special. I wasn't sure what the weird feeling in my chest had been when I saw the giant smile on Emmy's face as she hugged Riley.

Whatever, it was probably the hangover.

I looked at Emmy again. Everything I'd felt about her last night was still there.

I still thought she was beautiful.

I still wondered what she'd look like wrapped up in my bed sheets.

I was still pissed that she left with Wyatt, and I still wished she'd left with me instead.

I hoped she couldn't see all of that written on my face.

Shit, I was in dangerous territory.

Emmy Ryder had burrowed her way under my skin in a way I was not expecting.

What the hell was I supposed to do about that?

6

LUKE

After my last lesson group of the day, I started my walk back to the Big House. Today was a good late summer day. The kind that brought a little breeze to the ranch.

Rebel Blue Ranch was the best place on this green earth, and I never got tired of the path that led along the stream, through a cropping of aspen trees, and up to where the Big House was situated. It sat just a little higher than everything else, keeping an eye on everyone and everything—just like Amos Ryder.

My walks to and from my truck were usually my favorite parts of the day, but not today. Today, I saw the only thing in my life I ever thought was prettier than Rebel Blue, and that was Emmy.

What the hell was wrong with me?

Emmy had always been pretty, but I'd never seen her as anything more than my best friend's little sister.

The woman who walked into my bar last night walked taller than I'd ever seen Emmy walk. She was never that confident around anyone, let alone a guy. I might have hated that Wyatt had been the focus of that side of her, but I did like seeing her like that.

Amos said Emmy was too small for her britches, but from where I stood, those britches now fit her just right.

It was almost like Meadowlark was a low ceiling, and when she left, she could grow past its barrier.

So why the hell was she back here?

That was the question on my mind when the path rounded the corner to the small cabin. Emmy's truck—a baby-blue 1991 GMC Syclone—was out front. I remember when she bought it. Her dad had bought Gus and Wes their first cars, but not Emmy. She'd told him not to. Who the hell turned down a free car?

She did her ranch work and waited tables at the Main Street Diner to save up for it. She loved that ugly truck at first sight. I liked that she still had it, but I was surprised it was still running.

The cabin door was open and Cheap Trick drifted out. I got closer as Emmy came out. She had traded her jeans for a pair of tight black athletic shorts. *Fuck me.* Her tan legs looked a mile long.

She went to grab a box out of the back of the truck. It looked heavy. Gus would kill me if he knew how I was looking at his sister, but he would also kill me if I didn't offer to help.

Either way, I was going to end up dead, so I might as well try to get this whole thing with Emmy out of my system.

"Emmy, I got it," I said as I jogged up to the side of her truck.

She didn't even look at me as she said, "I don't need help from a big strong man to move a box." She let out a huff of air to move a piece of hair that had fallen over her face.

"You think I'm big and strong?" I asked.

"Shut up, Brooks." *Got her.* Now that I was closer to her truck, I could see it was packed full. She wouldn't have brought all of this if she was only going to be here for a week or two.

"Are you—" I started, unsure of how to phrase my question, "moving back here?"

Emmy stopped wrestling with the box I offered to carry. It stayed on the truck seat. Something had changed in her at my question. She let out a sigh and looked up at the sky. Then she shut her eyes.

"Yeah," she said, eyes still closed. "I am."

"What about racing?" I asked, equal parts curious and concerned. Emmy went rigid. It was like I could see the walls going up around her.

"What about it?" she said defensively.

"Are you done with it?" I asked. That was the only explanation. She couldn't ride competitively, the way she had for the past decade, from Meadowlark.

Emmy sighed again. It was the type of sigh that

could only come from a weight pushing down on you, hard enough that you had no choice but to let out a breath.

I knew all about those.

"I don't know." She still had her eyes closed and her nose toward the sky.

"Okay..." I didn't know what to say to that. *It's none of your business, Luke*.

The silence stretched between us for a few beats. "I'll help you unpack. Twice the people, half the work." I tried to make my offer sound transactional and not like I wanted to spend more time with her or anything. She looked at me, and after a few seconds, gave me a nod. "I'll start with the heavy box," I said, grabbing the box that started this whole thing.

Holy shit. It was heavy as hell. I thought about her packing up her life in Denver. Did she do it by herself? Or did someone help her? A boyfriend, maybe? My fingers tightened their hold on the box at that thought.

Even though I knew Emmy, I didn't *know* Emmy or what her life was like now.

But I wanted to.

Emmy grabbed a smaller box and led the way up to the cabin.

Inside the cabin hadn't changed since the last time I was in here. Gus, Wes, and I used to hang out here, usually with Coors and a joint. It was far enough away from the Big House that Amos wouldn't catch us, but close enough that we wouldn't be tripping through the ranch.

I'm pretty sure Gus lost his virginity in this cabin. I made a mental note to keep that to myself.

Emmy bent to set her box on the floor by the bed, and I couldn't help but look at her heart-shaped ass in her tiny fucking shorts.

I was going straight to hell.

"You can just set that anywhere," Emmy said, unaware of the fact that I was checking out her ass half a second ago.

"What the hell is in here?" I asked, setting the box on the ground inside the doorway. "Rocks?" Emmy let the slightest hint of a smile slip, and I felt like I'd won the lottery.

What the hell was happening to me?

"Close," she said. "Books. Have you ever read one?"

"Funny."

"Sorry, I know not knowing how to read is a tough subject for you." Her smile was growing. If giving me shit made her smile like that, I'd have no choice but to let her do it as often as she wanted.

"The Wyoming public school system failed me and countless others," I responded.

"You can't blame the school if you never actually went to school."

"I went to school," I protested, even though I really hadn't.

"Playing football and drinking in the parking lot

doesn't count." God, that smile. *Take that, Kenny*, I thought to myself, remembering how Emmy had smiled at him last night. *Look who she's smiling at now, asshole.*

"Damn. You got me," I conceded. She wasn't wrong. I did graduate, though.

"Thanks for ratting me out to Gus, by the way," she said. Her tone was still light, so I figured she couldn't be too mad about that, even though I did feel bad about it.

I knew what she looked like when she was mad, and it wasn't how she looked right now. She looked calm. Comfortable.

I liked that she looked that way while she was with me.

"You could've left out the Kenny detail, though," she continued. "Me being home without him knowing was probably enough to make that notorious forehead vein of his make an appearance."

Fuck Kenny.

"Did you"—again, I didn't know how to phrase my question correctly; Emmy had me all tied up— "have a good time after you left the bar last night?" *Smooth.*

Emmy laughed. "I can't believe Gus is trying to use you to interrogate me." *Yeah, it was Gus who wanted to know.* "Kenny gave Teddy and me a ride to Teddy's because, I'm not sure if you noticed, but we were blitzed."

Just a ride to Teddy's? She didn't go home with Kenny? Nothing happened?

Relief washed over me. I told myself it was because I didn't want to see my best friend's little sister get hurt again, which was true. It just wasn't the whole truth.

"Your very loud and very passionate rendition of *Islands in the Stream* might have given you away," I responded. The memory of Teddy pushing the lead singer of the house band out of the way and pulling Emmy onto the stage ran through my mind.

It was a little blurry, though, thanks to the shots I'd had behind the bar.

"Oh god." Emmy ran a hand over her face. "I blacked that out until now."

"You were honestly pretty good. Take a couple of singing lessons, and I'll give you and Teddy a set," I joked.

Emmy started walking back out to her truck to grab more of her stuff, so I followed.

"So it's true, then?" she called over her shoulder.

"What's true?" I asked.

"That you own The Devil's Boot."

"I do, yeah."

"How did that happen?"

It was impossible to bring up how The Devil's Boot fell into my lap without bringing up Jimmy. I stayed quiet for a second, preparing myself for the familiar ache that settled in my chest every time he got brought up.

"Do you remember drunk Jimmy?"

"Your dad? Yeah, I remember Jimmy." Emmy looked confused, and I couldn't blame her.

"Turns out he owned it the whole time. He left it to me when he died." I didn't really like talking about my dad. It wasn't that I thought he was a bad guy, but I knew he was a bad dad. The way I felt about Jimmy wasn't an open wound anymore, though. It was covered in scar tissue. That didn't mean there wasn't any lingering pain under the surface.

No matter how many years passed, I could never entirely shake the fact that my dad didn't want me.

He lived in the same town as me my entire life, and I saw him maybe once a year until I was old enough to pull off a fake ID and get into The Devil's Boot. Then, I only ever saw him in his regular spot at the bar. Sometimes he talked to me, sometimes he didn't.

I don't even know why he left me the bar and everything that came with it.

"I honestly didn't think anyone actually owned The Devil's Boot," Emmy said as she turned to grab another box. I was right behind her. "I mean, I guess I knew someone had to own it at some point, but I figured it was around so long that it just, like, transcended ownership."

"Honestly, the books made it look like there wasn't an owner when I took over. It was a disaster." Jimmy had run the bar into the ground. I hated to admit it, but when I saw how much damage he'd done over the years, I found it kind of comforting to know I wasn't the only thing my dad hadn't looked after. Still, I think he cared about the bar more than he ever cared about me.

Emmy and I set our boxes on the floor of the cabin. It was starting to fill up with her things.

"I don't think I ever said this to you," Emmy started. "I'm sorry your dad died. Grieving someone you never really knew is hard and confusing." My chest got that weird feeling again. I knew Emmy's words were genuine. Her mom had died before she was a year old. Riding accident.

"I appreciate that, Emmy." And I did. "Jimmy left me the only things that ever meant anything to him, and I guess that's worth something." I never talked about my dad like this. I didn't know why I was.

I just wanted Emmy to know me, I guess. And I wanted to know her, too.

We continued back and forth from Emmy's truck until Cheap Trick turned into Bruce Springsteen and all of Emmy's boxes made it into the cabin. After our conversation, we worked mostly in comfortable silence except for when Emmy told me where to put something or when she started absentmindedly singing the lyrics to the songs that were playing.

"I think that's it," She said as I brought in the last box, which had to be more books considering how goddamn heavy it was. What was this woman reading?

I set it down next to the others. "Thank you for helping me."

"Anytime," I said. And I meant it. As of yesterday, I would do anything, anywhere, anytime for Emmy Ryder. "You need anything else before I head out?"

I might as well have gotten on my knees and begged for her to let me stay a little bit longer. Jesus Christ, what was wrong with me?

She was trying to get out of where she was stuck in the middle of a pile of boxes. Before she could answer me, her foot snagged on the corner of a box and she went down hard. I instinctively reached for her, but I couldn't get to her before she hit the ground.

Goddamn boxes.

"Emmy!" I got around the boxes in my way as fast as I could and crouched down next to where Emmy on the ground. She had blood on her arm. *Shit*. "Emmy, are you okay?"

The panic in my voice took me by surprise.

"Yeah, I'm good. I stuck my arm out to stop the fall, and it went into a box. It's fine."

"Let me look at it, please."

"It's fine," she grumbled. *Stubborn woman*. Her head had always been harder than a horse's.

"Emmy, you're bleeding all over your box of shoes." She looked down at her arm. I didn't think she knew she was bleeding. She looked dazed.

"Shit," she breathed.

"Come here." I placed one of my hands on her

waist and one under her elbow on the arm that wasn't bleeding to help her stand up. "There's a first-aid kit under the sink. Gus and I just refreshed them a few months ago."

"God, I hate blood," Emmy said.

"Then don't look at it, Clementine."

"Wow. That's really good advice, Luke. You should be a doctor. Thank you." *Luke.* She called me Luke. She was bleeding out before my eyes *and* being a smart ass when she said it, but I liked the way it sounded on her lips.

"I'm serious, don't look at it," I said. "Here, sit down." There was a small kitchen table with two chairs near the back window. I led her to it, sat her down, and grabbed the first-aid kit before kneeling in front of her.

"I can't do blood, Brooks. I really can't," Emmy said. Her voice sounded hollow now. I looked up at her. She looked that way, too. She had her eyes on the blood coming out of her arm.

"Hey," I said, trying to keep my voice gentle. "Emmy, look at me." She kept her eyes on the cut, a vacant expression on her face. She looked like she was about to pass out. I didn't remember Emmy having this sort of aversion to blood. Cuts and blood weren't unusual on a ranch. Plus, I'd shown up at the Ryder's more than once looking worse for wear after a fight, so I felt like I would remember if Emmy's reaction to blood growing up had been this visceral.

I brought my hands up to either side of her face

and tilted it up. This forced her to take her eyes off her arm. "Look at me," I demanded.

Emmy's green eyes met mine. She *could* listen—who knew?

"Keep your eyes on me, okay? I'm going to take care of you, Emmy." She didn't respond, but she gave me a small nod. I kept my hands on her face longer than I should've, soaking up what it felt like to be close to her.

Jesus Christ. You are pathetic, I thought to myself. *She is literally bleeding dipshit.*

I moved my hands from her face and went to work on her arm. I had her set her hand on my bicep so I could see what I was doing. After cleaning the cut up, I was happy to see that it wasn't deep at all. It was just one of those "just right" cuts that bled like a mother-fucker until you got it under control.

I grabbed the rubbing alcohol from the first-aid kit. "This might sting," I said as I brought the soaked cotton pad to her forearm. She sucked in a breath, and the hand on my bicep squeezed. Hard.

"Shit. That did hurt," she said.

"Almost done," I said. I patted her skin dry with some gauze and put the biggest band-aid the over the cut. "There," I said.

I brought my arms to either side of her legs and let them rest there, against my better judgment. I looked up at her. She didn't look like she was going to pass out anymore—we were out of the woods.

Emmy had her eyes on me, and I instinctively

brought my hands to the bare skin on the sides of her thighs, right below the hem of her tight shorts. I watched her swallow. The way her throat worked made me want to grab her by it and pull her lips to mine.

I tried to remember the last time I'd felt this sort of pull toward anyone. I wasn't sure I ever had.

"Thank you," she said. Did she sound out of breath? Or was I making that up?

I slid my hands up a little higher and then brought them back to where they'd been, rubbing the sides of her legs. I told myself it was just to comfort her after the cut. Her breath caught, but she didn't stop me.

Her eyes darted to my mouth and then back up.

Fuck. I wanted to kiss her.

And from the way she was looking at me, I think she wanted to kiss me back. I knew what it looked like when a woman wanted that, but god damn, this wasn't just any woman.

This was Emmy.

Neither of us said anything–we just stayed where we were.

I looked at her mouth.

One kiss wouldn't hurt, right? Both of us were adults.

I was going to do it. I was going to kiss my best friend's little sist—

"Emmy!" Wes's voice shattered the trance Emmy and I were in. "I've got your bedding." I quickly snapped to my feet, and Emmy was right behind me as

Wes came through the front door. "Oh, hey, Brooks," he said. "I wondered why your truck was still outside of the Big House."

"Hey, man." I tried to keep my voice level so I didn't give away the fact that I was just about to plant one on his little sister.

"He was just helping me with boxes," Emmy said quickly. She sounded like a kid who just got caught sneaking a cookie.

Wes raised one of his eyebrows at her, and then at me. "That was nice of him," he finally said.

This was weird.

Emmy and I were being weird.

We had to stop being weird.

Nothing happened.

But it would've.

"Yeah," I said. "I saw her truck when I was walking back from the stables. Figured I'd lend a hand."

Wes stared at me for a second longer before he turned to Emmy and spoke. "Dinner is going to be ready in thirty. Riley wanted barbecue chicken. Brooks, are you staying tonight?"

"Thanks, but I gotta get to the bar. They're probably wondering where I am." That was true. The sun was starting to set, which meant people would start rolling into The Devil's Boot any minute, but Joe had it covered.

"Are you sure?" It was Emmy who asked. Did she...

want me to stay for dinner? There was a first time for everything, I guess.

"Yeah," I said. "Welcome home, Emmy. Wes, I'll be back tomorrow for the game." I always did Sunday football at the Ryders'.

I started making my way to the door and both Ryders gave me a wave. I waved back and hoped I didn't look as sheepish as I felt.

I basically ran to my truck. I couldn't believe I almost kissed her. If Wes hadn't come in, I would've.

If he hadn't yelled so we knew he was there, he would've walked in on me kissing his sister, and I would be dead right now. I rested my head on my steering wheel.

That couldn't happen again.

7

EMMY

It had been almost a week since I moved into the small cabin and whatever it was that happened with Brooks on its inaugural evening.

I tried not to think about it, but every time I let my mind wander, I came back to how his arm felt under my hand, the way his hands felt on my thighs and the way he looked at me like he wanted to devour me.

Brooks had always been a ladies' man. It had taken less than a minute of all his attention being on me to understand why.

He was intoxicating.

I can't believe I was so close to letting Luke Brooks —the man who had probably slept with over half the women in Meadowlark within spitting distance of his age—kiss me. Thank god Wes showed up when he did, or I probably would have.

Gross.

I'd seen his truck a few times on the ranch since then, but never him. I mostly stayed in my cabin, where I was currently halfway through unpacking my clothes. Wes was fine with me secluding myself in my cabin as long as I came up to the Big House and ate dinner with him, but Gus wouldn't be when he got back in town.

I should have been relieved that Brooks and I weren't crossing paths. I didn't even like him.

So why did I feel disappointed?

Snap out of it, Emmy. Remember how you broke up with your boyfriend via Post-it last weekend? You don't need to be kissing anyone.

Especially Luke Brooks.

The thought about my ex took me by surprise. Stockton and I weren't together very long—a few months. He lived in the same apartment complex as me. At first, I liked him because he wasn't like any man who had ever been interested in me. He was from a big city, he worked in tech, and he wasn't a cowboy.

He'd never even been on a horse.

He was nice, but over the past month and a half or so he'd started doing things I didn't like. He checked up on me constantly and would get really touchy whenever Teddy would call, so I wouldn't end up answering the phone. A few weeks ago, we went to a restaurant and he tried to order my food for me.

Not only that, he tried to order me a steak.

I didn't even eat red meat.

I would tell him that, and he would say, "Just try it."

I didn't need to "try it." I literally grew up on a cattle farm. But we weren't at a point in our relationship where I felt like I could talk to him about my sensory issues—especially if his response was going to be "Just try it."

Honestly, I would've broken up with him eventually anyway.

My injury and subsequent spiral just sped up the process.

There was a knock on my cabin door. Before I could answer it, Teddy came in like a tornado.

"Hello, lovey!" She had a few shopping bags. "I come bearing gifts!"

"Why?" I asked. I didn't mean to sound annoyed, but it came out that way.

"Because you haven't been answering my texts, so I needed to make sure you hadn't regressed to a *Sweet Home Alabama* situation"—I rolled my eyes at that— "and just in case you did: gifts." She held up the bags she was carrying.

Teddy loved gifts—buying them or getting them, it didn't matter.

"I love you, you know that?" I said.

"Obviously. And I love you, which is why I'm not going to say anything about the attitude you gave me a few seconds ago."

"I'm sorry," I said. I meant it.

"Accepted. Do you want to see your presents?"

"You know I do." Teddy gave an excited mini-squeal and clapped her hands together. She started walking toward the scene of the Brooks incident, otherwise known as the kitchen table, and I followed.

"First things first." Teddy reached into the biggest bag of the bunch. "New bedding! I'm assuming your attitude isn't great because you haven't been sleeping well. I know Wes probably brought you down the run-of-the-mill ranch set." She was right. "That shit is scratchy, and we know how you feel about scratchy textures against your skin."

The bedding Teddy brought was cream-colored and very, very soft. Sometimes I forgot how well Teddy knew me, but the lump in my throat was a good reminder.

"I love it, Ted. Thank you."

"We are just getting started," she said. "Also, I brought a mini coffee pot, your classic Folger's, a lot of dill pickle potato chips, and these new leggings that I think you're going to love. They literally feel like you're just walking around naked."

Teddy and I hadn't lived in the same place since college. Even though I could never forget what it felt like to be loved by Teddy, I think I did forget what it was like to be near her.

"You didn't have to do all of this."

"Blah blah blah." Teddy was a star at giving compliments and praise—not great at taking them. "I'm happy you're here, even when you don't answer my texts, and I just want you to know that I'm here for you, Em. Whatever you need."

Teddy was my best friend.

I could tell her anything. That was the whole point of having a best friend. Plus, I had to tell someone or I might explode.

"I wanted to kiss Luke Brooks," I blurted out. Teddy went totally still. I didn't even know she was capable of that.

"WHAT." Teddy's eyes almost burst out of her head. "Start talking, now."

Shit.

"It's hard to explain but there was an injury and adrenaline and his biceps are just so...you know, and his face isn't bad either and—"

Teddy cut me off. "Where did this happen?"

"Where you're sitting."

"Holy shit." Teddy leaned back in her chair and kept her eyes on me. "So you wanted to"—she paused for a second—"kiss him?"

I swallowed. "In the moment...kind of?"

"What about now? Like, now that the moment has passed?"

"Of course not." That was a lie. I was a dirty little liar.

"Okay. Okay." Teddy shook her head in disbelief.

For the first time in our lives, I think Teddy was at a loss for words. "I mean, I don't blame you," she finally said. "He's got that whole bad boy cowboy thing going for him, and you did just break up with someone, so it makes sense."

"It does?"

"No, but let's pretend it does. It'll make you feel better." Ugh. I buried my face in my hands. "So do you, like...like him?"

"No!" I said quickly. Too quickly. Teddy gave me a look that said she didn't quite believe me.

I didn't quite believe me either.

There was another knock at my cabin door—well, at the door frame, since Teddy had left the door open.

"Emmy, how many times have I told you not to leave the cabin doors open?" Gus made his way into the cabin, which was way too small for three people, especially when two of those people were Teddy Andersen and August Ryder.

"Sorry, Gussy," Teddy called. "That was me."

Gus's steps immediately halted as he shot daggers at Teddy.

If Gus were a few years younger—and smiled more—we could be twins. But my eyes didn't have his dagger-shooting ability.

Gus was even sporting a neatly trimmed beard that *really* made him look like a younger version of our dad. He didn't have that the last time I saw him. "Theodora,

I thought I banned you from Rebel Blue," he said. He was very obviously annoyed.

"I thought I told you if you called me that I would shove a fence post down your throat," Teddy said in a sickly sweet voice. "And that's the last thing you'd need considering you're looking a little worse for wear these days."

Teddy batted her eyelashes for good measure. She made that gesture look so condescending.

"If I get you a bridle, will you shut up?" Gus snapped.

"A bridle? Ooooh, August Ryder has a kinky side," Teddy responded.

"Okay," I interrupted. "It's not even 10:00 AM, so maybe let's cool it on the verbal warfare." Teddy and Gus both looked at me, remembering I was there. When they got like this, they could go all day.

"Yeah, I wouldn't want to make a loser out of Gus so early in the morning," Teddy said. She flipped her copper hair over her shoulder. "I just came to check on Maverick." Maverick used to belong to Teddy's dad, but he couldn't ride anymore, so Teddy looked after the horse. "I'll call you later, Emmy."

"Bye, Ted. Love you."

"Love you more." On her way out of the cabin, Teddy stopped in front of Gus. "What's that?" She pointed at his shirt, and like an idiot, he looked down. She flicked her finger back up and hit him in the nose.

Gus growled. Literally growled.

I heard Teddy's laugh until she shut her truck door.

"I really can't stand her," Gus said to me.

"Well, she can't stand you either." I looked at him for a second before rushing over and giving him a big hug. "Welcome home, big brother."

Gus gave me a squeeze. "You, too, little sister." He used one of his hands to ruffle my hair. Gus had the tough guy bit down pat, but underneath it all, he was a softy, even though he'd never admit it. If I said that to him, he would double down on being an asshole just to prove me wrong.

"How was Idaho? I thought you guys weren't getting home until later?" I was happy to see him, really happy. But I'd been hoping for a little bit more time to mentally prepare myself before seeing him and my dad.

"We got an earlier flight. Dad's dying to see you." Their early arrival did mean I got to hug my dad sooner, and that was something I needed. There wasn't anything a hug and a home-cooked meal from Amos Ryder couldn't fix.

"Where is he?"

"He's at the house making the world's latest breakfast for us. He told me to come get you. Ready?" I nodded, and we started toward the Big House. For Gus's sake, I made sure to put on a show of shutting the door and locking it.

While Gus and I walked up to the house, he told me about the conference he and my dad had gone to in Idaho. Apparently, Gus got a lot of information on guest ranches and horse rescues. From the way he was talking, it seemed like he was pretty into the idea of both. Rebel Blue had the space for them.

Wes was going to be stoked about this potential change of heart about the guest ranch.

"Is Riley here?" I asked.

"No, she's with Cam. I'll go get her tomorrow."

"I saw the last part of her lesson on Saturday. She's a natural," I said, thinking back to how brave and confident she looked while riding Cheerio. She looked how I used to feel when I was riding.

Thinking about that made my heart hurt. I wondered if riding was something that was behind me now, but Gus's response pulled me out of my head before I could make it too far down that spiral.

"Yeah, she's good. Brooks is a good teacher, too." Of course, Gus would bring up Brooks. I'd brought up the riding lesson, and I recognized bringing up the instructor was the natural progression of what we were talking about, but it still bugged me.

Luke Brooks was taking up enough of my head-space. I didn't need him taking up airtime in my conversations, too.

"I still can't reconcile Brooks the riding instructor with Brooks who was known for a different kind of riding," I said, mostly without thinking. Gus looked at me like I just grew a second head.

He was the second person who had given me a look like that today, and both times, it had to do with Luke Brooks.

"Gross, Emmy. I don't want to hear that coming out of my sister's mouth."

"I thought we were on this level, considering you're the one who asked me whose *bed* I was in last week," I retorted.

"Point taken." Gus changed the subject. "Wes tells me you've been sulking in your cabin," he said. It wasn't a question.

"Why does everyone always think I'm sulking?"

"You're a sulker, Emmy. It's what you do," he said matter-of-factly.

I scoffed. "You're one to talk." But it galled me that he was right and that he'd called me out on it. I was a sulker. It was just easier for me to retreat into my head than anything else. It was the path of least resistance— at least for a while. "But yeah, I have been spending a lot of time in the cabin. Just settling in. It's a big change."

"So you're moving back? This isn't just a 'break' like you called it on the phone?"

"It's still technically a break," I insisted. "But yeah. I think I'm moving back. At least for a while." I knew I was staying when I talked to him on the phone, but he didn't need to know that.

"You know I'm going to put you to work, then, right?"

I sighed. Of course he was. "I know."

"We're down a ranch hand, so between you and Brooks, you can fill in for that spot until we fill it. Okay?"

I didn't love the fact that Brooks and I were a pair in this situation, but I nodded anyway. If I agreed to work, Gus would be happy.

"Alright, then. I'm happy you're home," Gus said. *Predictable*. Work was always at the top of Gus's mind. The only thing that beat out the ranch was Riley.

We made it back to the Big House, and Gus pushed open the back door for me. And for the second time since I'd been home, I ran into a man's rock-hard chest.

My luck in avoiding Brooks had just run out.

I looked up at him. His face was mostly blank as he steadied me, just like he had after the first collision. Blank stare or not, I could drown in his deep-brown eyes.

This was truly the worst.

"Hey, Emmy," he said. Cool. Neutral.

Annoying.

I would honestly rather he use his arrogant voice. This cool indifference was infuriating, considering he'd been relentlessly occupying my thoughts for days. It really sucked that he was so good-looking. That shouldn't be allowed.

"Hi." Two could play the cool game.

"Spud? Is that you?" I heard my dad's gruff voice from the kitchen. It was the only thing that could pull me from my standoff with Brooks. I ran for my dad, and as soon as I saw him, I launched myself into him, giving him the biggest hug I could muster.

His arms circled me and he lifted me off the ground. Being in his mid-sixties had nothing on him. Amos Ryder was tough as nails.

Maybe it was the yoga.

His skin was weathered and his green eyes were dark. He was wearing his usual flannel button-down with the sleeves rolled up. He had a swallow tattooed on each of his forearms. After a lifetime in the sun, they were faded. I loved them.

Even though I'd been home for a week, it hadn't truly felt like it without my dad. Now I really was home. He laughed into my hair. It was hearty and gravelly. "I missed you, too, Spud." I wrapped my arms around him tighter for a second before I let go.

He lowered me to the ground.

I looked at my dad. He looked older than when I last saw him—a few more wrinkles around his eyes, and the salt in his hair had made it further up. It was more salt than pepper these days.

"Did Maple make it back okay?" he asked.

"Yeah, she's in the stall next to Moonshine." Maple made it back to Rebel Blue a few days ago. Her transport took a little longer than expected, but she made it.

I'd been riding Maple since the beginning of my

professional career. Before her, I had Moonshine. I had tried a few horses in between them because I was waiting for Maple to be ready to ride, but none of the other horses were the right fit for me. Most of them were still at the ranch, like Gus's horse, Scout.

Not every horse was built for the barrels, but Maple was. She was an expressive horse, and when we raced, I could tell she felt the same way I did.

The way I used to feel, anyway.

"I'm sure they're happy to be reunited," my dad remarked. They were. Moonshine was made to be a mother, and she loved Maple like she was her own.

Honestly, seeing them back together in the pasture almost made me want to ride.

Almost.

"They are. I've been letting them pasture together."

"We'll have to take them out for a trail ride soon. I'm sure Moonshine would rather ride with Maple than Cobalt." Cobalt was my dad's horse. He was a black-and-white American Paint Horse—easily the most beautiful horse on the ranch. Cobalt and Moonshine had a love-hate relationship. They both thought they were the alpha of Rebel Blue.

I couldn't bring myself to answer my dad's suggestion of a trail ride. It was our favorite thing to do together—at least, it used to be, so I just nodded.

The front door opened again. It was Wes. He was in his work clothes. This time of day was usually the boys' lunch since they were up at the ass crack of dawn.

"Weston, you're just in time. Food's ready."

I sat at my normal seat at the table. I'd forgotten it was the seat directly across from Brooks.

Great.

8

LUKE

I was starting to think Emmy was put on this earth to torture me. After the breakfast at the Big House yesterday, I was pretty damn convinced that was the case.

I didn't hear a thing Gus and Amos said about their conference, and I couldn't even give a damn that I'd agreed to help Gus with a bunch of extra work.

All I could do was try not to look at Emmy and try not to think about how her skin had felt under my hands.

She also did a damn good job of ignoring me, and that pissed me off.

I was ignoring her back, but still.

The best I could do was sneak a few glances when I thought she wasn't looking. Her hair was messy, as usual.

I wanted to be the one who made it that way.

That's what I was thinking about while I was mucking out stalls, which was one of the tasks I'd agreed to yesterday.

The Ryders had three stables on the property, but only two were currently in use. This one, which had the family's horses, also included the horses and ponies we used for lessons—about fifteen in total. The other stable was further down the way, where the ranch hands could keep their horses if they brought their own with them. That stable was the biggest, so it had horses whose owners rented space. I was grateful I wasn't mucking out stalls in there.

I started with Friday's stall. Friday was mine. He was a palomino Morgan that came to the ranch as a rescue when I was seventeen. The first time I saw him, I was listening to "Friday, I'm in Love" by the Cure in my truck. That's where his name came from.

Friday was close to Moonshine and Maple, Emmy's horses. Even though she'd been home for almost a week, I hadn't seen her at the stables once. I knew she had to have come to let all the horses out to pasture and bring them back in, but her tack stayed in the same place.

That meant she hadn't gone riding.

That wasn't like her. Not at all.

Amos typically had to fight to get Emmy off a horse. There was never any trouble getting her on one. Amos was one hell of a horse whisperer, but Emmy was close to having him beat.

I thought back to the fall in the cabin, the way she'd looked at the blood. I wondered if that had anything to do with her unexpected return home.

Yesterday, it was obvious Amos was so happy to have her home. He didn't care why. Wes, too. But I could tell Gus was worried.

I was, too. Not that I had any right to be.

I heard the stable door open, and Emmy came in. Of course she came in right when I was thinking about her. That's what I got for lusting after my best friend's little sister.

She was wearing her boots, black leggings, and a white tank top. Her hair was braided down her back and topped with a ratty baseball cap. Why did she always have to look so damn good? She was making her way toward Maple's stall but stopped when she saw me.

"Hey," I forced out.

"Hey. Stall duty?"

"Yeah. Friday and Moonshine are out to pasture, if you were looking for her."

"I'm here for Maple. Don't worry about Moonshine's. I can do it."

"Alright. Are you here to ride?"

There was a long pause. Emmy looked almost scared. Was she scared of Maple? Scared of riding?

"Yeah, I'm here to ride," she said finally. She didn't seem so sure about her response. I kept mucking out Friday's stall, but I couldn't help but sneak glances at

Emmy. I tried not to be obvious about it. She took Maple's halter into her stall. When she went to open the stall door, her hands were shaking.

What the hell?

She brought Maple out to the crossties and grabbed the grooming tools from the wall. I could still see her hands shaking when she started to brush Maple.

Emmy knew better than anyone that handling a horse by yourself when you were feeling nervous or scared was a bad idea.

Her back was to me. The longer she brushed, the less her hand shook, but she was still wound tighter than a drum.

"Emmy?" I said quietly as I approached her. She didn't answer. She just kept brushing. I noticed her shoulders were shaking slightly, too. "Emmy," I said more firmly. She still didn't answer me. I was right behind her now, so I reached out and put my hand over hers to stop the brush. Besides her shaky hands and shoulders, she went completely still.

I took the brush out of her hand and then wrapped my fingers around hers, and started to lead her away from Maple. I finally got her to face me when I put my hands on her shoulders. There were tears in her eyes.

Fuck.

I didn't want to see her cry.

"Talk to me, Emmy. What's going on?"

"I'm fine." One tear fell down her cheek. I wiped it

away without thinking about it.

"You're obviously not fine." I had never seen her like this. I hated it. "What's wrong?" I asked.

She was still for a second, but then she nodded slowly. I rubbed my hands up and down her upper arms, trying to calm her down.

"You can tell me, Emmy."

"I'm fine." She was still crying, but her voice was angry now.

"Emmy—"

"Don't. Leave me alone." Yeah, I definitely would not be doing that, but I didn't push her right then. I stood by her, letting her cry for a little while longer. Watching the tears fall down her face felt like a punch to the throat.

Something had to have happened to her. She came home out of nowhere and didn't tell anyone. Gus told me she hadn't really left her cabin, and now she wasn't riding.

What the hell happened to her in Denver?

I was going to find out.

"Emmy, why did you come home?" I asked. Trying to keep my voice soft, even though seeing her like this was making me feel weird, and that freaked me the fuck out.

"Why do you care?"

"Because I care about you," I said. That had always been true, but it sounded different now.

Emmy just scoffed. I decided to try another angle.

"C'mon, Emmy. You have to tell someone, and even if I told Gus, do you think he's going to believe you confided in me? You can't stand me."

I tried not to visibly deflate at that last part.

"You can tell me, Emmy."

Emmy let out a deep breath before speaking. "I...I got hurt. I got thrown," she said. Her voice was shaking, and more tears started to fall. "I got thrown, and it was into the fence..." She was talking faster now. It was like the words were a firehose. "I got knocked out and woke up with blood in my eyes. I hit my head just right, and I don't know what happened. I was riding a different horse. Just doing drills...I was thrown so far and I hit the fence so hard. I should've been hurt worse..." Her breaths were getting faster.

Dangerously so.

"I'm so sorry that happened, Emmy. I really am." Remember the throat punch from earlier? It was way fucking worse now. Of course she hadn't been riding. Going through shit like that would mess with anyone's head. I could only imagine how much worse it was for Emmy, considering how she'd lost her mom.

Even if she didn't relate those events together, I bet her head did, whether she acknowledged it or not.

"I woke up, and I tried to get back on. I really did... but I couldn't. I couldn't do it, and I haven't been able to since." Emmy's breathing didn't slow at all. "I don't know what to do. I don't know what to do. I don't know what to do."

"Emmy, hey, it's okay. It's okay." I kept rubbing her arms. Her whole body was shaking now, and she brought her hands up to her neck and started scratching like she was trying to escape from her own skin.

"Emmy. Tell me what you need. Tell me what I need to do."

"I need..." she said as best she could between breaths. "Can you...?"

"Anything, sugar."

"Squeeze. Please." She shut her eyes and wrapped her arms around herself like she was giving herself a hug. I got it.

I pulled her into my arms and lowered us to the ground. I held her tight to my chest and started gently rocking back and forth. I felt her tears dampening my shirt.

"Emmy, breathe with me, okay?" I started exaggerating my breaths, in and out, so Emmy could feel them and hear them. "You're safe, Emmy."

We stayed on the floor of the stable for a while. Emmy's breathing started to slow, and I let my grip on her loosen as I felt her relax. I kept my breathing the same. Slow and steady.

After a few more minutes, Emmy pulled her face away from my neck. Her face was red, and her eyes were glassy.

"I'm sorry," she said. "I'm so sorry."

"Emmy. Please don't. Has that happened to you

before?" She just nodded. "For how long? Since the throw?"

"A few times before that, but it's been happening more since then."

"Does it happen every time you try to ride?"

"Almost every time." Fuck. If there was one thing everyone knew about Emmy, it was that she loved to ride. Not just race, but ride. She was probably the only person who had actually ridden every trail through Rebel Blue—not just the main ones. Multiple times. Knowing she wasn't able to ride devastated me in a way I wasn't expecting.

Everything I'd been feeling for her was unexpected.

I wanted to help.

"And you've been trying to ride every day?"

She nodded.

"Emmy, why are you doing that to yourself?" Her eyes welled with tears again. Shit.

"I thought it would get better. I really thought it would get better."

"It will get better, Emmy," I said. "But the saying 'get back on the horse' doesn't work if it's giving you panic attacks."

"I don't know what to do, Brooks." Seeing Emmy hurt was fucking terrible. I wanted so badly to make it stop for her.

Maybe I could. I had an idea.

"You've put up one hell of a mental block, Emmy.

You're a damn good rider—you just need to learn to trust your skills again."

"How?"

"We're going to start from the beginning."

She tilted her head at me. "We?"

"Yeah. I teach people how to ride, Emmy," I reasoned softly, trying not to puncture the bubble we were in. At this point, I would've done anything to be close to Emmy, but this was more than that. I wanted her to get back on the horse, and I wanted to be the one who helped her.

I wanted her to be able to do what she loved.

"You're offering to teach me how to ride?" she breathed. Her voice was shaky and unsure.

"Why not?"

"We're not friends, Brooks." Ouch.

"Why can't we start now?" I wanted to be more than her friend, but she didn't need to know that. No one needed to know that.

Emmy looked down, not making eye contact with me. I watched her eyes dart back and forth across the ground. She did that when she was thinking. She always had.

After what felt like forever, she said, "Fine. But you can't tell Gus or Wes what's going on. I don't want them to know." Yeah, I definitely would not be telling them anything that was related to Emmy and me.

"Deal. We'll start tomorrow after whatever Wes has you doing. Eight AM?"

"Sure," she said. I realized we were still tangled together on the floor of the stable, and Maple, who was apparently the world's best horse, was still content on her cross ties. Emmy seemed to realize this at the same time I did and basically jumped off my lap.

I stood, too.

"Thank you. For that," she said, motioning to the ground. "I've never been with anyone when that's happened. It was...helpful. Thank you." I smiled at her, and I could've sworn she blushed.

It was probably just a trick of the light.

Emmy turned to Maple and started untying her. "I got her," I said. "You go. I'll let her out and do her stall."

"You don't have to—"

"It's fine, Emmy. Go."

"Thank you, Brooks. For everything. I really do appreciate it." She turned to head out the stable door.

"Hey, Emmy," I called. She turned back to me. The sun was shining at her back as she stood in the stable door. She looked like a fucking angel—an off-limits angel.

"Yeah?"

"Friends, then?" I asked. She seemed to chew on that for a moment.

"Friends," she said.

When it came to Emmy, I was playing with fire, but I would happily walk into the flames for her.

And I'd have a smile on my face the whole damn time.

9

EMMY

Riding lessons with Brooks were actually going okay. He hadn't asked me to mount a horse yet, but I was able to fully tack Maple up yesterday without giving into the little panic monster inside me.

I felt like I should have been more embarrassed about Brooks seeing me in that state, but I wasn't. Every time I thought about that situation, the actual panic attack didn't really cross my mind, but the way Brooks had comforted me without questions or reservations did.

"What do you need, sugar?" I replayed those words in my head over and over again. I'd never heard him talk like that—soft. In the moment, his words held me together just as much as his arms had.

He took care of me like it was the most natural

thing in the world, and that's what was heavy on my mind–not the panic attack.

Neither of us had brought it up, and I didn't think either of us ever would, but that didn't make me any less grateful I hadn't had to go through it alone that day.

The fact that someone else knew what happened was weirdly freeing. It was like, now that he knew, the whole situation didn't just exist in my head—it was real. The pain it caused me was real. The aftermath was real.

And if the fall was real, the rise could be, too.

So far, Brooks's riding lessons consisted solely of tacking up and untacking our horses together. Then, we would take them out to the riding corral and walk them. When we returned to the stables, we untacked and then let Maple and Friday out to pasture.

He had to be bored of that. How did he have the patience to do all the work of getting our horses ready just to take them on the horse equivalent of walking a dog around the block and then bringing them back?

I felt like he was wasting his time with me, but I was grateful he was taking it slow, not pressuring me to mount Maple...yet.

I knew it had to be coming.

While we were doing our tack-and-walk routine, Brooks and I talked. This guy had been hanging around my house since I was born, yet this was the first time I'd ever had any one-on-one time with him. And we talked. Like, *actually* talked.

And when we were talking, I wasn't thinking about my accident or the aftermath.

It helped. Probably more than I wanted to admit.

I'd learned a lot about Brooks over the past few days. His favorite movies were *Dead Poet's Society* and *National Treasure*—two movies I definitely wasn't expecting. I thought he would be more of a *No Country for Old Men* type of guy.

His favorite band was Bread, but if he had to choose a second favorite, he would pick Brooks & Dunn or The Highwaymen.

I learned other things, too. Things that were sprinkled into our conversations that he probably didn't realize he was telling me. Like that his half-brothers didn't speak to him at all anymore. He hadn't seen his mom in years because of his stepdad, John. A few years ago, someone at The Devil's Boot offered him their condolences on his mom's health, and that was how he found out she'd gone through treatment for cancer in her esophagus.

She was okay now, but he still hadn't seen her.

He tried to a few times right after she went into remission, but John wouldn't let him in the house.

Growing up, I knew Brooks's home situation wasn't great. That was why he spent all his time at the ranch. But hearing about it as an adult was different. It held more weight for me now.

And if it felt heavy for me just hearing about it, I could only imagine what it felt like for Brooks. He was the one who had to carry it.

He deserved better.

It was weird, spending time with Brooks this way. I'd known him nearly my entire life, but I didn't actually *know* him.

Before recently, the main thing I knew about Brooks was that he was *always* around. I used to get so jealous he got to be part of the Ryder Boys Club with my brothers and my dad, and he wasn't even a Ryder.

I wish I'd known then how much it meant to him to be a part of something like that—to be a part of us.

We had another lesson today, but not until later in the morning. Gus was taking advantage of the extra hands Brooks was willing to provide, so I took the opportunity to eat breakfast with my dad. I hadn't seen him nearly enough since I'd been home—he was a busy guy.

As we sat at the kitchen counter, me with home-made chocolate chip pancakes, him with a green smoothie—Wes really wasn't kidding about the health thing—I asked about Brooks.

"Dad?" My voice was quiet, timid, even.

"Yeah, Spud?" he replied without looking up from his morning paper. I knew what I was about to ask would raise some flags with my dad, but I needed to know what he saw in Brooks.

"What do you think about Brooks?"

"Luke? He's a good man. Why?" *Because he sat on the stable floor with me for an hour the other day, and I need to know if that's normal.*

"I guess I'm just wondering why you basically took him in when we were kids."

My dad took off his reading glasses and set his paper down. "Why the sudden interest?" *Flags: raised.*

"I don't know. Just curious."

The look my dad gave me told me he wasn't fully convinced of my answer, but he answered my question anyway.

"Luke is fearless. When Gus brought him home from school when they were kids, I knew he was either going to be great or he was going to become his own worst enemy, like his dad." My dad continued, "I knew Jimmy pretty well back in the day. He was fearless, too. But no one ever had any expectations for him. What started out as being fearless just turned into being reckless as he got older."

That made sense to me. Jimmy Brooks wasn't really known for being a responsible or stable guy.

"But Brooks was reckless, too," I said, thinking back to all the times he'd gotten himself hurt or done something stupid. Like when he bought a piece of shit motorcycle, sped through town without a helmet, and wrapped himself around a tree all in the same day. It scared the hell out of my dad and Gus. When I got home, a bloody and bruised Brooks was getting one of Amos Ryder's famous talking-tos.

Knowing what I knew now, I wondered if Brooks had ever had anyone care enough to yell at him the way my dad did that day.

Since being home, I was constantly trying to wrap my brain around this man who was way more caring and dynamic than I'd ever given him credit for.

"Luke isn't reckless. He has never been. He's been careless sometimes—impulsive and hasty—which is probably why he's ended up with his nose broken more times than I can count. But it's hard to care when you don't have anyone or anything, and there's no one around to care about you."

I didn't know what that was like. I'd always known I was loved.

"Luke is kind of like a stray dog," my dad continued. *Nice,* I thought. "Rough around the edges, in need of a little structure and a healthy dose of love. He has good days and bad days. Granted"—my dad clicked his tongue—"I haven't had to bail his ass out of jail for a few years, which I'm pretty damn pleased about."

I remember my dad having to bail Brooks out of jail for fighting three times, and those were just the times I knew about.

Luckily, this was a small town, and Amos Ryder had gone to school with the sheriff.

"It took a long time for him to trust me, to trust Gus and Wes, when we said he was welcome here, but we never stopped showing up for him, and eventually, he showed up for us–and has every day since."

I thought about the time Brooks was supposed to pick me up from rodeo practice because no one in my family could. I would've rather walked home, but Gus insisted it would be fine.

Brooks was late. He couldn't drive because he'd had a few beers, so when his truck rolled around the corner, whatever girl he was screwing around with at the time was in the driver's seat.

Back then, the whole situation pissed me off, especially because I had to sit between the girl and Brooks on the bench seat. He had to stick his head out the window while she was driving to get some air on his face.

Looking back on it now, I realized he still showed up for me that day.

Albeit tipsy and late, but I didn't think there were many people a twenty-year-old Brooks would've done that for.

I felt the smallest of smiles tug at the corners of my mouth, thinking about Luke Brooks having to ask that girl to drive him to go pick up his best friend's little sister.

"I never thought about what it must've been like for him—living in a house where he wasn't wanted," I said. I felt bad for being such an asshole to him. "Do you think if he didn't meet Gus, he would be different?"

"Maybe. I don't think we can take all the credit. The kid's got a heart the size of the Rocky Mountains. He likes having people to care for, and he needs people to care for him. I think he would've found his way eventually, maybe with a few more shitty pit stops."

I thought about that for a second. I was still trying to connect the two versions of Brooks I had in my brain: the careless teenager who'd pushed my buttons and the man who'd sat with me on the floor of the stables for an hour while I was having a panic attack.

It was hard to believe they were the same person. I didn't know if he had changed or if I just hadn't seen him clearly before.

"I guess he's okay," I said, trying not to give anything away in front of my dad.

He smiled at me, and there was an expression on his face I couldn't place. "He is," my dad agreed. "Thanks for having breakfast with me, Spud."

"Is your time up?" I asked.

"It is. I'm headed into town today to pick up some inventory and a new part for one of the hay balers. Do you need anything?" He started clearing his area at the counter and taking his dishes to the sink.

"I'm okay. I've gotta get down to the stables."

"Enjoy your day, Spud," he said as he pulled his cowboy hat from its hook in the kitchen. "Love you."

"Love you," I responded. Now that my dad was back at the ranch, I was grateful for the time I had with him. The time I was spending with him now was different than when I used to come home for the holidays or when I had breaks in my schedule. During those times, my dad planned around me, so we could spend a good chunk of time together.

Since I was home longer, I cherished these smaller moments with him. It meant there was no pressure for us to spend time together. We got to just exist in each other's orbit–without a deadline on our time–for the first time since I was eighteen.

The small moments made me realize how much I missed him while I was gone and how much I needed him.

And, in an unexpected turn of events, how happy I felt to be home.

I STARTED WALKING DOWN to the stables, and my phone buzzed. I pulled it out of my back pocket and saw it was Kenny. We had talked a little bit since I saw him at The Devil's Boot, but nothing crazy. He'd been fun to flirt with that night. It had been nice to see him, he was kind, and I really appreciated him giving Teddy and me a ride home so we didn't have to sleep in the bed of the truck outside the bar, but I didn't have any interest in him.

It had nothing to do with the man I was going to meet.

Probably.

I also had a few texts from Stockton. I hadn't read them, and later, I knew I would delete them without doing so. I sighed and slid my phone back into my pocket without responding to Kenny.

I saw Brooks before he saw me. He was in the doorway of the stables, and he had some tools out. He was probably fixing the hinge that was driving Gus up the wall.

For the first time since I got home, Brooks was wearing his signature muscle tee. It looked like this one used to be an INXS t-shirt before he took a pair of scissors to it.

As annoying as it was to admit, Luke Brooks was hot as hell, and so was the muscle tee. God, what was wrong with me? Historically, I was staunchly anti-muscle tee, and now I was drooling over Brooks and his exposed arms. The way his biceps flexed and bulged was enough to get anyone hot and bothered.

And don't even get me started on the fucking backward baseball cap he was sporting today.

Damn.

Damn. Damn. Damn.

You are weak, Clementine Ryder, I thought to myself. One backward baseball cap, and I was throwing all my opinions on muscle tees out the window.

And my opinions on Luke Brooks were being thrown out with them.

He must've heard my boots on the dirt because he looked up from his task. He smiled as big as he could, but he was holding a nail between his teeth, keeping it handy if he needed it.

Why was that hot, too?

"Hey," I called out. He pulled the nail out of his mouth and dropped it in the bowl at his feet.

"Good morning," he drawled. I used to hate his mountain drawl, but now I wanted to wrap myself up in it. I watched his eyes track me up and down, but he did it fast, like he didn't want me to notice. My cheeks heated, and I tried to will it away.

"Do you think you're ready to mount today?" he asked. There was a joke in there somewhere, but I wasn't touching it. The last thing I needed was to make mounting jokes with Luke Brooks.

The thought of getting on Maple made my heart beat a little faster, but it wasn't anywhere near what my reaction had been like a few weeks ago.

"I think I can give it a go," I said. Brooks smiled again. When he smiled big like that, he got these wrinkles around his eyes. They were stupid cute.

"Let's go, then." He used two of his fingers and motioned for me to join him in the stable. We walked side by side back to Maple and Friday's stalls, but Maple's was empty.

"Where's Maple?" I asked.

"I let her out this morning," he responded. Okay?

"So...am I not mounting today, then?" I was confused. Maple was my horse, so if I was going to ride, why wasn't she here?

"You are, but we're going back to basics."

"So?"

"You're going to ride Moonshine." Huh. I hadn't thought about riding a horse other than Maple, but Moonshine made sense. Moonshine was bombproof— the perfect horse for a beginner.

And I was a beginner again.

Why didn't I think of that?

"Okay," I agreed. "Moonshine it is."

"I'll get her and Friday on the cross-ties, and we'll get started, yeah?"

"Yeah." My heart started to kick against my ribcage, and the early feelings of panic were all too familiar at this point. Brooks had his eyes on me, probably to gauge my reaction. Instead of focusing on the feelings of panic that were creeping their way up my chest, I focused on him. I focused on how secure I'd felt when his arms were wrapped around me, and the way his breath had felt against my cheek.

If he was here, I was going to be okay.

I pushed the panic down, locking it firmly at the base of my throat. I felt it prick at me as I moved to start the tacking process, but I didn't let it overcome me.

I could do this.

I wanted to do this.

I grabbed the grooming tools off the wall as Brooks secured the horses, and we fell into the routine we'd been doing for the last week or so. I started to brush Moonshine, and I think it made her happy. Her tail was swinging freely.

"So, what should we cover today?" he asked. I liked that he wanted to talk to me, that maybe he was enjoying our conversations as much as I was.

"Hmm..." I said out loud. I thought about it for a second. What did I want to know about Luke Brooks? "Who was your first kiss?" I asked.

Brooks looked surprised, but he just smiled and said, "Interesting question, Ryder."

"So answer it," I said. "Or can you not remember the long line of women who got their hearts broken by Luke Brooks?"

He laughed. It was a deep, genuine laugh. "My first kiss was Claudia Wilson."

That name—well, the last name—rang a bell in my head immediately. "Didn't you sleep with her mom?" I blurted out.

"You keeping tabs on me, Ryder?" he said with a smirk.

"No," I said defensively.

"Sure." He was still smirking, and I didn't even find it annoying, which was annoying in itself. "I had my first kiss when I was thirteen. It was at some junior high dance. You know, the ones where they play "Yeah" by Usher and then hit you with, like, "Open Arms" by Journey and warn you not to get too close?" I knew exactly what he was talking about. "And those poor teachers have to monitor a room full of tweens who could spontaneously start grinding on each other at any moment?" I couldn't help but let out a giggle.

Those dances were a universal experience in
Meadowlark.

"Anyway, it was one of those. During a slow song,
we snuck into the boys locker room, and I kissed her in
the showers. I wasn't very good at it. I nearly knocked
both of our front teeth out and tried to use my tongue
before I was ready."

I laughed louder at that.

"And to answer your other mildly invasive question, yes. I did sleep with her mom." He flinched, but at
least he was honest. "But that wasn't until I was in my
twenties; I didn't know who she was until a few months
later, and it was only once."

Huh, interesting.

"And for the record, the rumors about my sexual
exploits involving people's moms—and my sexual
exploits in general— are exaggerated." It was funny to
me he knew those rumors were out there but never
addressed them. He just kept on rolling, not caring
what anyone thought of him.

"So, how many moms have you slept with, then?"

"Just the one, smartass." Someone told me it was at
least ten. I guess you can't believe everything you hear
through the Meadowlark gossip hotline.

The lore surrounding Luke Brooks in Meadowlark
was deep-rooted. It used to bother me that everyone
besides me just put up with him.

"You're really peeling back the curtain for me,
Brooks."

"Do you like what you see?" he asked jokingly, but I was honest when I answered.

"Yes." He paused what he was doing–cleaning Friday's hooves–and looked up at me. I couldn't quite place the expression on his face, but it was...intense. It left as soon as it came.

"So, who was yours?" he asked, returning to his task. "First kiss, I mean."

"It was Colton Clifford. Sophomore year. It was during the fireworks at the Fourth of July rodeo." I thought back to that day. I was fifteen, and all I could think about was that there were only three years until I could get out of Meadowlark.

I wondered if fifteen-year-old me would be disappointed that I was right back where I started.

"Damn. Smooth." I could hear the smile in Brooks's voice as I got some stubborn dirt out of Moonshine's shoes.

"It honestly was," I said. "Until I found out he kissed another girl later that night."

"You're kidding." Luke's voice was truly shocked like he couldn't believe a guy would do that to me. When my heart kicked in my chest again, it had nothing to do with panic and everything to do with him.

"Nope," I responded. "I caught him under the stands with a freshman."

"I know where he lives. I will go down there and kick his ass right now."

I laughed, but he might have been serious. "Teddy took care of that years ago," I said, smiling.

"Good," he replied.

Both of us finished grooming and went to grab our tack. My heart rate started to kick up again. As if Brooks could sense it, he said, "It's okay, Emmy," and placed his hand on my lower back as he led me back to Moonshine. The heat that coursed through my body at his touch distracted me from my anxiety about mounting her.

I went through the motions of tacking her up. This was second nature. I'd done it thousands of times in my life. That wasn't an exaggeration.

Saddle pad. Saddle. Girth. Bridle, starting with the bit. I repeated the words in my head over and over again as I went through the motions, trying to keep my mind on the task at hand and not what would come after.

After Brooks finished on Friday, we walked the horses out of the stable to the corral. Brooks secured Friday on one of the posts and came up to me.

"Let's do this, Ryder. Need a boost?" Honestly, a boost couldn't hurt. Based on my reaction when he'd put his hand on my back, I figured his touch might distract me, so I nodded.

Something shifted in the air, like giving him permission to touch me, changed something between us.

"Alright." He put his hands on my waist first, which

was not how you helped someone get on a horse. We both knew that, but I didn't care. I could get on Moonshine myself, but I wanted him to touch me. "Left foot in the stirrup, sugar." The term slipped off his tongue effortlessly. It didn't sound demeaning anymore, though he probably called every woman that.

"One hand on the pommel." Did his voice get lower? Was that possible? A shiver oozed down my spine.

I followed his instructions, even though I knew what I was doing. But not having to think about it, to just be able to listen, was freeing.

The distraction worked. When we got to the point where he was supposed to boost me up, I felt him lean down to me.

"I know you can get on this horse by yourself, Ryder." His hands were still on my waist, and I could feel his breath on the back of my neck. He gave my waist a squeeze, and then let go. "So do it."

I did.

Before I even realized what happened, I pushed my right foot off the ground and swung my leg over Moonshine.

I was in the saddle.

Holy fucking shit.

I was in the saddle, and it was okay.

I looked at Brooks—he was beaming, and his smile warmed me all the way through.

"There she is," he said.

It was almost like he had trouble taking his eyes off me as he went back to Friday.

Luke Brooks did a lot of sexy things, which was getting less annoying, but I don't think there was anything quite as sexy as watching him, in his backward baseball hat and muscle tee, mount his horse.

Damn.

Once he was situated, he said, "We're going to take it slow, okay? A few walking laps around the corral, and then we'll be done for the day."

I nodded. I saw Brooks give Friday's middle a small squeeze with his calves, asking him to start going forward, which he did.

I took a deep breath and did the same to Moonshine. She went.

"Breathe, Emmy. You know Moonshine will take care of you. She always has." He was right. I took a deep breath and relaxed my white-knuckle grip on the reins.

Moonshine followed Friday, just like she was supposed to.

Brooks kept looking back to check on me. The smile never left his face.

We did three laps around the corral before Friday stopped. I gently pulled on Moonshine's reins, but she would've stopped without it. Brooks dismounted and secured Friday to the post again. He walked back to me, and the smile on his face was so contagious I smiled right back.

"How do you feel?" he asked.

"I feel amazing," I said. Truthfully.

"You look amazing, too." This man and his ability to make me blush was still annoying.

"Shut up, Brooks," I said. He just kept smiling.

"Let's quit while we're ahead. Ready to dismount?"

The dismount went smoothly, and when my boots hit the ground, it was like I couldn't contain the joy anymore. I secured Moonshine to the post next to Friday and turned to face Brooks. I couldn't help it—I flung myself into him and wrapped my arms around his neck.

He was stunned still for a moment, but then he wrapped his arms around me and lifted me off the ground for a second. We laughed together. I pulled back so I could look at him.

"Thank you, Luke." I hoped he could hear my sincerity.

"You did this, Emmy. It was all you."

"I wouldn't have done it without you." Yeah, mounting a horse and taking a few walking laps was way different than barrel racing, but it was something. After having nothing for so long, I felt like I was on top of the world.

"You would have. I know it." He brought his hand up, tucked a stray piece of hair behind my ear, and then kept his hand on my face. His eyes flashed to my lips, just like they had that night in my cabin. Unlike that night, he moved his thumb and brushed it over my bottom lip. I wanted to take it into my mouth.

This was it.

I wanted him to kiss me. I wanted it so badly.

He didn't.

Instead, he pulled away, untied both of our horses and started walking them back to the stable.

10

LUKE

In less than two weeks, I almost kissed my best friend's little sister not once, but twice. I wanted to kiss her so badly it was pathetic.

I tried to tell myself it was just because Emmy was pretty and I hadn't kissed a woman in a while. I hadn't wanted to. But I knew that wasn't true. There was something between us.

And Emmy wasn't just pretty. She was extraordinary.

Sometime in the last two weeks, Emmy started looking at me like I was worth something, and I was high on the feeling it gave me.

Watching the way her confidence grew with every lap around the corral yesterday had made my jeans tighten. And the way she threw herself at me afterward?

I was a fucking goner.

The next day, I texted her and told her I had some business at the bar, so I couldn't ride. It was true. I didn't usually work at the ranch on Fridays because I spent the day getting The Devil's Boot ready for the weekend.

I told her I had a busy couple of days, and that we would get back to it on Tuesday. That should give me enough time to get my head on straight and stop thinking about what it would be like to touch her...everywhere.

I felt bad bailing on Emmy, but I needed a few days to get my head right where she was concerned. If I saw Emmy while I was feeling the way I was right now, there was no doubt in my mind that I would kiss her. I'd do more than kiss her.

I wanted to make Emmy mine in every single way.

I wanted to know everything about her, including how she'd sound moaning my name.

If I thought we were in dangerous territory before, I didn't even want to know where we were now.

I sighed and ran my hands down my face. I had a million things to do, and all I could think about was Emmy.

This morning, Joe asked me why I was so distracted, and I didn't know how to answer. Joe was a good guy. He had worked at The Devil's Boot longer than I had been alive, and he was the sole reason the bar survived being owned by Jimmy Brooks.

When my dad left the bar to me, I wanted to give

fifty percent of it to Joe. He deserved it, but he'd refused. We settled on a forty-five/fifty-five split. That seemed to make him happy, and I got a damn good partner out of it.

It also allowed me to keep helping out at Rebel Blue, and that meant everything to me.

I almost didn't accept the bar. I didn't want anything from my dad. When he died a few years ago, I had made it over thirty years without needing anything from him and hadn't wanted to start then. But when the bank explained to me it probably meant the end of the bar—the end of something that meant so much to so many people, even if it was just the place where they sang country classics at the top of their lungs—I decided to take it.

I also took the house—a single-story bungalow that was nestled in the trees behind the bar, about a thousand yards away. The land I owned was no Rebel Blue, but one hundred acres that had a house and a business wasn't too shabby for someone like me.

I didn't quite know how all of this had ended up in Jimmy's hands, but I'd be lying if I said I wasn't grateful.

There was a knock on my office door. I looked up, expecting to see Joe. Instead, I saw Teddy Andersen.

Why was Teddy Andersen at my bar at 10:00 AM on a Friday?

Why had Joe even let her in the front door?

"Are you busy?" she asked. Her hair was pulled up

in her signature ponytail, but the look on her face was unfamiliar. She looked mad.

Teddy was one of the last people on the planet I'd want to piss off. Her and Gus were probably tied in that regard. Yesterday, when Emmy told me the story of her first kiss and mentioned Teddy "took care of it," my first thought was that she probably cut off that guy's dick and fed it to him.

"What's up, Teddy?" I asked. Teddy crossed the threshold of my office and shut the door behind her.

"What's going on between you and Emmy?" She didn't pull punches, I guess. *Fuck.*

"What are you talking about?" I responded. I kept my voice neutral. Or tried to, at least.

"Cut the shit, Brooks. She told me about the almost-kiss in her cabin, and now you're giving her riding lessons? She's a professional barrel racer. I don't think she needs any tips from you."

Emmy told her about the cabin? She wouldn't tell her best friend unless it meant something to her, right?

That's not the point, you idiot.

"You can play with any girl you want. Why are you messing with Emmy?" she pressed, clearly not taking my indifference as an answer.

"I'm not messing with her," I answered honestly. I wasn't *messing* with Emmy. If anything, she was messing with me. From the second she walked through the door of my bar a few weeks ago, it was like she had branded herself onto my brain and practically demanded I think about her 24/7.

I wasn't supposed to get feelings for anyone, let alone my best friend's little sister. "Emmy and I are friends."

Teddy didn't look convinced. Probably because my answer wasn't convincing. Emmy and I were friends, but only because that was all we could be.

"Friends?" she asked.

"Yeah. I like spending time with her."

"And the riding lessons?"

"More of a riding refresher, and you're going to have to ask her about that." I preoccupied myself with some papers on my desk. It wasn't my place to tell anyone what Emmy was going through. I just wanted to be there for her.

"Do you have tension-filled almost-kisses with all of your friends?" *Tension-filled?* Is that how Emmy described it to her?

I tried not to smile. I didn't think it worked, so I brought one of my hands up to cover my mouth in hopes of hiding what I was feeling from Teddy.

Maybe Emmy was just as affected by whatever was happening between us as I was.

I couldn't think about that. I couldn't let my mind wander down that path and think about where we would end up if that were true.

"No," I responded simply. I'd never had tension-filled anything with anyone. Just Emmy.

"Wipe that stupid smirk off your face, Brooks. Tell me what's going on."

"Look, Teddy, I'm not messing around with Emmy. I promise. I would never do anything to hurt her. We're friends, and I like spending time with her, that's all. Okay?"

Half of that sentence was true, but it seemed to work.

I watched Teddy think about my words for a minute before her features shifted from mad to amused.

"What?" I asked.

"Nothing. I get it now." A small smile stretched her mouth.

"Get what?"

"I just get it." Teddy's smile was getting bigger. "Thanks for clearing everything up for me."

"Teddy, what the hell are you talking about?"

"Nothing." God, she was being annoying. She started toward the door of my office, and as she opened it, she said, "See you around, Brooks." Before she was completely out of sight, I heard her say, "If you hurt my best friend, I'll cut your dick off and feed it to you."

I had a bad feeling, somehow, Teddy knew exactly how I felt about her best friend.

11

EMMY

My phone rang at the ass crack of dawn. I assumed it was Teddy since she was the only person who was calling me lately. I answered without looking at the screen.

Big mistake.

"Hello?" I said. My voice was groggy.

"Hi, there. Is this Emmy Ryder speaking?" The voice on the other end of the phone was definitely not my best friend. Even Teddy wasn't that cheery in the mornings.

"This is she."

"Good morning, Emmy. It's Wendy from the Women's Professional Rodeo Association." On the list of people I didn't want to talk to on a Monday morning, the rodeo people were pretty high up there. Especially Wendy with her cloyingly sweet voice. "I'm calling because I wanted to know if you'd be competing when we come to Meadowlark next month."

"Um, I don't know. I'm taking a break from the circuit right now."

"Yes, we're aware of your situation." Great. "I wanted to call and let you know that we understand those things can be hard to work through, and we want you to do so, but we also would love to have you with us in Meadowlark. That's your hometown, correct?"

"Yeah," I said blandly.

"Well, we've never brought the circuit there before, and we think having you on the roster would be great for us and great for your town." What about what would be great for me?

"I'll think about it."

"Great! I'll call in a couple of weeks to check-in. And, Emmy?"

"Yeah?"

"If there's anything we can do for you, please don't hesitate to reach out. We appreciate you and we love having you as part of our crew. You're a great racer."

"Thanks." *Where were you when I was holed up in my apartment for a month?* I thought to myself. Wendy had been in charge of barrel racing at the WPRA for years. I'd known her for a long time. I didn't blame Wendy for anything, but my accident was reported to her right after it happened, and this was the first time I'd heard from her.

And the first thing she asked me was whether or not I'd be willing to race.

"Alright, we'll talk soon. Have a great day!" Wendy said. Her voice really was like nails on a chalkboard, especially this early in the morning. I hung up the phone without responding.

That wasn't the way I wanted to start my morning.

So far, all I'd done on a horse since I'd come home from Denver was walk laps around a corral. I couldn't even take Moonshine out to one of the riding paths that weaved through the ranch.

It felt too unfamiliar right now, which was hard to reckon with, considering I'd spent my entire life riding those trails.

I couldn't think about that right now.

Last night at dinner, a dinner from which Brooks was notably absent, Wes asked me if I could help him with a project. I agreed.

Even though Brooks wasn't able to ride with me for a couple of days, I still went down to the stables and did a few walking laps with Moonshine every morning. It wasn't as easy without him there, but I could do it.

It was amazing how much our trivial conversations while tacking up calmed me down.

I wasn't brave enough to take Moonshine to a trot yet, so I hoped whatever Wes needed help with didn't require too much riding, or else today would not be a good day.

I forced myself out of bed and into a warm shower.

It was that point in the summer when the mornings were getting colder, but not cold enough to justify starting a fire in the cabin. Those days would probably be approaching soon, though.

Usually, a few weeks after Teddy's birthday, which was this week, it started to get cold earlier in the evening and stay cold later in the morning. That didn't mean it wasn't still hot as hell during the day.

It wasn't Wyoming if you didn't experience at least three of the seasons per day.

After my shower, I slid on a pair of Wranglers, a black tank top, and an oversized Carhartt hoodie. I pulled my hair back into a braid, and just as I slipped my boots on, Wes knocked at the door.

"Emmy? Are you ready?" His voice was muffled through the door.

"Yeah, come in!" I responded. He opened the door, and the cool morning air made its way into my cabin. The hoodie was a good call.

"Hey, morning. Are you okay if we take the side-by-side?" He had no idea how okay I was with that.

"Yeah, that's fine." We walked out my cabin door, and I made sure to shut it tightly. *You're welcome, Gus.*

Wes had driven the side-by-side down to my cabin, so I made my way to the passenger side and hopped in. "So, what's this big project you're on about?"

Wes smiled while keeping his eyes on the dirt road ahead of us, dimples on full display. "You'll see." There was a fork in the road, and Wes took the one that went

to the left. This led to the older part of Rebel Blue–
well, the part that had the most original structures.
Since there weren't a ton of working structures over
here, a lot of cattle roamed through. It was the part of
the ranch where you were most likely to get blocked by
them, but it didn't look like we were going to this
morning.

"So, how's being home?" Wes asked as he drove.

"It's nice. I didn't realize how much I missed being
here," I said. It was easy to be honest with Wes. Well,
about some things.

"Here as in Meadowlark or here as in Rebel Blue?"

I thought about that for a second. "Both," I
answered truthfully. "I thought I would only feel that
way about the ranch, but Meadowlark isn't as bad as I
remember."

"Somebody check the weather in Hell," Wes
responded, and I smiled. "What about that boyfriend
you mentioned when we were on the phone last
month?"

"Not important," I said. Harsh, but true.

"Ah, got it." Wes let it go. I appreciated the way he
didn't push me on things. Like Gus, I really didn't like
to talk about what I was feeling. Wes made me feel like
I could talk about things, but he never pressured me to
do so before I was ready.

"What have you been doing with your time here?"
he asked.

"I've been at our stables mostly." This was true. I

hadn't really been anywhere else in Meadowlark, or even at Rebel Blue. But it wasn't where I was that I was hiding from Wes–it was who I was with and what I'd been starting to feel about him.

"Doesn't Gus have Brooks on those?"

"Uh, yeah. I've just been helping out."

"Well, he's busy with the bar, so that's probably nice for him." We came to a stop in front of the structure that used to be the Big House before any of us were born. It was technically bigger than the one we lived in. It was just a hell of a lot older. Our dad built our Big House when he was in his twenties because the plumbing in this one was less than ideal.

Unlike ours, this one was built more like a normal house. It was a ranch-style Craftsman. Its blue paint was faded and the front door was boarded up, but it was still beautiful.

"What are we doing here?" I asked.

Wes wore a giant smile, and I could feel the excitement radiating off of him. Something big was going on in that golden retriever brain of his.

"This is going to be the center of our guest ranch."

"Wait, wait, wait," I said, trying to get my brain to catch up with my mouth. "Dad and Gus gave the go?"

"Not yet, but they will," he said. "When they came back from Idaho, Gus asked me if I was still interested, which I obviously am, and we're going to vote at dinner sometime this week."

"Well, you know my vote," I said.

"I know. Thank you." I looked at the old Big House. It was maintained as well as we could maintain it, but it didn't take priority, especially since I don't think anyone thought it was ever going to be a working structure again. If we'd needed the space, my dad probably would have just torn it down.

"So tell me, how are you going to take this house, that's basically a ruin, and turn it into a place that people actually want to stay?"

"Well, the entire project will probably take at least eighteen months before we're ready to welcome guests, with the actual construction hopefully taking six to nine months," he said. I knew he'd been working this plan out in his head for years. "The entire house needs to be gutted and brought up to code. But as far as the layout, on the west side of the house there are six bedrooms. Two of those will turn into large suites and the other four will turn into a set of suites, each with a bathroom between them. We'll create a large kitchen and dining area, and a living area for people to relax after a long day."

Wes was a dreamer. Neither Gus nor I had the ability to dream the way he did—in the way where it felt like anything was possible. I never could have come up with this vision, but when Wes laid out his plan, I could almost see it.

"I love it. This is going to be fantastic, Wes. I'm so proud of you." And I was. I wanted this for him.

"Thanks, Em."

"Okay, so why are we out here today?"

"We're going inside. We need to document the state of the house. As soon as Dad and Gus give their formal go-ahead, I want to start looking for a designer and contractor."

"Let's do it." Wes and I walked up to the door.

"Have you ever been inside of here?" Wes asked.

"No. I'm not in the habit of going inside abandoned buildings like you." Wes liked adrenaline. It was the only thing about him that sometimes got him in trouble.

"Boring," Wes said as he pulled the plywood from the front door and opened it. I looked inside. God, this place was in bad shape. Wes, and whoever he hired, had their work cut out for them.

AFTER A NEAR-DEATH EXPERIENCE having to do with the kitchen ceiling and a lot of rodents, both dead and alive, Wes and I boarded back up the door.

"Wes, I know you can do it, but goddamn. Are you sure you don't just want to tear the whole thing down?" I asked, shaking my head. After seeing the inside of the house, I was one hundred percent certain starting from scratch would be easier.

"I'm sure." Wes smiled. He was undeterred by the state of the house. "Gus gets the ranch," he continued. "You left Meadowlark and made something of yourself all by yourself," he continued. "This is mine."

Wes put his hands in his front pockets and looked back at the house. He looked at it like it was already finished. His ability to see potential in things was something I admired.

"It's going to be beautiful, Emmy."

"I know. If anyone can do it, you can." That was true. Neither Gus or I could ever pull something like this off. We wouldn't even try. Wes threw an arm over my shoulders and we walked back to the side-by-side.

"Speaking of dreams, are you going to race in divisionals when they come to Meadowlark next month?" Goddamn. Was nothing sacred in this town?

"How do you know about that?"

"It was in the paper." Of course it was. I swear, Meadowlark was the only town left that had a thriving local paper. It was publicly funded, and everyone got a paper—whether they donated to it or not—and its biggest donor happened to be Amos Ryder.

Good for Meadowlark for supporting local journalism, I guess.

"Do you want the real answer?" I asked him.

"Always," he said.

"I don't know. Honestly, Wes, I don't know what my dream is anymore." Wes stopped walking. I took a few more steps before stopping and turning back to face him.

"You'll figure it out. You always do." That was the thing. I usually did, but I didn't know how to do *this*— how to give up a part of myself, how to start over.

"This time I'm not so sure."

"I am," he said. He looked at me, and how much he cared about me was written all over his face. "Everything ends, Emmy. Whether you choose to keep racing or not, I do want you to know that I would love to see you ride one last time in the town that built us."

That was what Wes left me with as we made our way back. He dropped me at the family stables, and I got started on my work for the day.

I tried not to think about how badly I wanted to talk to Brooks about what Wes had said, or about how quiet the stables were without him.

12

LUKE

I didn't sleep at all last night. After hours of tossing and turning, I took the loss and just got out of bed. I threw on a pair of running shorts, grabbed my running shoes, and headed out the door. I needed to get my mind right.

It was still dark, so it was probably around four in the morning. Every morning, I ran the trail that made a circle around my house and led to The Devil's Boot. I knew it like the back of my hand, so even though it was dark, I started down the path.

I couldn't stop thinking about Emmy. I hadn't seen her for a few days, but it felt like weeks. I didn't know what this feeling was. I'd never had a woman consume my every waking moment like Emmy did.

I listened to my feet hitting the trail, using the familiar rhythm of my run to try and slow my thoughts down. I didn't run with headphones, just all the voices in my head.

There were so many things in my thoughts I wanted to sort through, most of them having to do with Emmy, and by association, Gus.

I had always cared about Emmy, and she had been in my life for as long as I could remember. But before these last few weeks, Gus had been a barrier between us. Not a bad one, but still a barrier. Other than a few rides home from school, I really had never been alone with her.

Until now.

Being alone with Emmy was like taking a quick trip away from reality. It was just the two of us, Luke and Emmy. Not Brooks, the Meadowlark screw-up, and Emmy, the Meadowlark sweetheart. What I felt when I was with her was quickly becoming the best thing I'd ever felt.

I'd spent the past few years trying to be something, and there was something about Emmy that made me believe I could get there. Because when she wasn't being a smart ass, she was thoughtful, kind, and a hell of a listener.

This Emmy was new to me, and I couldn't help but think it was because I usually brought out the worst in her. I was a fucked up kid. That usually led to me being impulsive and looking for attention—any kind of attention. Getting cut up by Emmy's sharp tongue included.

I still liked that version of her, honestly.

I didn't like the way I teased her relentlessly about everything, but I liked the way she fought back. Growing up, people probably would've described Emmy as sweet and shy.

Not me. She didn't show me that side of her.

I would've used phrases like "pain in the ass" or "bullheaded."

When we were younger, even when we weren't at Rebel Blue, Emmy would always appear near me. If I took a girl out to dinner, Emmy would be at the diner studying with Teddy. If someone threw a house party, Teddy would somehow sneak the two of them in, even though everyone there was at least five years older than them.

It annoyed the hell out of me, and I made sure Emmy knew it.

There was one bonfire night where I saw Emmy mucking it up with a guy who lived a town over and was older than me. Emmy was seventeen, so he was being a fucking creep.

When he got up to go get her a drink, I went up to him and told him if he ever looked at her again, he'd be sorry. After he scurried away, I went to Emmy and said some pretty terrible things—stuff about her dressing like *that* to get the wrong kind of attention, calling her a stupid kid, and telling her to leave in front of everyone.

I thought I'd been a big enough asshole to knock

her down a peg and get her to go home. I knew she was embarrassed. If anyone else had said that stuff to her, it probably would've had the desired effect, but since it was me, Emmy came right back and lit me up.

In so many words, she called me a good-for-nothing fuck up and stormed off.

She wasn't wrong.

Whenever she burned me like that, I wanted her to do it again. I didn't know what it was—her honesty, her vitriol, or even just having someone see me for who I thought I really was—that made me so desperate to piss her off.

Now, I was getting to know a different side of Emmy, but I could still see parts of the girl with the razor-sharp tongue in the woman with the tempting mouth.

It was like I had spent my life getting pieces of her, and now I was finally putting the pieces together.

Guess what? There wasn't any piece of Emmy I didn't like.

I was so fucked.

I had no idea what to do. On one hand, Emmy was off-limits. Gus would freak out if he found out anything was going on, or had ever gone on, between us. Given my track record with women, I couldn't even blame him.

It wasn't like I treated women badly. To be honest, I was never with them long enough to treat them any sort of way. I saw the way my stepdad treated my mom, and early on, I decided I would never be that guy—the guy who constantly needed to have the upper hand, needed to have all the power.

I hated that guy.

Instead, I became the guy anyone could call for a good time.

I mean, who wouldn't want their little sister to end up with a guy like that?

Not that Emmy and I were ending up together or anything. That wasn't what I meant.

Gus was my best friend. Who knows what would've happened to me if he hadn't fed me half of his peanut butter sandwich in second grade when I didn't have a lunch.

I didn't want to fuck up our friendship, but I also didn't want to miss out on what could happen with Emmy.

Something about her just felt different. It felt *good*. I wanted to know where it could go, where *we* could go.

Even if we just ended up being friends. I wanted her in my life, more than the way she already was. That way wasn't enough anymore.

The first signs of sunrise were peeking through the trees, and I slowed to a stop right outside The Devil's Boot. The trail ended here, so I would have to turn around to get back home. In the early morning light, The Devil's Boot almost looked haunted. Honestly, it probably was. At the very least, it was haunted by bad decisions. It was like pieces of the night clung to it, refusing to make way for the light.

There was a big part of me that couldn't believe it was mine.

I stared at its faded paint. I got this place out of the hole Jimmy had dug for it. There would've been a time I would've dug the hole even deeper, and believe me. It was fucking tempting to run everything into the ground, to self-destruct. But I didn't do that anymore. At least, I was trying not to. It wasn't much, but it was something.

This part of me, who wanted to build a life that was different from my father's and had done a damn good job in doing so—at least so far—was a different piece of me Emmy didn't know. I wanted her to.

I wanted to give her pieces of me, too.

I'd started my run trying to figure out how to stay away from Emmy. I ended it with the decision that I wasn't going to stay away from her. At least, not yet.

Not today.

Today, I was going to give Emmy a piece of me she could hold onto.

EMMY

The next morning, there was yet another knock at my cabin door. It woke me up, which meant it had to be pretty goddamn early, considering I set my alarm for six o'clock. Why did everyone on the planet insist on waking me up?

The knock came again. I let out a groan and rolled out of bed, then padded toward the door, the hardwood floors cold under my feet.

I opened the door to none other than Luke Brooks. His eyes widened when he took in my appearance. At that moment, I realized I had crawled into bed last night in only a thin white tank top and a pair of panties. *Shit*.

"One second," I said and slammed the door in his face. Shit, shit, *shit*. I couldn't even say good morning to him now because my nipples beat me to it.

I rummaged through the pile of clothes on my floor, looking for something that would give me even a *little* coverage. I found an old, oversized flannel and threw that over my chosen pajamas.

I went back to the door and took a deep breath before opening it again. Brooks was still there. Now that I was semi-decent, I had time to take in his appearance. Another pair of perfectly worn jeans, a mutilated t-shirt, and a backward baseball cap. His chosen uniform. I was a big fan of the Brooks uniform these days.

Traitor, I thought to myself.

"What are you doing here?" I asked.

"It's eighty-thirty. I've been waiting at the stables for you for an hour." Oh shit. Had I really slept through all of my alarms? "And I've been knocking for ten minutes. I was about to barge in just to make sure you weren't dead."

"Shit, I'm sorry. Give me a few minutes, and I'll get ready."

"We're not riding today," he said.

"What?" Then what the hell were we doing?

"I want to take you somewhere. A swimsuit is probably a good idea."

I folded my arms over my chest. "I have work to do, Brooks."

"One of the ranch hands is stationed over here today because I'm usually not around, and his schedule didn't get changed with you coming home. You're good." Oh. That was okay.

I guess.

"Tell me where we're going."

"No. I already told you more than I should with the swimsuit, but I figured you wouldn't want to swim in your underwear."

"So you were thinking about me in my underwear?" His eyes narrowed, probably not appreciating me flinging sarcasm at him this early in the morning. Well, I didn't appreciate him showing up at my cabin door and telling me what to do.

"Get dressed, Emmy," he said firmly. He reached inside the cabin and shut the door, my cue to do what he said.

God, he was so demanding sometimes. I wondered if he was like that in bed.

Get a grip, Emmy.

I looked around my cabin, unsure of where I would even find a swimsuit. This place was a fucking disaster. I wasn't very good at keeping things clean. Sometimes, it was just easier for me to live under the piles rather than face what might be in them. It wasn't logical, but my brain didn't really work normally.

It took me a few piles, but I found a red two-piece. The top was sporty, and it had a square neckline that made my collarbones look good.

I slid on a pair of denim shorts and a cropped band t-shirt and made my way back to the door. When I opened it, Brooks was right where I left him, truly looking like a Wyoming poster boy.

"What shoes should I wear?" I asked. Brooks took that as an opportunity to give me a once over. Heat flooded my body as his gaze tracked from my toes all the way up to my eyes.

"Your boots are fine," he said.

They were by the door, so I turned away from Brooks and bent to put them on. "Ready," I said as I turned back around. His eyes were still where my ass would've been when I was putting my boots on.

His gaze met mine. I raised my eyebrows at him, and Luke Brooks did something I didn't even know he could do—he *blushed*.

"Let's go," Brooks said. He moved to the side and put his arm out, motioning for me to go in front of him. I shut my cabin door and walked toward his truck,

which was parked next to mine. Brooks caught up
to me.

"You've been riding the past couple of days, right?"

"Yeah. How'd you know?"

"Lucky guess. I figured you could use a day off." We
made it to the passenger side of the truck, and I went
to open my door, but Brooks beat me to it.

I couldn't remember the last time a man had
opened my door for me. I climbed into the cab, and he
made sure I was fully in before shutting the door.
When he climbed in on his side, he grabbed a pair of
aviators off the seat and slid them on.

As if he couldn't get any hotter.

"That coffee is yours." He nodded at the cup in the
cup holder closest to me. It was from the only coffee
shop in Meadowlark. Apparently, he could, in fact, get
hotter. I took a sip. It was perfect.

"I didn't know if your coffee order changed, so I just
got what I remembered. Drip, lots of cream, no sugar."

"It's perfect," I said. I couldn't even think of a time
when Brooks was around to hear how I took my coffee,
but here he was, remembering it like it was nothing. I
held the coffee in both hands and let it, and the
thoughtfulness that came with it, warm me through.

Brooks's Chevy K-20 only had a front bench seat,
and there was a bag in the middle. Even though I didn't
eat bacon, I recognized the smell. "And there's a veggie
breakfast burrito in there for you."

"And one with extra bacon for you, I'm guessing?"

Brooks had eaten enough meals at my home that I knew the man loved bacon. He and my brothers were bottomless pits when it came to food. When we passed dishes around the dinner table, my dad always made sure I got them first because if I got them last, there was a good chance there wouldn't be anything left, even with the giant portions we made.

"Obviously," he said.

I pulled my burrito out of the bag and started eating. Damn, the coffee shop had really stepped up their breakfast game. This was delicious. "When did you get rid of the C/K?" I asked.

Brooks smiled. "I still have it, but unfortunately, she's no longer in fighting shape. I bought this one off of a Devil's Boot patron last year."

"I like it." It fit him. It was classic and masculine.

"I do, too. Gus tried to talk me into getting a newer truck, but I'm not ready to give up the manual transmission or the windows that actually *roll* down," he said. "I'm happy to see you still have your truck."

Now it was my turn to smile. I loved my truck. I worked hard for it, and it was the first big thing I ever bought myself. "I'll drive that thing until I physically can't drive it anymore, and even then, you'll have to pry the keys out of my cold, dead hands," I said.

"You know that thing is ugly as hell, right?" he said with a grin.

"So are you," I quipped. I would not stand for this vehicle slander. "Where are you taking me, anyway?"

"You'll see," he said, his grin getting bigger. "I think you're going to like it."

"What gave you the idea for the field trip?"

"Since you've been home, you've only been to three places: the ranch, The Devil's Boot, and Teddy's house." He was right.

"All great places," I said. "Except for The Devil's Boot. I'm a little iffy on that one." Brooks flashed me a pointed look.

"Anyway. If you're going to be in Meadowlark, you might as well find some places to love in Meadowlark," he said. "I know it wasn't easy for you to come home, and even though you love your family and you love the ranch, those can't be the only things you love if you're going to stay here and be happy."

A small lump formed in my throat. That was thoughtful. Instead of talking, I took Brooks's breakfast burrito out of the bag, unwrapped it halfway so he could eat it while driving, and handed it over. It was a small gesture, but I hoped he'd get the point: thank you.

He gave me a quick smile before turning his eyes back to the road, breakfast burrito in hand. How the man could drive a manual transmission and eat a burrito at the same time was beyond me.

I thought about something my dad said the other day: Luke Brooks had a heart the size of the Rockies. I was starting to think it was true, and I wondered why I didn't notice it before.

Brooks and I drove for a while, probably thirty minutes. I absolutely housed my breakfast burrito but took a little more time with my coffee, savoring both the drink and the gesture. We made our way through town, which was basically just one road. From there, he got onto the highway.

A few miles later, he took an exit that led to a mountain road. Once we were off the two-lane, he slowed down enough that we could roll the windows down. I was grateful he waited until we were going slower. Usually, windows down on the highway made me a little overstimulated. There was just so much impenetrable noise. But having the windows down at this pace was heaven.

Wyoming summer air flooded through the truck, and the sun glinted off the hood. Brooks & Dunn was playing on the radio—one of Brooks's favorites.

I wondered if his name had anything to do with it.

He drove until the blacktop ended and then kept going down the dirt road that followed. It went up. We were going into the mountains. After a few switch-backs in the road, Brooks pulled his truck off to the side.

"We've gotta walk for a minute. Is that okay?"

"Are you bringing me out here to kill me?" I asked.

"Yep," he said neutrally.

"Damn. You could've at least told me to wear boots with some tread so I could go out with some dignity," I said. "Now I'm going to be slipping and sliding all over the place while I try to run away."

"Had to make sure I could catch you," he said. Why did that make me all...tingly? "But don't worry, it's a short walk, and it's mostly flat. We drove up the steep part."

Brooks got out of the truck, and I was close behind. There was a footpath that led into the trees. It was cooler up here but still warm.

Brooks and I walked in comfortable silence for a few minutes. While we were walking, I looked up. I didn't think there was anything that felt more magical than the way the sun broke through the trees.

We made our way out of the trees and into a small clearing. It was lush and green with patches of wildflowers throughout. I bet the entire clearing would be full of wildflowers if you came up here in April.

I could hear water running over rocks, so I searched for the source. On the far end of the clearing, there was a small waterfall that broke through the trees. The water from it flowed until it pooled in a spring.

Everything about it was serene. It was like a painting.

"How did you find this place?" I asked. My voice was awestruck.

"Luck. I found it pretty soon after I got my driver's license." He was beaming, the wrinkles around his eyes making an appearance as he started walking toward the pool of water. I followed, fighting the urge to run and jump into the crystal-clear water.

"How often do you come up here?" I asked.

"As often as I can. Summer is the best because you can swim, but in the winter, the waterfall freezes. It's incredible."

"Do you normally come up here by yourself?" I asked. *Translation: Do you bring a lot of women up here? Because this would be a damn good place to bring women.*

Brooks looked at me, his gaze earnest.

"This place is mine. You're the first person I've brought here."

"Oh," I said dumbly.

"Yeah, oh," he said with a smile.

"Not even Gus?"

"Not even Gus." I got this feeling in my stomach that was becoming a normal occurrence when I was around Brooks. I didn't know what to think about it or about the way he was looking at me. After a second, the look on his face changed into something more mischievous, and my stomach flipped.

What was happening to me?

He grabbed the hem of his shirt and brought it over his head. His hat came off with it. He threw it at my face. His shirt smelled like clean laundry and spearmint.

Why was he stripping? Not that I was opposed.

Not even a little bit. God, I was *so* weak.

It took me a second, but I remembered I was wearing a swimsuit. That was why he was stripping. We were swimming. He slipped off his boots and pulled his jeans down his legs. I tried not to stare, but damn.

Brooks had one of those bodies that was honed by hard work. His muscles weren't bulging, but they were well-defined, corded, and toned.

Don't even get me started on the fucking veins running down his forearms.

You couldn't get a body like his in the gym.

I took him in. Why didn't he have any tan lines? Was he just naked-baking in the sun? A vision of a naked Brooks flashed through my mind. I couldn't even chastise myself. I was shameless.

Someone should sculpt this man, I thought.

"Your turn," Brooks said, pulling me out of my quickly devolving train of thought.

"W-what?" I stammered. I was still staring at his body, not making eye contact.

"You're not going to swim in all your clothes, are you?" he asked.

Oh. Right.

I started unbuttoning my shorts, but the way Brooks was looking at me, combined with the fact that he'd brought me to "his place," made this entire situation feel weirdly...intimate.

I locked eyes with Brooks as I slid my shorts down my legs and stepped out of them. I watched him inhale sharply, and his eyes stayed on me as I pulled my t-shirt over my head and dropped it on top of my discarded shorts.

Was I imagining it, or did his nostrils flare?

"You ready?" he asked. His voice had definitely gotten deeper. I just nodded, afraid I would squeak like a mouse if I tried to speak. Brooks stretched his hand toward me. I took it, locking my fingers with his, trying not to think about how good it felt. "Fair warning," he said, "the water is going to be cold as fuck."

I let out a laugh.

Brooks wasted no time in pulling me toward the pool, breaking into a jog. I laughed again, louder this time. I reveled in what it felt like to be so free.

When we reached the edge of the pool, I didn't even think about it. I just jumped.

So did he.

Hitting the water was intense and wonderful.

Brooks was right—it was cold as fuck.

When my head went under the water, I couldn't hear anything. All I could feel was the water all around me and Brooks's hand in mine. After the war I'd been having with myself since I got thrown off that horse, my head finally felt quiet.

I made my way back to the water's surface, and when my head broke through, I took a deep breath. Brooks broke the surface shortly after me and used my hand that he was still holding to pull me to him. I instinctively wrapped my legs around his waist and felt my stomach flip.

Damn, he was smooth.

He had water dripping down his face, and he was smiling bigger than I'd ever seen. It made the crinkles around his eyes deepen, and it made me dizzy.

"Thank you for bringing me here," I said sincerely. I'd been here for five minutes, and I already loved it.

"It's nice. Someone else being here," he said. He didn't try to move me, so I stayed in the water with my legs around his waist. We were toeing a line I was desperate to cross. I tried not to think about the way my body was reacting to being with him like this. "How has riding been going the past few days?"

"It's been going okay. I want to try walking in the barrel pattern, but I don't know how I'm going to feel, and I know Maple is itching to fly, but I don't feel like I'm ready yet."

"Are you going to race when divisionals come to Meadowlark?" God, first Wes, now Brooks. Why were all of the men in my life reading the paper?

"I didn't know you read the paper."

"I'm a local business owner. I have to be well informed on Meadowlark happenings," he joked.

"I think I want to," I said. "Race, I mean." Admitting it to him at the same time I admitted it to myself. I didn't know how I would do it, but something about racing in my hometown called to me in a way I never thought it would.

"Then you should. You can do it, Emmy. Getting back on the horse is the hardest part." That felt like something a parent would tell their kid when they fell off their bike. I'd fallen off bikes and horses plenty of times, but this time was just different.

This time had shaken me in a way I didn't know was possible.

"But I don't just want to do it," I said, knowing just racing to race wouldn't be enough for me. "If I do it, I want to win." I always wanted to win. It was a problem.

"Then win." Brooks was still smiling, but this one was more thoughtful.

"You say that like it's a no-brainer."

"You're Clementine Ryder. You broke fifteen seconds in a race last year. It is a no-brainer." How did he know that?

"Yeah, and I'm currently averaging like five minutes to make a circle," I argued. "Just a slight difference."

"Two weeks ago, you couldn't get on a horse, so I like your odds," he said. "Besides winning, why do you want to ride?"

That was a hard question. Not because I didn't know the answer but because I did. I had no doubts about it. I wasn't sure what it was about this man that pulled out all the words that usually existed solely in my own head, but I wanted to tell him.

"I want a chance to say goodbye," I admitted quietly. I didn't even know if Brooks could hear me over the water.

"You deserve that," he said simply. The way he was looking at me made me want to stay right here, with my legs wrapped around his waist and his arms holding me to him, forever.

"You're not going to hound me about why I'm giving up my career or tell me I'm making a mistake?"

"No," he said. "Honestly, I'm curious about it, but the only person who needs to feel good about your decision is you, Emmy." From the look on his face, I think he really meant that.

"I don't know how I feel about it, honestly. All I know is I love to ride, but I don't want riding to be my everything anymore," I admitted.

"You know, if you don't like the road you're on, you can always pave a new one."

"Who said that? Robert Frost?"

Brooks smiled and shook his head. "Dolly Parton," he responded.

"Ah, God herself," I said with a laugh. "I feel like this decision has been a long time coming. My therapist in Denver was worried I was burning myself out."

"Were you?"

"Yeah. But in a different way than you're thinking," I said. He gave me a small nod, giving me permission to keep talking. "A few years ago, I was diagnosed with ADHD. I've always felt like I've been doing a million things at once, and I felt like I had to give all of those things all of my attention." I thought about the way being diagnosed had changed things for me. All of the sudden, I could explain why I did things the way I did. It was a revelation for me. It had made things different, but not in the way I expected. I'd hoped the diagnosis would be a fix-all, that I would no longer feel so desperate to be in complete control all the time, and that I would stop making impulsive decisions based on the fact that it made me feel like I was in charge of my own life for a minute.

That didn't happen. Instead, I would kind of know why I was doing something, but I wouldn't be able to stop myself from doing it. I kept on doing too many things and fixating on the things that made me feel like I had power.

"For a while, doing all of these things would feel incredible. It felt like I could accomplish a million things and not drop any balls. I did it in high school, I did it in college, and I did it in my riding career. I went too hard, too fast. It's like this cycle of hyper fixation. Riding has been more consistent than anything, but when I broke fifteen seconds on that record-breaking ride, my relationship with riding changed completely."

Brooks hadn't taken his eyes off me, listening to everything I had to say.

"It didn't bring me any joy, but I was still doing it because I couldn't stop. It was almost impulsive, the way I was training and riding in the months leading up to my accident. About a week before, I hit the wall.

"I lost my motivation. I was too overwhelmed; I was done. I withdrew into my head. My heart wasn't in it, and I wasn't riding to my level. If I was, I probably could've done something about the fall. Maybe not stop it completely, but I could've at least lessened the blow."

"The fall wasn't your fault, Emmy. Shit like that could happen to anyone," Brooks said. His tone was earnest.

"I know, but I've bailed off a horse a million times. I know how to do it safely, and I should've done that instead of letting the horse take me for a ride." I winced when I thought about what it had felt like to hit the fence, and I felt Brooks's thumb under the water make small circles on my ribcage. His touch was comforting.

"And the past few months, I've just been so damn tired. I've slept through my alarm more than I ever have. I stopped taking my ADHD meds. I sat in my apartment and didn't move, letting my life pile up around me, and I didn't even care."

"So, what made you come back home?" Brooks asked.

"Poor impulse control," I said honestly. He looked confused, and I felt like I needed to explain. "When I get the impulse to do something, it's hard for me to control when everything is normal. It's especially hard when I feel out of control anyway."

"But does it make you feel more in control?" he asked thoughtfully.

"For a minute, yeah."

"So, do you regret coming home?"

That was a damn good question. I thought about it. Honestly, I thought I would regret coming home, but I didn't.

"No, I don't. No matter how I came to that decision, it was the right one." I saw his shoulders relax the slightest bit at my answer. I didn't realize they were tense until then.

"Emmy, I want you to know I'm happy you're here." He was looking at me that way again. Like I was the only person on the planet like I was the only thing that mattered.

I could get drunk off that look.

My legs were still wrapped around his waist, and he was holding me to him. I could feel the heat of his hands on my skin, even under the water. I leaned in and rested my head on his shoulder.

"You know," he said. I could feel his lips in my hair. I wanted them everywhere. "I've learned more about you over the past two weeks than I have in twenty years."

"Ditto," I said. I wanted to know more. "Tell me something else."

"What do you want to know?" he asked. I wanted to know when he'd changed, but I didn't think I could ask about it outright. Mostly because I didn't know if he *had* changed if I had just never actually known him, or if it was a combination of the two.

Instead, I said, "You seem different."

"And?"

"I guess I'm just wondering when that happened." He was quiet. I hoped I hadn't said the wrong thing.

"Five years ago," he said finally. "A bunch of things happened to me at once. Riley was born, Jimmy died, I inherited a bunch of shit I didn't know my dad even had, and I got put in jail after a pretty bad bar fight.

"Your dad came to bail me out. He said I either be myself or be Jimmy, but I didn't get to be both. I don't know, it's like that just kind of connected something in my head. I think most things about me are the same. I just stopped actively working against myself."

My dad told me Brooks was his own worst enemy, so I could see how having something to work for could change that for him.

"Did you at least win the bar fight?" I asked, lightening things up a little.

"Obviously," he said. "But that fucker did break my nose."

"Ah, that's why it's so fucked up," I said. I felt his chest vibrate with a laugh. He moved his hands from my waist and unwrapped my legs from around his. *Damn*, I thought.

"You're a smart ass. You know that?"

"Me? Never." Brooks gave me a pointed look. I took that opportunity to hit him with the biggest splash I could muster.

"You little sh—"

Before Brooks could finish his sentence, I started swimming away, knowing he would come after me.

He did.

I lost track of time, but we spent the next while swimming in the springs, taking turns on the rope swing Brooks set up years ago, and talking the whole time.

We were sitting on the shore of the spring drying off when my stomach growled loudly, and Brooks said, "We should probably get out of here."

I didn't want to go, but I probably had a million missed calls from Teddy, wondering where I was. Brooks handed me my t-shirt and shorts from the ground. We dressed in silence and started our walk back to the truck.

Brooks laced his fingers through mine. At that moment, I made my decision. I was going to kiss this man.

Today.

13

LUKE

s we walked back to my truck, I couldn't
help but slide my fingers through Emmy's.
She intertwined her fingers with mine, and
damn, I felt like I was floating. I wasn't sure when we
crossed the line that led to this being okay, but damn,
I'm glad we had.

Today was the best day I'd had in a long fucking
time.

I opened her door for her but stopped her before
she got in by snagging one of her belt loops with my
fingers. I wasn't sure what I was going to do, but I
needed to do something. This woman took up every
piece of spare space in my brain, and I didn't want to
stay away from her any longer.

Honestly, I didn't think I'd be able to stay away
from her, no matter how hard I tried.

Emmy Ryder was just...more. She was more than anyone was, or than anyone would ever be.

She was kind and brave. She was also so fucking beautiful. It was getting more difficult not to let myself think of what it would be like to touch her, to claim her.

When she wrapped her legs around my waist in the water, I could feel the heat simmering underneath my skin. My attraction to her was intense, and I wasn't sure how much longer I could tamp it down.

"Emmy—" I started but didn't get to finish because she gripped my shirt in both of her hands and pulled my face to hers.

The second our lips met, it was like I was on fire. I was too shocked to do anything but stand there with one of my fingers in her belt loop, and her hands fisted in my shirt.

Emmy pulled away too soon, but she pressed her forehead against mine. "You've chickened out on kissing me twice, so I did it myself," she said. Her voice was breathy and perfect. The way she sounded made me overlook the fact that she'd just insulted me.

But she was right. And I hated that. Since when was I too shy to kiss a woman I was interested in?

I was going to have to make up for that. Immediately.

I needed to say something to her. Anything to keep her right here where I wanted her.

But I couldn't. Emmy Ryder had just willingly put

her mouth on mine. My brain was a pile of hay. Her grip loosened on my shirt, and she started to pull away. Her cheeks were red. Was she...embarrassed? *Shit. No.* That wasn't what I wanted. I wanted her mouth on mine. *Move, Luke, move.*

I couldn't let her get away from me. It was her almost doing so that finally forced me to kick my dumb ass into gear.

I pulled on her belt loop again. On instinct, I brought my hand up to her throat and hauled her mouth back to mine.

This time, I didn't just stand there.

I fisted my other hand through her still-damp hair, and she wrapped her arms around my neck. I couldn't get enough of her. This was everything.

She was everything.

I traced my tongue along the seam of her lips, begging for entry.

I would take whatever this woman would give me.

She let me in, and I dominated her mouth. Our kiss was hot and frenzied. She was clutching at my shirt again like she couldn't get close enough to me.

I was way ahead of her. I brought both of my hands down to cup her perfect fucking ass and lifted her off the ground. She wrapped her legs around my middle the same way she had in the water. It drove me insane then, and it was driving me insane now. I was already hard for her.

Emmy bit my lower lip, and I couldn't hold back any longer.

I turned us around so her back was facing the inside of my truck. I didn't break our kiss as I carefully moved both of us inside, pushing her along the bench until she was laying down, legs still wrapped around me, and I was on top of her.

Exactly where I wanted to be.

Her legs fell open, and I nestled myself between them. My mouth was still glued to hers. I was taking everything I could from her. Her body felt like it belonged under mine.

Between this and having to watch her in that goddamn swimsuit all day, I was probably about forty-five seconds from blowing in my pants like a fucking fifteen-year-old.

But I didn't care.

All I cared about was Emmy, about being close to her, about the fact that I finally had her in my arms.

She trailed her hands down my spine over my t-shirt, and I broke her kiss only so I could bring my lips to her neck. I could feel her pulse under my tongue. Her heart was beating as fast as mine.

I kissed a trail down to her collarbone, and she moaned. I wanted to memorize everything about her, with my mouth, my hands, my tongue.

"Fuck, Emmy," I said. My voice was hoarse. "You're so fucking perfect."

She moaned again, and I couldn't help but thrust

my hips into her. She brought her hands to my hair, knocking my hat off. I kissed my way back up her neck and to her lips again.

"Oh my god," she said against my lips. "More, I need more." I thrust again, and she moaned. I kissed her harder like I was trying to swallow her moans.

I traced my hand down over her breast and squeezed. Her breath hitched when I did it. I wanted that breath hitch imprinted on my brain.

"Emmy," I breathed. "If we keep going, I'm not going to be able to stop." She pulled away from my kiss and brought her hands to my face. She was looking me dead in the eye when she said:

"I don't want you to stop, Luke." I swallowed. Was she...? Did she want this like I did?

"What do you want, Emmy?" I asked. She was quiet for a moment. I could almost hear both of our heartbeats.

"I want you to fuck me in this truck. Please." *God damn*. Who knew Emmy Ryder had a mouth on her? One thing was for certain. I wanted her mouth all over me. It was like a switch flipped in my brain at those words. Any sort of reservation I had about doing this flew out the window. I wasn't just crossing the line–I wanted to blow that line the fuck up.

"That's what you want, sugar? For me to fuck you out here in the open?" I said, needing her to say it again. I needed her to tell me she wanted me.

"Yes, Luke. I want it so bad. Please." The way she

said my name sounded desperate. Just when I thought I couldn't get more turned on by her. The part of my brain that was determined to claim this woman took over.

"You want to feel me inside of you?" She moaned at my words.

"Oh god, yes. Please."

"*Fuck*." I kissed her again. This kiss was all teeth and tongues. We would have plenty of time for softness, but right now, all I could think of was how badly I wanted her.

She brought her hands to the hem of my t-shirt and started to drag it up my body. I pushed up her crop top so I could see the tops of her perfect tits.

I was about to lower my mouth to them when Emmy's phone rang.

Absolutely fucking not.

I sucked on her nipple over the fabric of her godforsaken red swimsuit. "Ignore it," I growled. She picked it up off the floor of the truck anyway. *Brat.*

"It's Gus," she breathed.

Well, shit.

I stopped what I was doing. Gus calling was the only thing that could distract me from the mission I was on right now, and that was to fuck Emmy senseless.

His little sister.

God fucking dammit.

I lifted myself off of Emmy. I took in how she

looked. Her hair was still damp and messier than usual, but *I* was finally the one who'd made her hair messy. Her lips were swollen from my kisses, and she had red marks on her neck from my mouth.

She was fucking devastating like this.

Her phone stopped ringing, and I took that as my cue to pick up where we'd left off. I was about to do just that, but then my phone rang.

I had a sinking feeling I knew who it was.

I pulled my phone out of my back pocket, and the screen showed Gus's contact.

"You have to answer it," Emmy said. "If you don't, he'll start looking for both of us."

She was right. I took a deep breath and brought the phone to my ear. "Brooks, here." Apparently, this was my go to greeting for Gus after I was just doing things I shouldn't be doing involving his little sister.

"God, the job interview greeting again?"

"I like it," I said. Emmy giggled and pushed herself up on her knees across from me. I gave her a warning look, but she just gave me a smile that made my cock twitch.

"You're getting weirder as you get older," Gus said on the phone. "Have you seen Emmy?"

You know, let me think, Gus. As a matter of fact, your baby sister just licked my fucking neck.

Jesus Christ.

This woman.

"No," I croaked out. "Why?" Emmy dragged her

nails softly down my chest and torso, stopping right above the waistband of my pants. My cock was hard for her, and there was no way she couldn't see exactly what she was doing to me.

"She's not in her cabin, and she's not at the stables. She's been helping you out down there, right?" Emmy, who was apparently a fucking succubus from hell, chose that moment to cup my dick through my jeans.

Fuck.

I bit down on my lower lip, but I couldn't control the small groan that came out. I grabbed her wrist and shot daggers at her.

"Yeah, but I haven't seen her today," I said. Emmy's wrist was still locked in my hand, but she wasn't deterred. She went back to kissing my neck.

"Huh. That's weird. She hasn't really left the ranch since she got here." Gus's voice was both concerned and annoyed.

"She's probably with Teddy," I said, trying not to think too deeply about the fact that I was lying to my best friend.

"Yeah, you're right. I'll try calling her again later."

"Is everything okay?" I asked, immediately unsure of why I would say anything that would extend this phone call.

"Yeah. We're just doing family dinner on Thursday. You can come if you want."

"Sounds good. I'll let you know if I see her." I felt Emmy's soft laugh against my neck.

"Okay. Are you out for a run or something?"

"No, why?"

"You sound out of breath." *No shit, Gus. I was three seconds away from tearing your little sister's clothes off when you called.* Emmy ran her nails down the front of my chest again, and I had to stifle a groan.

"Nope, just doing projects around the bar. I'll talk to you later, yeah?"

"Sure. Bye."

I hung up without saying anything, and Emmy laughed again. At a normal volume this time. I loved that sound.

I fisted her hair in one of my hands and pulled, forcing her head back so she was looking at me.

"I'm going to punish you for that, sugar," I said.

"For what?" she asked sweetly.

"For being a fucking cocktease while I'm on the phone."

"I can take it," she responded and then kissed me again. *Christ.* She was something else.

Was this my world now? Did I just get to kiss Emmy Ryder?

"I need to get you home," I said reluctantly. She pulled back from our kiss and gave me a pout. *Damn.* One near-fuck in my truck, and this woman had me wrapped around her finger.

Who was I kidding? I'd been wrapped around her finger since she walked into my bar.

"Don't look at me like that," I said.

"Fine. You can take me home, but you're going to have to make it up to me," she said, then planted a firm kiss on my mouth.

"Done," I said against her lips. I felt her smile.

I knew exactly how I was going to make it up to her, and when that happened, I wouldn't be rushed.

14

EMMY

"So was the phone call from your brother before or after you told Luke Brooks to 'fuck you in his truck?'" Teddy asked on the phone.

"Ted. You are absolutely not helping," I said. I wish I could say I regretted telling Teddy about what happened in Brooks's truck, but I was physically incapable of keeping this to myself. It was better to tell Teddy than accidentally blurt it out at dinner or something.

There was already so much I wasn't telling her—why I came home, the panic attacks—and I needed to balance the scales a bit.

"Just for some additional clarification," Teddy continued. "The 'fuck me in this truck' situation is a direct quote, yeah?" God, she was loving this. "I need to know so I can cite you when I write about this in my journal later."

"I regret calling you," I said.

"No, you don't. Plus, it's my birthday week, which means you're legally and contractually obligated to tell me everything concerning you and Luke Brooks."

"I don't remember signing this contract."

"Your dad signed it on your behalf when he started the monthly friendship payments."

"You're hilarious, and that joke isn't overdone at all," I said in my best monotone.

"We're getting away from the point," Teddy said. "I need to know the exact order of events if it was a direct quote, and what kissing Brooks is like."

I sighed. Teddy was like a dog with a bone. Once she had her goal in mind, there was no stopping her, so I might as well tell her what she wanted to know.

"It was before the phone call, yes, that is a direct quote from yours truly, and he is a very good kisser." More than a very good kisser. Hands down, the best kisser I've ever kissed. It was honestly irksome.

"Of course he is. There's no way he wouldn't be." I knew Teddy didn't mean it the way I took it, but it stung anyway. It was a reminder of who Luke Brooks was, and who he'd always been.

Yeah, I'd seen a different side of him recently, and I wanted to believe he didn't take other women to his favorite place—breakfast burritos and perfectly ordered coffee in tow.

But Luke Brooks had always been a playboy.

This was the man who told me a few days ago that he'd slept with his first kiss's *mom*. I had done some social media sleuthing after his admission, and I had to give it to him, Claudia's mom was hot.

"Emmy," Teddy said over the phone. "Where did you go?"

"Nowhere," I lied.

"Emmy, I didn't mean it that way." Damn. I forgot Teddy was an actual mind reader.

"No, I know, but it's true. Of course he's a good kisser because practice makes perfect." I thought about the way he grabbed my throat before pulling my lips to his.

I wasn't usually the type of girl who made the first move, but in this case, I was happy I did. It was like, as soon as I kissed him, it gave him the permission he needed to just let go.

He'd been so confident, so sure. The way he'd handled himself—the way he handled *me*—in that moment was just as intoxicating as the kiss itself.

"Do you want to know what I think about this whole situation?" Teddy asked.

"I'm sure you're going to tell me."

"I think you need to give Brooks more credit." Well, shit. That wasn't what I was expecting. At all. "He's obviously attracted to you and likes spending time with you. Have you ever known Luke Brooks to do something he didn't want to do?" She had a point.

"No," I sighed.

"Did you have a really nice day today?" she asked.

"Yes," I admitted.

"Do you like the way you feel when you're spending time with him?"

"You are so frustrating," I said into the phone. I dragged my hand down my face. Even though Teddy couldn't see me, I hoped she could sense the gesture.

"Answer the question, Clementine."

"Okay, fine. Yes, I like the way I feel when I'm with him," I snapped.

"Exactly. So maybe this is something and maybe it isn't, but you'll never know if you keep trying to fit Brooks in the same box you've had him in since we were thirteen. This version of him might be new, but I think it's worth getting to know."

Leave it to Teddy to make sense out of this distinctly nonsensical situation.

"What about Gus?" I asked.

"What about him?' Teddy responded, her tone bored.

"Brooks is his best friend. He is to Gus as you are to me, and I don't want my brother to lose that," I said. "I don't want Brooks to lose it either. Best friends are hard to come by."

"Listen," Teddy started, "I know Gus has that whole silent-but-deadly protector thing going on, but you can't let what Gus might think stop you from doing something you want to do. And I'm ninety-nine percent sure you want to do Brooks." That pulled a smile out of me. "Seriously, Emmy. It's okay to invite a little positive chaos into your world."

"Maybe for you," I said. Teddy loved chaos, but she could handle it. Teddy was the queen of rolling with the punches, or, when the situation called for it, punching right back.

"For you, too. Listen, if Gus finds out and throws a shit fit, I'll deal with him," she said. "I don't think there's any harm in getting to know Luke Brooks a little better."

"And when this entire situation blows up in my face?"

"I'll shield you from the wreckage," she said. I sighed, but Teddy was undeterred. "You know," she said, "you're sure sighing an awful lot for a woman who just got to have a good ol' fashioned make-out with one of the hottest men in Wyoming." Teddy had a point, yet again.

"He is hot, isn't he?" I said.

"He is. And so are you. You guys deserve to be hot together," she said. "Just don't overthink it, Em. If Luke Brooks turns out to suck, which I am *very* confident will not be the case, at least you got a hot make-out session and a burrito out of it."

"The burrito was good," I said. "The Bean has really stepped up their game."

"I know. I literally go there for lunch almost every day." Teddy worked at a small clothing boutique in town and sold her own designs on her website. "I would've taken you there, but apparently you only leave the confines of the ranch with Brooks."

"That's not true."

"It is, but I'll let you off the hook since you haven't been home very long. As long as you're leaving with someone."

"Why are you so pro-Brooks all of the sudden?" I asked.

"I have my reasons," she responded.

"Care to share?"

"Nope." She emphasized the 'p' with a pop. "I gotta go. I'll see you on Friday for birthday bevvies. Love you!"

A few minutes after I got off the phone with Teddy, Gus stopped by my cabin with Riley in tow. Riley wasn't great at knocking, but I didn't mind. She made it from my door to laying beside me on my bed in three seconds flat.

"Auntie, your cabin is really small," she said. "Dad's is way bigger."

"Well, both of you have to fit in your dad's cabin. This one is just for me," I responded.

"You don't have a friend like my mom? He lives with us now. They're getting married." Gus had told me Camille was getting married. He was happy for her, and so was I. Gus and Cam brought us Riley, but it was obvious to everyone, including them, that they weren't destined for romance. They were close friends and great co-parents.

"I don't have a friend like that, but it's good that your mom has one."

"Dad doesn't have a friend, either," Riley said matter-of-factly. Gus cleared his throat by the door.

"Where were you earlier today?" he asked. "I tried to call you."

Because I couldn't tell him I was making out with his best friend, I said, "I went into town. Got some coffee, had some alone time."

"Do you really need more alone time?" Gus asked pointedly.

"Dad, you said alone time is important," Riley chimed in. "That's why I can tell you when I feel like I need some."

"Yeah, *Dad*. Alone time is important," I teased.

"You're right, kiddo, but Auntie Emmy has alone time all day, every day."

I shot him a dirty look. Riley and I were still laying on my bed. She rolled onto her side so she could face me.

"Auntie, do you need me to visit more?" she asked. Her tone was so serious. It was adorable.

"You know," I said, "I do need you to visit more." Riley kissed her hand and then touched my face. It was a gesture she learned from Gus. He said our mom used to do that, but I wouldn't know.

"Okay, I'll visit more," she said. "But I won't bring Dad," she whispered. I laughed.

"What's so funny over there?" Gus asked.

"Nothing," Riley and I responded simultaneously. Gus looked at the ceiling as if asking for strength in that moment. I loved annoying him.

"Anyway," he said, "I just came down here to tell you we're having dinner tomorrow. It looks like Wes is going to get his guest ranch, but you know Dad won't sign off until we vote on it."

"I'll be there," I said.

"Good. Riley, let's go. I've gotta take you back to your mom's." I gave her a quick squeeze.

"Bye, sunshine. I love you."

"Love you, Auntie!" She bounded across my cabin and back to the door. Gus put a hand on her shoulder and started to guide her out.

"Oh, and Brooks is coming tomorrow, so please try to behave."

15

LUKE

W hat the fuck were you supposed to wear
when you were having dinner with the
girl you like's family, but that family was
also your best friend's family, and his dad was the
closest thing you ever had to one?

I had never once worried about what I was wearing
at the Ryders' or even in general. But this felt different.

Everything felt different after kissing Emmy.

I was still having a hard time believing that what
happened in my truck was real, or even that the entire
day had been real. I still couldn't get the image of her
laughing in the water out of my head or how she'd
looked underneath me.

Fucked. That's what I was: fucked.

I felt like I was going to walk into the Big House,
and all the Ryder boys were going to know I kissed
Emmy like someone wrote "I KISSED YOUR SISTER"

on my forehead with permanent marker without me knowing.

I ended up in my least worn-out pair of jeans and a plain black t-shirt. I spent thirty minutes agonizing, and this was what I came up with? Great.

I did decide to forego any sort of hat, which was a bigger decision than someone might think.

I quickly looked at my phone. It was already six fifty-four. Shit. There was no way I was going to make it on time. I might have grown up a little bit, but being on time was never going to be my strong suit.

I slid on my boots and headed out the door.

It took about fifteen minutes to get from my gravel drive to the front door of the Big House at Rebel Blue. I drove with the windows down and the music loud to drown out my thoughts.

I'd had dinner at Ryders' house a million times.

Everything was going to be fine.

When I pulled up, I noticed Teddy's truck was here, too. I'm sure Gus was thrilled. Wes was outside with his dog, Waylon, a big white Pyrenees. He was a marshmallow, inside and out. He was completely devoted to Wes, and he was a damn good farm dog.

"Hey, man," Wes called.

"Hey," I said. Waylon trotted up to me and dropped his tennis ball at my feet. I picked it up and gave it a solid throw into the trees. He took off like a shot.

"Only ten minutes late," Wes remarked. "Impressive." I gave him a small smile and shrugged my shoulders. Luckily, I'd always been a man of few words, so me not talking his ear off wouldn't be weird.

"Why aren't you inside?"

"Dinner won't be ready until seven-thirty, and Waylon kept whining by the door."

"The dinner timing was on purpose, wasn't it?" I asked. Wes just smiled. The Ryders were well-versed in Brooks Standard Time.

Gus was my best friend, but I was close to Wes, too. I fell right in the middle of their ages, so the three of us were together a lot. They were so different, though. Sometimes, it was hard to believe they were related, but one of their common denominators was how much they loved their little sister. They just showed it in different ways.

"Waylon!" Wes shouted. "Let's go inside." A white fluff ball darted out of the trees, and I followed Wes into the house.

When I walked in, I was immediately hit with the smell of home cooking. My mouth was already watering, and I hadn't even seen Emmy yet.

One set of tiny footsteps came charging toward the front door.

"Uncle Brooks!" Riley exclaimed as she jumped into my arms. I lifted her up past my shoulders and did a little toss. She squealed with excitement.

"Hey, what about me, kid?" Wes asked. She had run right past him. I loved this kid.

"I saw you already," Riley said. We walked toward

the back of the house. Gus was setting the table, and Amos was working in the kitchen. Rebel Blue had a cook, Ruby, who made breakfast and lunch for everyone on the ranch. There was a fridge and pantry that were open to the ranch hands, and they got a weekly grocery stipend since they had kitchens in their cabins. Ruby would leave dinner or leftovers for Amos, but he usually preferred to make his own. He liked to cook.

"Hey, Luke," Amos called from the kitchen. "Glad you could come."

"Wouldn't miss it," I responded. "It smells like heaven in here."

"Smothered chicken, mashed potatoes, and veggies are coming your way."

"I suggested a beef roast," Gus chimed in.

"Emmy doesn't eat red meat, though, right?" I said without thinking. *Shit*. Was I supposed to know that? Had I always known that? Was it weird I knew that?

"No, she doesn't, and Gus should know that," Amos responded. "And he should probably stop eating beef at every meal." He shot a pointed look at Gus. "You're getting old, and your cholesterol isn't what it used to be." I stifled a laugh.

"I'm thirty-four!" Gus exclaimed.

"Dad, you're *that* old?" Riley said. Everyone laughed except for Gus.

At that moment, the back slider opened, and in walked Emmy. It was a good thing I was still holding

Riley because if I wasn't, I probably would've dropped to my knees.

She was beautiful. I wondered if there would ever be a time when she didn't cause my heart to go from zero to one hundred in one second flat.

Her hair was pulled back away from her face. She was wearing an old, faded Broncos crewneck and denim shorts. I think it was the first time since she'd been home that she wasn't wearing her boots, just a pair of sandals that she slipped off when she came through the door.

"Hey, Spud!" Amos called from the kitchen. Emmy gave him a mock salute. It took her a second to notice Riley and me, but when she did, her eyes stopped on us for just a breath too long.

I got this weird feeling in my chest when she looked at me.

Maybe I needed some fucking Tums or something.

I saw Teddy come through the slider in my peripheral, but I still had my eyes on Emmy as she gave Wes a hug. When I pulled my eyes away from her, I noticed Teddy staring at me with a smug look on her face.

This was the second time she'd caught me staring where I shouldn't be staring: right at Emmy.

"Hey, Brooks," Teddy said. Her tone was amused.

"Teddy." I nodded at her.

"You look nice," she remarked. "Any particular reason you've chosen to forego the ratty-ass t-shirt and hat you're so fond of?"

Ruthless. Teddy was ruthless.

"Any particular reason you keep breaking your life-time Rebel Blue ban?" Gus chimed in before Teddy could hurl another missile my way.

"Yeah, to murder you in your sleep." Teddy had changed her tone to her sickly-sweet one—the one she reserved solely for insults.

"I would like to remind everyone that there are little ears present." That was Emmy. I looked over at her. She was standing next to Wes, and she had her arms folded. Her eyes were on Teddy, and she looked like she was trying to yell at her with her brain.

Considering how close those two were, I wouldn't be surprised if Teddy could hear her.

"Dad," Riley started, "what's a murder?"

"It's a group of crows, sunshine. Like a herd of cattle, but it's a murder of crows," Gus responded without pausing. Damn, he was quick on his feet.

"Why is Teddy getting you crows?" Riley asked.

"Because Teddy thinks she's funny."

"Teddy *is* funny," Riley said, her tone pretty damn matter-of-fact for a four-year-old. Everyone in the room laughed again at Gus's expense. He looked like he had just suffered the deepest betrayal.

Amos gave a single clap from the kitchen, getting everyone's attention. "On that note, let's eat. Everyone come grab a dish and bring it to the table."

I sat Riley down, and she scampered over to Amos. He gave her the salad. I started to walk over, but Emmy bumped against my shoulder. Her touch stopped me dead in my tracks. I looked down at her. She was giving me a small smile.

"Hi," she said.

"Hey." She linked our pinky fingers for half a second before continuing to the kitchen, stopping beside her dad, putting her palms up, and saying, "Dish me, daddio." Amos handed her a massive bowl of mashed potatoes. Her favorite.

Apparently I'd been storing a lot more information about Emmy over the years than I thought.

We all took our regular seats at the table. I was next to Wes, who was beside Riley. Emmy was across from me, and Teddy took the spot on her right. Amos and Gus took each head of the table. It was physically impossible for me not to look at Emmy. I hoped no one noticed the goofy smiles we couldn't help but give each other every few minutes.

We all talked for a while. Gus gave Amos some updates on a few ranch operations: estimates for baling season, which ranch hands were staying for the winter, and calving season. Wes had updates about irrigation and fences.

"Emmy," Amos started, "how are things going at the stables? Maple all settled in?"

"Yeah, she's good. The vet is coming over the next few weeks for everyone's end-of-summer check-up. She's doing the boarded horses, too."

"Anything we should be concerned about?"

"Whiskey's skin is really dry, so I've preemptively started her on some high protein feed." Whiskey belonged to Emmy's mom. She was old but still healthy.

"Good. Anything else?"

"Nope. Brooks does a good job down there. They're all taken care of." It was a pretty basic compliment, but coming from Emmy, it felt like I just won a Nobel Prize.

Amos turned his attention to me. "Any other updates, Luke?"

"No, sir. The last riding lesson of the summer is on Saturday, and we'll move them to the indoor arena in November," I said, stumbling over the first few words.

"Good. Teddy, I trust you don't have any updates for me?" Amos asked, making sure no one was left out of the conversation. Gus groaned at that.

"None directly related to the ranch, sir," Teddy said with a smile. I saw Emmy hit Teddy's leg under the table. Amos looked at both of them for a minute, obviously confused, but brushed it off.

"Alright. You all know we're here because we're seriously considering the addition of a guest ranch to Rebel Blue. Is anyone voting no?" The three Ryder children shook their heads.

Wes was beaming.

"Weston," Amos said with his best ranch-owner voice, "this is your project. You owe a budget and proposal to August, Clementine, and me by the end of next week. Deal?"

"Deal," Wes responded. You could almost see the excitement radiating off of him. Amos gave a firm nod.

"If the numbers don't add up, we don't do it. If they do, you're going to be expected to carry this project from start to finish. Are you ready?"

"Yes, Dad. I'm ready." There was no doubt in my mind Wes would blow this out of the water.

"Alright." Amos picked up his beer. "Cheers to the Rebel Blue Guest Ranch."

"Cheers," everyone said as they lifted their glasses, including Riley with her grape juice.

"Hey, Teddy," Wes started. "Do you think you could help me find someone to do the design work on the old Big House?"

"You know I design clothes, right? Not houses?"

"No shit. But you're, like, artsy and connected and stuff. Whoever you find is going to be better than who I come up with. I want this to be unique."

Teddy thought about it for a second. "Yeah, I actually know someone who I think could be really great for something like this. Let me reach out to her and see if she's open. When do you want to start?"

"Barring any hiccups with my proposal"—Wes shot a pointed look at Gus—"after calving season."

"Sounds good. I'll keep you updated."

"Thanks, Teddy."

The rest of the dinner was nice. With all of the business talk out of the way, conversation flowed. After dessert, Amos's famous peach cobbler, we migrated to the living room. Emmy and I ended up on the same couch, something that definitely did not escape Teddy's watchful eye, and it took all of my concentration not to touch her.

When the clock in the entryway struck half past nine, Gus stood from his chair. Riley was already asleep in his arms, with hers wrapped around his neck.

"We better head out so I can get this one in her own bed. Thanks for dinner, Dad." Amos gave Gus a handshake as Gus passed his chair and headed toward the front door.

A few minutes later, Teddy got up to go.

"Teddy, I saved some plates for your dad. They're in the fridge. There's enough for him and the nurse that's helping him out tonight," Amos said.

"Thank you, Mr. Ryder. I know he'll appreciate it." I didn't know much about Teddy's dad, but I knew he and Amos had been friends for a long time. Both of them were single dads who were just trying to make it work for their families.

"Tell him I'm going to come see him on Saturday, alright?"

"Yes, sir."

"Wes, help Teddy get all the food out to her car." Wes, who was laying on the floor with his cowboy hat over his face, let out a sigh and rolled himself up.

"Dramatic, much?" Emmy said with a laugh.

"I was almost asleep under there," Wes yawned. Emmy stood up and gave Teddy a hug before she and

Wes went to the kitchen and then out the front door. Teddy was saying something to him about an interior designer she knew.

"I should probably go down to my cabin, too." Emmy gave her dad a kiss on the cheek.

"Luke, make sure Emmy gets down to her cabin, okay?" I looked at Emmy. She looked like she didn't know how to respond to that. I didn't, either.

"Dad, it's 500 yards," is what she settled on.

"It's pitch-dark outside, and I haven't gotten around to adding some solar lights along the path. Just give your old man some peace of mind, eh? Luke doesn't mind. Does he?"

"Not at all, sir."

"Good," Amos responded. Emmy had a look on her face I couldn't place. She looked...nervous, maybe? "Have a good night, Luke. Goodnight, Spud."

"Night, Dad."

Emmy and I walked back to the slider. I opened it for her, and she slipped out first. We walked in silence for a minute before I intertwined my fingers with hers and gave her hand a squeeze.

She squeezed my hand back.

"Did you have a good time tonight?" I asked her.

"Yeah, I did. My first family dinner back. I missed it."

"Your dad was a ball of light tonight. I think he missed you, too." She was silent for a second. Maybe that was the wrong thing to say?

"Can I ask you something?" she said finally.

"Shoot."

"I feel like I need to start this with the disclaimer that I'm not asking you for anything, but what is this for you? Are you just messing around with your best friend's little sister?" I had to work hard to not let that sting. The truth was, I didn't know how to do this. I didn't know how to give Emmy what she needed, or how to be in any sort of relationship. I'd never done it before.

I'd never even wanted to try, but with Emmy, everything was different.

And it scared the hell out of me.

"God, no. Emmy, I would never do that to you or think about you as someone I would just mess around with. I want to spend time with you. Okay?" I was met with silence again.

We were approaching her cabin. I could see her porch light.

She didn't say anything until we were at her front door. "Okay," she said softly. "I want to spend time with you, too."

I turned to face her. "I'm serious, Emmy. I don't know when it happened, but I like you. I like you a lot more than I fucking should, and I know we shouldn't do this because a million things could go wrong, but you feel so *right*."

She looked up at me. "Okay."

"Good." I put my knuckles under her chin so I

could tilt her head up toward me and kiss her forehead. Emmy folded herself into my arms, and I held her for a minute. She fit in my arms like she was made for them. I'd like to think she was.

I wanted to tell her how much she meant to me, how much the past few weeks had meant to me, but I couldn't. Not yet.

Not when I felt like this whole thing could slip away at any moment. She could wake up tomorrow and decide I was nothing more than the screwed-up kid she knew and that I wasn't worth her time.

I didn't even know if she was planning on staying in Meadowlark. She could drive back to Denver before I'd even known she'd gone.

And Gus could kill me if he found out about us. That could happen.

"I should get to bed," she said. "I need to rest up before the Teddy Andersen birthday extravaganza tomorrow." I chuckled at that but didn't want to let her go.

"Teddy doesn't do anything halfway, does she?" Emmy shook her head.

"I'll see you on Saturday? I'm coming to Riley's lesson."

"Okay," I said. I wasn't ready for this to end. I wanted her so badly. I'd driven myself crazy not being able to be near her all night. She looked so perfect in her little denim shorts. It was like everything about her was designed to drive me crazy.

Emmy pulled away, pushed her door open, and turned back to me.

"I like you, too, Luke." Those words hit me hard enough to knock the wind out of me. "Goodnight."

I couldn't untangle my tongue fast enough. "Goodnight," I responded, but not until a few seconds after she shut the door. *Nice*.

I turned and started walking toward the Big House in a daze. I paused and looked up at the big Wyoming night sky. It was incredible how many stars were up there.

I couldn't believe the universe was so big, and I got placed on this random floating rock at the same time as Clementine Ryder.

Before I even knew what I was doing, I was turning around and starting back toward Emmy's cabin as fast as I could.

I wanted her, and I'd be damned if I was going to let her get away from me.

16

EMMY

Saying goodnight to Brooks had been a good decision. A smart decision. After I'd been staring at him all night, it was honestly a miracle I didn't try to tear his clothes off as soon as we walked out the back door.

Literally, the first thing I saw when I walked into the Big House was him holding my perfect niece in his giant arms. My ovaries didn't stand a chance.

And don't even get me started on his hair. For someone who liked hats so much, you'd think he was hiding a receding hairline or something, but no. He had a full head of hair, and he looked just as good without a hat as he did with one.

It was no secret Brooks in a backward baseball cap was my kryptonite, but there was something about being able to see his full head of dark hair that just did it for me tonight.

Me salivating over Brooks's appearance? That was expected. I'd been doing that forever, even when I didn't like him. Brooks telling me he liked me? Unexpected. Me believing him? Also unexpected but not unwelcome.

The way his face looked when he said it had been so intense and earnest. There was no way I couldn't believe him.

Was I stupid to let him walk away tonight? That could've been one of those moments. The ones that seem small but turn out to be big. The ones that change the course and alter your path.

I wanted that. A new path.

I wanted him.

I didn't think before I swung my front door back open, ready to chase after him.

But I found Brooks right where I'd left him. But now, his chest was heaving like he had left and run back, and his arm was raised like he was about to knock.

We stared at each other, and I decided *this* was the moment. Not the moment that could've been if I hadn't closed the door on him, but a better one—a moment both of us chose to come back for.

That's the thought I was mulling around in my brain when Brooks said, "I can't stay away from you anymore."

He took a step forward, grabbed both sides of my face, and kissed the hell out of me. When his lips were on mine, I couldn't think at all.

I fisted my hands in his t-shirt and tried to get as close to him as humanly possible. He started walking me back through my door, and I let him. I was desperate to know where this would take us.

Once we were both inside, he pushed the door shut with his foot. He moved his hands from my face and dragged them down my body—down my neck, over my breasts, and around my waist until he cupped my ass and lifted me off the ground. I wrapped my legs around his middle, clinging to him.

He turned us around, so my back was against my front door. His tongue was in my mouth, taking and taking. I wanted him to take it all. I moved one of my hands from the front of his shirt to his thick hair.

God, I wanted him.

It took some effort, but I pulled back from his mouth. He was undeterred. He just moved his mouth to my neck and started kissing me there. I couldn't help but let out a small moan. It was like he knew exactly where to touch me.

"Luke," I breathed. He didn't answer, just tightened his grip on my ass. He had changed the position of his hands. They weren't over my shorts anymore but under them. It was his skin on mine, and the sensation of it was intoxicating. "Luke," I said again. He pulled away this time. His eyes were on fire.

"Do you want me to stop?" he asked.

"No, I—" I stumbled a little bit. "I don't want you to stop. I want it all." His eyes burned brighter.

"Are you sure?" he asked.

"I'm positive." And I was. I didn't know the last time I felt so sure about something.

"I don't have a condom with me." Luke Brooks wasn't just packing around an industrial-size box of condoms? That was a bummer for everyone.

"I have an IUD," I said. "And I had a doctor's appointment a few days before I left Denver. I'm all clear."

"So am I."

Thank god.

"Are you sure?" he asked again. "I don't want to pressure you into this."

"You're not," I promised. "I want this. I want *you*." I cupped his face in my hands when I said it, his stubble scratching at my palms in the most wonderful way.

"If you change your mind at any point, you tell me right away, okay?" He turned his head to place a gentle kiss on one of my palms.

"I'm not going to," I said.

"Say that you'll tell me if you change your mind." His voice was firm. I loved it.

"I'll tell you."

He took a deep breath, like hearing that was the thing that might snap the tether he had on himself.

"God, Emmy, I want you so fucking bad."

"Then have me," I said. He didn't think twice. He

crushed his mouth to mine again and started carrying me to my bed.

I was a tall woman, and most of the men I'd slept with hadn't been much taller than me. I didn't know I minded until I was with Luke. The way he was able to pick me up and fucking manhandle me was hot as hell.

Before we made it to my bed, he set me on my feet.

"Strip," he said. His voice was low and gravelly, and it shot straight through me. "I want to see you." He took a few steps back, and I could see his dick straining against his jeans.

Seeing that he wanted me filled me with a confidence I didn't normally have.

I started with my crewneck. I had a tank top underneath it, but no bra. "Take your shirt off," I said to Brooks. My voice was breathy and almost unrecognizable. Brooks immediately did what I asked, whipping off his black t-shirt. The hard muscles of his stomach and chest were lightly covered with dark hair. It was cliché, but up until now, I had been with boys. Luke was a fucking man.

"Keep going, Emmy," he said. "Let me see you."

I unbuttoned my shorts and slid them down my legs. I thought back to the springs and how I was so nervous to take my clothes off and be in my swimsuit. Now, I couldn't wait for Brooks to see all of me.

I took my tank top off, and I heard Brooks let out a low growl. I'd never understood the phrase "his eyes darkened" that was in all the romance books Teddy loaned me, until now.

The way he was looking at me was all-consuming. Brooks started toward me, but I stuck my arm out to stop him. He stopped immediately.

"Your pants. I want them off."

Brooks's large hands went to his belt, and his jaw tensed. "That's the last command you give me," he said. Fuck, I knew he'd be this way in bed. "I'm in charge tonight. Do you understand?" Everything about him was all-consuming, and I didn't trust my voice to answer him.

I nodded my head. I wanted him to be in control. I trusted him to take care of me.

"I asked you a question, sugar." He wasn't going to let me get away with just a nod.

"Y-yes. I understand."

"Good." He undid his belt, dropped his jeans, and stepped out of them. His dick was straining against his black briefs.

"Stop staring at my cock like that, sugar."

My eyes shot back up to Brooks. "L-like what?"

"Like you want me to put you on your knees and shove it down your throat." *Jesus*. I licked my lips as I stared at him. "Would you like that, sugar? My cock in your hot little mouth?" I would. I definitely would.

I nodded.

He was on me in an instant, grabbing my throat and devouring me with his kisses. He picked me up again before sitting on my bed, so I was straddling him. I could feel his hardness against my blue panties, which were so soaked it was almost embarrassing.

I ground against him, and he groaned.

"Fuck. You're so fucking perfect," he said against my lips. I couldn't help but continue to grind against him, wishing there wasn't anything between us, but I didn't want to stop. This felt so *good*. I could probably come from this friction alone. He rubbed his hands up and down my back. "That feel good, sugar?" he asked, his breaths short. "You rubbing your pussy all over my cock?"

"Yes," I moaned. He pulled away from my mouth and bit my neck. I let out a yelp, and he smoothed his tongue over the bite.

"Keep going, Emmy. Make yourself come like this." I mean, if he said so. I started moving faster. The friction was delicious. I put my hands on his shoulders for balance. God, I was feeling so many things at once. I didn't remember the last time I was so turned on.

Or the last time I felt so desired and wanted.

"That's right, sugar. Keep riding me." Brooks's words of encouragement spurred me on. So did his hand on my ass and the other on my breast. "So fucking perfect. I can feel how wet you are." I was so close. I went faster, chasing what he was offering to me. When he gave my ass a light smack, all sense of rhythm left me, and I rode him with reckless abandon.

"I know you're close. C'mon, sugar, let me feel you come."

A few more seconds, and I was breaking apart at the seams. My body was racked with shakes as pleasure coursed through me. I'd never come so hard, and neither of us had even taken our underwear off.

I looked down at Brooks, and his eyes were on me. He knotted his fingers in my hair and kissed me. It was hot and rough.

"You're so beautiful when you come." He stood up and threw me on the bed. Literally threw me. "I can't wait to watch it again," he said.

He stood at the bottom of my bed and finally took his briefs off. His dick jutted out from his body. I could feel he was big, but seeing it was different. I couldn't wait for him to be inside me.

He got on the bed and crawled his way up my body. The way his muscles flexed as he held himself to hover over me almost sent me over the edge. He stopped his journey at my stomach so he could lick all the way from my ribs to my breasts.

He circled my left nipple with his tongue, and my back arched off the bed. He bit down softly before moving to the other side. He continued switching between them while one of his hands made its way down to my underwear.

He brushed his thumb over my clit above my panties, and I jerked. I could feel his smirk against my breast. "Feeling sensitive, sugar?" he asked.

"A little," I breathed. He answered by moving my panties to one side and pushing one of his fingers into me. We both groaned.

"*Fuck*, you're so wet. Is this all for me?" I let out a sound he must've correctly interpreted as a yes because he pushed another finger inside me. The sounds of his fingers pumping in and out of me were obscene.

Between his fingers and his mouth on my breasts, I was so close to coming again. It had never been like this for me. I didn't know how to handle it.

He licked all the way up my neck before kissing me again. When he pulled away, he also pulled his fingers from me, and my body ached at the loss. He was hovering over me, looking directly into my eyes as he brought them to his mouth and sucked.

His eyes closed as if he were savoring the taste. Then he brought them out of his mouth with a lewd pop. "You want a taste?" he asked me. Being with Luke felt erotic and freeing. I'd never done anything like this before.

To my own surprise, I nodded.

He pushed his fingers into me and pumped a few times. My back arched off the bed, and my body started to grind of its own accord, but he removed his fingers again. God, he was so frustrating.

He wiped them over my lips before putting them in my mouth.

"Suck," he said. I did. I sucked myself off his skin

like a mad woman. "Good girl." The heat that flooded my body at his praise was unexpected but not unwelcome.

"You taste like a dream," he said. "I need more." He started moving down my body again, situating himself between my legs and draping one of them over each of his shoulders. Spreading me out like his own personal feast.

"Luke..." I started.

"Yeah, sugar?"

"You don't have to do that," I said, feeling the insecurity that sometimes crept up on me during sex start to rear its ugly head.

"Eat your perfect pussy?" he asked. He looked up at me from between my legs, and I wished I could take a picture. I blushed. I had stripped for him, ground on his dick until orgasm, and sucked myself off his fingers, but this made me blush?

"Y-yeah, that."

"I want to. Badly. But I won't if you're not comfortable with it."

"I-it's not that." He studied my face, waiting for me to keep talking, but I didn't.

"Talk to me, sugar."

"I-I've n-never come that way, so it's just not worth your time." The men I'd been with before had done it like it was just the last pitstop before getting all the way into my pants, and it always turned me off.

"Not worth my time?" He sounded...angry? "I don't

know what type of men you've been sleeping with, sugar, but devouring your perfect cunt is always going to be worth my time." I gulped and felt heat flood me again.

"I'll tell you what. If it's okay with you, let me fuck you with my tongue for a few minutes, and if it isn't doing anything for you, we'll move on. Yeah?" That sounded...reasonable.

"Okay," I agreed. Even though I knew this wouldn't do anything for me. It never had.

"Hand me a pillow, and then lift your hips." I did what he said. He slid the pillow under my hips. Luke kept his eyes on me as he lowered his mouth to my pussy, and as he gave me one long lick all along my seam. Then, he started doing exactly what he said he was going to do: he devoured me.

He slid his fingers back in me as his tongue swirled and flicked at my clit. He used the pad of his tongue to replicate the pressure I'd felt when I was grinding on him. Between that and his fingers, the pressure was starting to make its way down my spine.

This had never happened to me before.

Holy shit.

Usually, I came from getting on top, so I could feel pressure against my clit–or I just didn't come and would finish myself off later.

Luke kept going. He was a man on a mission, and nothing was going to stop him. I had my hands in his hair—one of their favorite places to be, apparently—

and my hips started to buck, and everything I felt was too much. I knew I was moaning loudly and incoherently, but I didn't care.

"Oh...Luke...I'm going to..." I looked down and noticed Luke was thrusting against the mattress.

Was this...turning him on? Did that happen?

It was that thought, that Luke was turned on by the fact that he was bringing me pleasure, that sent me over the edge. For the first time ever, I came from someone going down on me. Not just anyone–Luke Brooks.

I wasn't convinced this man didn't have magical powers.

He looked up at me and licked his lips before crawling back up my body and kissing me hard on the mouth. He was hovering over me, and that would *not* do. I wanted all of his weight on me. I reached down and put my hands on his hips, pulling them down to meet mine.

We both gasped when his dick made contact with me. "I need you inside of me," I said.

He used one of his hands to trace my jaw. "My greedy girl came all over my tongue, and now she wants to come on my cock?"

"Yes, please, Luke. Please," I pleaded.

"Fuck, baby. Your begging is going to make me come."

"Then you better get inside of me."

Luke kissed me again. "Needy girl," he said. I was. I

didn't care. Luke reached down and positioned his dick at my entrance. He looked at me as he started to work himself in. Fuck. He was big. Just the head of his cock stretched me more than I was used to.

"You're so big," I said.

"You can take it, sugar. I'll go slow." I nodded. He pulled out and worked back in, going a little further, stretching me a little more. He did that again, and again, and again.

Finally, I felt him seat himself fully inside of me. The pillow was still under my hips, giving him the ability to get deeper than he would've otherwise. He groaned into my neck. God, adjusting to his size was going to take a second.

"You feel so good wrapped around my cock." A man had never talked to me like this. Usually, when someone tried to talk dirty with me, it just sounded weird. But all of Luke's dirty words just made me hotter, which I didn't even know was possible at this point.

"I feel so full," I breathed. When he was inside me, I could feel everything. Every sensation was amplified —the way the cool air felt on my hot skin, the slight burn left behind by his stubble, the way the hair that fell over his forehead brushed against my cheeks.

"God, you're perfect."

I started grinding my hips, trying to get him to move.

"Give me a second, baby," he breathed. "I've gotta

make this last." I pulled his mouth back to mine and kissed him, tangling my tongue with his. After what felt like an eternity, Luke pulled out a bit and then thrust back in slowly. He did it again. And again, picking up a little speed each time.

"Fuck, Luke. Yes. Yes."

"Emmy, you were made for me." He found his rhythm, and fucked me relentlessly. The pressure started building in my spine again, making its way down as Luke fucked me. It was going to happen. This man was going to make me come three times, which had never happened to me.

"I want you to come again, sugar. I want to feel you come while you're wrapped around my cock. Can you do that for me?"

"Y-yes," I groaned. Like he knew exactly what I needed, Luke kept the same rhythm but increased the intensity of his thrusts, almost moving me up the bed with each one of them. The pressure in my spine hit its peak, and I came with a cry.

After I came, Luke picked up his speed and pounded into me. I clutched at his shoulders, over-whelmed by everything I was feeling. Every nerve in my body was alive.

"God, I can't wait to fill you up," he said huskily.

I couldn't wait for that either. I wanted to feel it. I wanted to feel *him*.

"Please," I begged. "I need it." At that, his thrusts became sporadic and uneven. He was close. "Come inside me, Luke." He groaned, and his body shook as he emptied himself.

He collapsed on top of me and buried his face in my neck. "Fuck," he said before sliding his arms underneath me and rolling us so I was on top of him.

I laid my head on his chest and listened to his heartbeat, like a kickdrum, start to slow. "That was incredible," I said.

"You're incredible," he said. "I could bury myself inside of you every second of every day and never get tired of it."

"Is that a promise?" I asked as I lifted my head to look at him. After-sex Luke should be put in a museum. His dark hair was mussed, and his brown eyes were bright and intense. His smile climbed all the way up to his eyes so the wrinkles on the outside of them appeared. I was such a sucker for those.

"Do you want it to be?"

"I wouldn't mind." And I wouldn't. I'd never had sex like this before. I didn't think I was having bad sex before, but after having sex with Luke, I wasn't convinced.

He was dragging his fingers up and down my back gently.

"I can't believe that just happened," I said. "My thirteen-year-old self would be levitating right now."

Luke's chest vibrated with laughter underneath me. "Yeah? Was she a fan?"

"A fan of your looks, yes."

"Ouch."

"Don't worry, twenty-seven-year-old me thinks you're moderately less annoying." I pushed up on my elbows to kiss him. He wrapped one of his hands around the back of my head, cradling it. This kiss was slow and exploratory. It was our first kiss like this. I knew it wouldn't be our last.

AN HOUR LATER, after a bathroom break, maxing out the number of people who could fit in my shower, and another orgasm for each of us, I fell asleep in Luke Brooks's arms.

For the first time in a long time, I felt safe.

17

EMMY

I woke up to the sun streaming through my window. It took me a minute to realize the weight draped over my waist was a human arm. It took another minute for me to remember who it belonged to.

I slept with Luke Brooks.

And it was fucking incredible.

He must've felt me stir because his arm tightened around me before he kissed the back of my neck.

"Good morning, sugar," he said. Damn, his morning voice was definitely the hottest of all his voices.

"Good morning," I responded as I turned my neck just enough for him to give me a sweet good morning kiss. "Did you sleep okay?"

"Like a rock. You?"

"I slept okay, but I had this huge cowboy wrapped around me."

"That so?" He continued to kiss at my neck, and the hand at my waist started rubbing circles up to my ribcage.

"Yeah," I replied. "It was like sleeping in the same bed as a boa constrictor." I felt his chest move against my back with a small chuckle.

"Must be one needy cowboy," he said. He moved his circles under the tank top I'd put on before bed. They were larger now, going over my ribcage, to just under my breasts, and rounding out right above the front of my panties before going back to my waist and starting again.

And he had called me a tease?

His kisses traveled from the back of my neck to my ear, and I could feel him hardening behind me. "You really are a needy cowboy," I breathed, getting more turned on by the second.

"Says the woman who's pushing her ass against my cock at seven in the morning."

"You started it," I retorted.

"I plan to finish it, too." God, his *voice*. I should make him read a scene out loud from one of the books Teddy and I read last month. He continued his slow and frustrating circles, getting closer and closer to where I wanted him.

After what felt like an eternity, his pinky finally

dipped below the waistline of my panties, but his hand kept moving.

Two could play that game.

I arched my back and pushed my backside into his hardness. He groaned. *Good.*

This time, when his circle made its way back to my panties, his hand dipped inside and stayed there.

"You're already so wet for me." He started to toy with my clit. "So fucking wet." Two of his fingers dipped inside me, but he kept his palm against my clit so I could feel the friction as his fingers moved in and out.

My hips started moving of their own volition, and he started to grind harder against my ass. Fuck. I was already aching for release.

"That's right, sugar. Ride my fucking hand."

I moaned. "Luke, I need you inside of me."

"Beg for me again, sugar."

The effect he had on me was almost embarrassing. I would beg for him as much as he wanted.

"Inside of me, please."

"Fuck, you beg so pretty. I could get off on just that."

He pulled his hand out of my panties, and I hated the loss. He put some space between us, but only for enough time for him to get his briefs off. I slid my underwear off at the same time. A second later, his front was pressed against my back, and one of his arms moved under me and grabbed my breast. I could feel his hard cock against me. He trailed his fingers down my spine, leaving fire and goosebumps in their wake, then over my ass and between my legs from behind. He lifted my leg and snaked his arm under my bent knee.

"Can I fuck you like this, baby?"

"You can fuck me any way you want." I was very serious about that.

He guided himself inside me from behind, slowly. It'd been less than five hours since we last did this, and it felt like too long.

"God, I can't believe you let me fuck this pussy bare." This man and his dirty mouth. He started to move behind me, and the arm that was holding my leg came to stroke my clit.

He fucked me and stroked me in tandem, his fingers and his cock working in sync to bring me to oblivion. I didn't know which way was up or down. All I knew was I never wanted this to end.

"Yes, Luke. Oh, god. Yes," I whimpered.

"You like the way I fill you?"

"Yes. Yes." When he was inside me, one-syllable words were my only option. My whole body started to clench while Luke pounded into me. I let out a cry.

"That's right, Emmy. Take my cock. Take it every time. It's yours as long as you want it." I was so close. So fucking close, and he knew. "Tell me what you need, sugar. Tell me what you need and it's yours."

I moved one of my hands to rest on top of his hand that was stroking my clit. I pushed down, applying more pressure, and started grinding my hips against him for more friction. "*Fuck*, Emmy."

Both of our movements were becoming more and more frantic. Luke's words devolved into moans, and I came apart. I felt him stiffen behind me, but he kept his fingers on my clit and stroked me through my orgasm, wave after wave.

After a few minutes, we both came down from our high. Luke clung to me. Our bodies were sticky with sweat. I turned to face him. He had a lazy smile on his face that made me want to jump his bones...again.

Luke lifted his hand to my face and tucked my hair behind my ears. "You are something else, Emmy Ryder." His eyes were soft, content. Like he could stay here with me all day. The way he was looking at me turned my heart upside down.

If I wasn't careful, I could fall head over heels for this man before I even knew what was happening.

We were jolted out of our bubble by a knock at my cabin door. Why were people always fucking knocking?

"Emmy? Are you awake?" It was Wes's voice. Shit. Shit. *Shit*. Both Luke and I looked at each other like deer in the headlights. "Emmy?" Wes called again.

I snapped into action, throwing the comforter off of me and bolting out of bed. Luke was right behind me. I found a t-shirt on the ground and pulled it over my head, along with a pair of pajama shorts. "Hide in the bathroom. Now," I said to Luke as he was doing that little jump thing to get his jeans all the way on.

Everything he did was hot.

I started toward the door. "Hey," Luke whisper-yelled. I turned back toward him and he came up to me, giving me a quick peck on the lips before flashing me a smile that turned my heart into a puddle at my feet. "Okay, you can answer the door now."

It took a second for me to remember what he was talking about. Oh yeah, my brother was at the door.

"One sec!" I called. I waited until I heard my bathroom door click before swinging the front door open.

"Good morning, sunshine," Wes said with a hint of sarcasm while taking in my appearance. *Shit*. I hadn't even looked in a mirror. I probably looked like some sex-crazed heathen. "Long night?"

"Why do you say that?" I hoped my voice was even.

"Because you look like you just rolled out of bed, and your hair is a mess. Like, more of a mess than usual."

"Oh, yeah. I didn't sleep a lot last night." That was the understatement of the century.

"Looks like it. I've been trying to call you."

Whoops. "I forgot to plug my phone in last night. What's up?"

"Three of our ranch hands caught a stomach bug, and I've got a shit-ton of broken fence on the south side of the ranch. Mind helping your favorite brother out?"

I hadn't been over that way since I'd been home. "Sure. It's Teddy's birthday, though, so you're not roping me into anything else."

Wes put his hand over his heart. "I swear. I would never get in the way of Teddy and her birthday." He'd known Teddy long enough to know her birthday might as well be a national holiday.

"Okay. Let me get dressed, and I'll meet you at the stables." *Translation: please leave so I can sneak one of your friends out of my cabin without anyone seeing.*

"'Kay. I'm going to go down there and see if Brooks can help, too."

My heart dropped. "Oh, is he down there?" I asked. Neutrally, I hoped.

"Well, his truck is at the Big House, so he must've got here early. He's normally not here on Fridays, so gotta take advantage of it while I can."

Oh god. Luke's truck. We left his truck up there for my family, who all literally wake up at 4:00 AM because they're ranchers, to see.

"Got it. See you down there?"

"Yeah. Thanks, Em."

I gave him a mock salute before shutting my door and resting my back against it.

What a fucking morning.

Luke poked his head out my bathroom door.

"All clear?" he asked.

"All clear." He walked toward me and wrapped his arms around my waist. How did he smell so good in

the morning? Like spearmint and...man. I wanted to
bottle it.

"We should talk about that," Luke remarked.

"Talk about what?" I asked, even though I knew
what was coming.

"Your brother. Your *brothers*."

"What about them?"

"If we're going to do this, I don't want to hide from
them, Emmy." The feeling in his voice kicked me in the
back of my knees and made me feel unsteady. "I've
been people's dirty little secret before, and I didn't care
because I didn't care about them, but I care about *you*."
His voice was firm, but still soft and kind. I didn't want
him to be my secret, but I didn't even know what this
was yet.

I needed a second.

"I understand. Just give me a little more time,
okay?" Luke's face fell slightly, and a knife in the hand
probably would've hurt less than watching that
happen. We regarded each other in silence for a while.
I watched his mind work through what he wanted
to say.

Finally, he said, "Okay, but we're going to talk about
this again."

That was the best response I could've gotten.

"Okay." I pushed up on my toes and kissed him.
"You should get going. You've gotta figure out why your
truck's here but you're not at the stables, and I've got
fences to mend."

"Thanks for the reminder. I'll talk to you later?"

"Yeah."

He kissed me again. It was so easy to get carried away with him.

Luke pulled away and pressed his forehead against mine. "Before I go, I need something from you."

"What's that?" I asked, secretly hoping it was something dirty.

"My shirt."

18

EMMY

I rolled my truck into Teddy's driveway around four in the afternoon. I had strict instructions to not bring any "going out" clothes for later, which meant Teddy already had something in mind and she would not be deterred.

Teddy loved to make clothes, and she was good at it. She started embroidering flowers on the back pockets of our jeans in junior high.

In high school, she started selling reconstructed vintage denim jackets out of the bed of her truck at the Meadowlark farmers market.

In college, she majored in business but tacked on a double major in fashion merchandising.

She was insanely talented, and tenacious. If anyone could make it, it was Teddy.

I knocked on the door before letting myself in. The entry to the Andersen home led right into their living room, where Hank, Teddy's dad, was sitting in his chair watching *That 70's Show* reruns. His long black hair was mostly gray these days, but his blue eyes were as bright as ever.

Hank was a rockstar—literally. He was on tour as a drummer when he met Teddy's mom. They had a magical night before going their separate ways. Eleven months later, she showed up at a show with a month-old baby who she hadn't even bothered to name.

According to Hank, he loved Teddy from the moment he saw her. He named her after a famous jazz singer: Theodora King. He left his band and took his baby girl to a small town he had passed through in a tour van a few years earlier. He got a job, and the two of them started their life as a family of two.

The town was Meadowlark, Wyoming, and the job was at Rebel Blue Ranch.

Neither of them ever saw Teddy's mom again.

I wondered what my life would have been like if my dad had decided not to take a chance on the wide-eyed drummer with a baby and absolutely no ranch hand experience.

"Hey, Emmy. How the hell are ya?" Hank's gruff voice was cheerful.

"I'm good, Hank. How are you?"

"I'm survivin'." He meant that literally. Hank didn't say things he didn't mean. That's where Teddy got it from.

Before Teddy, Hank lived the "sex, drugs, rock n'

roll" life. At this point in his life, it had resulted in a lot of health issues. He currently had at-home care and used an oxygen tank.

That's why Teddy decided to live at home after college. She didn't want to leave him.

"And looking damn good doing it." Teddy appeared in the hallway. When she made eye contact with me, her eyes became laser focused. "You look particularly glowy today, Clementine." God dammit. I truly couldn't get anything past Teddy. "What did you get up to last night?" The tone in her voice told me she already knew.

"Teddy, she just got here," Hank chimed in. God bless him.

"Yeah, Teddy, I just got here," I said innocently.

Teddy continued to stare at me pointedly. "We're going to talk about this when we're no longer in my father's company."

"I appreciate that," Hank said. "I don't need to know about any dalliances having to do with Emmy and Luke Brooks."

My jaw dropped and my eyes shot to her. "Are you kidding me, Teddy?!"

"I didn't tell him, I swear." Teddy's eyes were wide, and she raised up her hands in surrender to emphasize her point.

"She didn't tell me," Hank admitted before turning to Teddy. "But you should consider shutting your door when you're on the phone."

I slapped both of my hands over my face, wishing I could crawl into a hole and disappear. Teddy let out a quiet "whoops."

Hank just laughed. Reveling in his keen ability to embarrass the hell out of Teddy and me. "Your secret is safe with me, Emmy. Just don't keep it a secret for too long."

Jesus. Had Hank heard mine and Luke's conversation this morning?

"I won't," I responded. I hoped I meant it.

"Well, on that note," Teddy said, "I thought we could make dinner and dessert together before the evening portion of the birthday extravaganza."

"That sounds great, Ted." Teddy and I made dinner for her birthday every year. It started when we were in college. It was our freshman year, and we had moved in the day before.

We made her entire eighteenth birthday meal with a microwave and a drip coffee maker. It was the worst pasta either of us had ever eaten, but we had such a good time that it didn't matter.

Teddy walked over to her dad and helped him out of his chair. He struggled, but he tried not to show it. Once he was up, Teddy gave him a kiss on the cheek. She looped her arm through his, and they started walking toward the kitchen. I followed.

Once Hank was settled in a chair at the counter, Teddy turned to me and gave me a big hug. "Sorry for accidentally ratting you out to Meadowlark's biggest gossip," she said into my shoulder.

"Forgiven." I pulled back from the hug. "How does it feel to be twenty-seven?" I asked.

"Like I'm just getting started." She flashed me a signature Teddy smile.

Teddy had all the supplies to make chicken cutlets and pasta with a spicy vodka sauce, sticking with the pasta tradition–but now we made dinners that were edible.

I was on sauce duty, Hank was masterfully tossing together a Caesar salad kit from the grocery store, and nothing could come between Teddy and her focus on her chicken. That was fine with me. Even though I ate chicken, I couldn't stand touching any raw meat.

Touching it made my gums feel weird. It didn't make sense to anyone but me, but Teddy never pushed on it. Being an adult with sensory issues was a weird thing. How could I tell someone that if I touched a piece of chicken while the music was too loud and I could hear somebody breathing, it would send me into a spiral?

Hank had turned on the Eagles. "Peaceful Easy Feeling" floated through the bluetooth speaker in the kitchen, and the smell of garlic and onions had me counting down the minutes until dinner was ready.

There was just something about food and the way it brought people together. That's why my dad loved to cook, even after he spent the whole day working on the ranch. Growing up, family dinner was a non-negotiable. Both Hank and Teddy used to join us at least once a week after Hank finished his day at the ranch.

"How's baling going at the ranch, Emmy?" Hank asked as we all sat down to eat. Hank worked at Rebel Blue as my dad's right-hand man until he physically wasn't able to, so he knew the schedule as well as Amos Ryder himself.

"We're actually a little behind, which is driving Gus up the wall, but he's got a plan to catch us up next week."

"He runs a tight ship," Hank remarked.

Teddy groaned. "Dad, please don't launch into your 'Gus Ryder is a fine young man' speech on my birthday, *please*. Today is sacred."

"Hey now, I've watched Amos run the ranch for years. I used to be the right-hand man, so I know what it takes to be good at it, and Gus is going to do a fine job of it. That's all I was going to say."

"He does a good job," I said. "Dad wishes he would loosen up a little, though."

Hank let out a hearty chuckle. "He is a bit of a hard ass, isn't he?"

"Understatement of the century," Teddy mumbled. "Oh, by the way, I sent Wes an email about a designer I think would be good," she continued, changing the subject. "She was in a few of my fashion classes before she transferred. She's talented and has a huge following on social media. Having her on the project might also be a good way to get your name out there as a guest ranch."

"Wes didn't mention anything today, so I'll poke at him. I don't even know if he uses his email." Which was true. We all had a Rebel Blue email, but I think Gus was the only one who regularly used it. He's the one who insisted on them.

"What's her name?" I asked.

"Her name is Ada. She's great. Remind me to show you her socials later." Hank, like Amos, had a strict "no phones at dinner" policy.

The three of us chatted for a while longer before Hank clapped his tattooed hands together. He had "theo" on one set of knuckles and "dora" on the other. He was covered in tattoos, but I knew those were Teddy's favorite, even though she never went by Theodora.

"Emmy, can you help me up?" Hank asked. "I've got a surprise for the birthday girl."

Teddy started to get up. "Dad, I can help yo—"

"Sit your ass down, Theodora. It's your birthday." I went to help Hank out of his chair.

"Where are we headed?" I asked.

"Just to the pantry." We walked in that direction, and Hank opened the pantry door. He moved a cereal box to reveal a plate of what I assumed were oatmeal chocolate chip cookies, Teddy's favorite. I grabbed the plate and handed it to him so he could be the one to put them in front of Teddy. "Thanks, Emmy," he said.

We went back to the table where Teddy was impatiently waiting. Hank set down the plate of cookies in front of a smiling Teddy.

"When did you even have time to make these?"

"While you were at work yesterday. I had to open all the windows to make sure you couldn't smell them when you got home."

"Thank you, Dad."

"It's been a while, so they might taste like shit."

Teddy picked up a cookie and took a huge bite.

"They're perfect," she said. Her voice was tight like she was holding back tears. "Dammit, Hank." She wiped a tear from the corner of her eye. "Love you, old man."

"Love you, too, Bear. Now, both of you ladies grab a cookie and go get ready. The birthday beverages at The Devil's Boot aren't going to drink themselves." Hank leaned down and gave Teddy a kiss on her temple before grabbing his cane that had been hanging on the back of his chair. Both Teddy and I got up and watched him get to his chair in the living room before we walked down the hallway to her room.

Teddy's room was an extension of her. It was a decor maximalist's dream. One of her walls was inspired by a gallery wall, but it didn't have any actual frames or art pieces hanging on it. It was just paintings of frames, filled with things she painted herself.

She had a black-and-white checkered rug on the oak floors, a deep emerald bedspread, an excess of multi-colored pillows, and more stacks of books than the Meadowlark library.

"God, leave it to my dad to make me cry over a batch of cookies," she said, trying to shake off the tears.

"I'm going to cry over the damn cookies and they weren't even for me," I said.

"Don't think tears will get you out of telling me what happened with you and Brooks last night."

I groaned. I was hoping she forgot.

Wishful thinking.

I flopped onto Teddy's bed and draped my arm over my face. She was not deterred.

"Spill," she demanded.

"Why do I have to tell you if you already know?" I whined.

"Because it's fun to make you admit things. Plus, it gets more real after you say it out loud." She paused, waiting for me to do exactly that.

"Fine. I slept with him." She was right. It did get more real after I said it out loud.

"Slept with who?"

"You are literally so annoying. Did you know that?"

"I'm just trying to make sure you're not throwing me a curveball." I rolled onto my back and looked my best friend in the eye. "I slept with Luke." It was out in the open now, and I couldn't shy away from it. Not that I really wanted to, but all of this just felt so new to me. I was expecting some sort of regret or uneasiness to bubble under my skin when I told Teddy about me and Luke, but it didn't.

All I felt was…happy. Content, even.

"I fucking knew it. You nearly blinded me with your afterglow." Teddy put her hands over her eyes like she was blocking out the sun.

"That's not a real thing," I argued, pushing her hands away from her face.

"It absolutely is," she replied, grabbing onto my hand so I had one less arm to cover my eyes with. Teddy wasn't going to let me hide from this. "And you have it. How many orgasms did it take to achieve? Three? Four?"

"Five," I mumbled.

"Five?!" Teddy shook her head in disbelief, and I couldn't help but breathe out a laugh.

"It could've been more," I started, "but things came to an abrupt end when Wes knocked on my cabin door this morning." Teddy's eyes widened, and her mouth dropped open. "Please tell me your brother did *not* catch Brooks in your bed. I'm assuming he didn't, considering I haven't heard anything about a murder today. Not that Wes would murder anyone, but he would tell Gus, and that would be that."

"No, I made Luke hide in the bathroom, but I answered the door wearing his shirt without realizing it." Teddy's jaw was still on the floor. "You're lucky he went for the plain black t-shirt yesterday, or you would've been fucked. In a bad way. Not the good way you obviously were last night." I felt a blush creeping up my neck. She wasn't wrong about either of those things. "So what are you going to do now? Are you and him, like, an item?"

I'd been dreading that question, but I knew it was coming.

"I don't know," I said. Recalling how Luke had said he cared about me and that he didn't want to be my secret. "He said he wants to see where this goes."

"What else did he say? You're holding back." I loved her, but damn, her human lie detector was annoying as hell sometimes. "How do you know that?" I demanded.

"Because you look like you're constipated." Okay, fair. "He said—" I hesitated for a second. "He said he didn't want to be my 'dirty little secret.'"

Teddy plopped down on the bed next to me. "Is that what you want him to be?"

"What? No, of course not." And I meant that. I didn't really know what I wanted Luke to be, but it definitely wasn't that. "This whole thing is just a lot. Three weeks ago, Luke Brooks was the one person I would've punched in the face on demand. But now, he's telling me he cares about me, and the way he kisses me makes me feel like I'm floating, and I just don't know how to deal with it."

The words poured out of my mouth without giving me a chance to breathe. Once they started, I couldn't stop them. I covered my eyes again.

"I don't want him to feel like he's a secret, but I also

don't want to announce this to the world and watch his friendship with my brothers implode while I'm still trying to figure out what the hell is going on. Because the reality of the situation is, I don't actually know him that well, and I don't know if this whole thing is as real as it feels when I'm with him."

Teddy let out a low whistle. "So, that's a lot to unpack, yeah?"

"Yeah," I sighed.

"He didn't ask you to run and tell your brothers right away, did he?"

"No."

"Good, because it's reasonable for you to want some time, and it's reasonable for him to tell you about his concerns. Right?"

I finally uncovered my eyes and looked at Teddy's ceiling. "Right."

"Okay, then. This is what we're going to do. We're not going to worry about it tonight. I know you feel like you have to make a decision right away, but you don't. Everything looks different after a few days, so just give it a little time to work itself out in your brain. Okay?"

"Okay." I turned my neck so I could look at Teddy, who was lying right next to me on her bed. "Sorry I had a mini freak out."

"I think you should have more of those. They're healthy. I'm happy you're talking to me about this, Em. You don't have to go through this season on your own—coming home, figuring out your next move, and unexpectedly catching feelings for your brother's best friend is a lot for anyone to deal with at one time."

And Teddy didn't even know the half of it. Guilt gnawed at me over all the things I hadn't told my best friend.

I just needed some time.

"Do you want to go somewhere else tonight? Get some space?" The plan was to go to The Devil's Boot with Teddy and a few of her friends from the boutique.

Maybe I should have wanted some space from Luke, but I didn't. I wanted to see him, get a glimpse of him through the dusky Devil's Boot interior. I wanted to go there. Even without Luke in the picture, it was the only place that could be counted on for a good time, and I knew Teddy loved it.

The duality of Teddy was that she could simultaneously be the center of attention while constantly focusing on other people's needs and comfort. I needed to be better about paying attention to hers. She would gladly give up The Devil's Boot and all of her birthday plans if she thought for even a second I didn't want to go, but I did.

I shook my head at Teddy, telling her I didn't want to go anywhere else.

Her mouth stretched into a smile. "Good. Wait until Brooks sees you in the dress I made."

"Isn't it weird to you that you made *me* a dress for *your* birthday?" Teddy looked at me like that was the stupidest thing to ever come out of my mouth. "Alright, never mind."

Teddy walked to her closet and pulled out a black garment bag. She brought it over to the bed and laid it in the spot she had just moved from.

"Open it before I explode," Teddy said.

I sat up and pulled the zipper on the garment bag down. I was immediately met with a beautiful, rich crimson color.

I pulled the entire dress out to find a simple, but beautifully constructed, sundress. It looked like it would hit a little below the middle of my thighs. The bodice was tight with a square milkmaid neckline and thick tank top straps. Teddy knew I liked the way necklines and straps like these looked against my collarbones—just like with the swimsuit I wore to the springs with Luke. Teddy is the one who helped me pick it out.

"Teddy, this is beautiful. I love it."

"I knew you would. Red is your color, but you don't wear it nearly enough." I couldn't even think of another red thing I owned besides my swimsuit. Maybe one of Gus's old Budweiser t-shirts? Definitely not anything like this. "And I know linen scratches your brain in the wrong way, so the top is lined with jersey knit. It's light, though, so you shouldn't get hot or anything."

"I seriously love it. Thank you." I gave Teddy a hug. "I'm dying to put it on."

"Not yet." Teddy said. "We have a whole birthday slash rom-com-getting-ready-montage to complete before you can put it on. It's the finale."

"We do?"

"Yes. We need to make sure I get the present I wanted."

"And what's that?"

"Watching Luke Brooks fall to his knees the minute he sees you."

19

LUKE

I spent the day at The Devil's Boot in a daze. I dropped more than one chair as Joe and I took them off the tables, miscounted part of the liquor inventory, and almost dropped a rack of clean pint glasses. I couldn't believe what happened last night. And this morning.

I was a goner for Emmy Ryder.

Before yesterday, I could've denied it, but not anymore. It was more than just the sex, which was obviously fucking phenomenal; it was the way I felt when I woke up with her tucked into me this morning and how I could've stayed there all day.

I didn't wake up with women. I was gone before the sun was up, and I never regretted leaving. Not with Emmy. I wanted to wake up next to her every day.

Don't even get me started on the way she looked in my t-shirt.

I would've spent the entire day in her bed if it weren't for Wes knocking on her door.

That was a close fucking call.

But I'd rather Wes catch us than Gus. I wanted to live to see forty.

"Where's your head at today?" Joe's voice broke through my thoughts.

"W-what?" I asked. I was stocking glassware under the bar, and Joe was giving the tables one last wipe-down before opening.

"You've been distracted all day. What's on your mind?"

"Nothing. Just didn't get a lot of sleep last night."

Joe smirked at me. "So it's a girl, then? That's what's on your mind?"

I let out a sigh. "Yeah. It's a girl."

"I don't think I've ever seen you all worked up over a girl. She must be special."

"She is," I said without hesitating. Emmy was everything.

"Does she think you're special, too?" He said it sarcastically, but I still hesitated. I didn't know. Joe spoke again before I had a chance to answer, "Ah. So that's what's got you all twisted up. You don't know how she feels about you."

"Something like that." Joe raised his eyebrows at me, waiting for me to keep going. "I just think I pushed her too hard."

"You're not giving me much to go on here, kid."

I didn't know how to explain to Joe that I was falling for the one woman in the world I wasn't allowed to fall for.

"The whole thing is just really, really new. For both of us. But I think I'm just ready for more than she is, and I don't want to rush her."

"Well, I'll be damned," Joe said as he shook his head.

"What?"

"You really like her." The look on Joe's face was a mix of happiness and disbelief. *Believe me, Joe. I feel the same way.*

"I do," I conceded. I liked Emmy. A lot.

"You want my advice?" Joe asked. "Granted, it might not be worth much."

"I'll take anything." Considering the person I would normally talk to about things like this—if things like this ever happened to me—would be Gus.

"She might not be ready, and that's okay. Just keep showing up. Instead of telling her how you feel, keep showing her. Actions speak louder than words and all that shit."

I could do that. I would do that. I wasn't very good with words anyway.

"That's actually good advice. Thanks, Joe."

"No problem. Now, get your head out of your ass. We open in twenty minutes."

. . .

THE DEVIL'S BOOT was a fucking mad house. Fridays were always busy, but damn, this was something else. The band was late, but they were finally set up and said they were going to start playing in the next five minutes.

If my patrons didn't get some Waylon Jennings soon, I would have a riot on my hands.

I had an extra bartender tonight, which I was grateful for. That left me free to bus the tables and run back and forth with different things the bar needed. While I was running, I noticed a flash of red at one of the tables.

It was Emmy.

Holy *shit*.

She was wearing a dress that was the same color as the swimsuit that drove me crazy at the springs. It clung to her breasts and her torso before flaring out slightly at her waist. Half of her hair was pulled away from her face, but in true Emmy fashion, pieces were falling out around her face.

She had on a pair of brown cowboy boots, different from the black ones she wore that first night I saw her in my bar.

The dress she was wearing looked like it was made for her, but the thing that really got my attention were her blood-red lips. I'd never seen that on her before.

I wanted to ruin those red lips, either with my mouth or my cock. I wasn't picky. My jeans tightened. I'd already had a hard enough time controlling my body's reaction to Emmy before we slept together, but now that we had—fuck—I wanted her so bad.

I shook my head. Emmy was at a table with a few other girls. I recognized them from town, but I couldn't tell you their names. I didn't see Teddy, but that meant she was probably swindling men at my bar.

I tore my eyes from Emmy. She hadn't noticed me, and I wanted her to have a good time with her friends tonight. It was Teddy's birthday, after all.

I made my way back to the bar, where sure enough, Teddy was flirting with my regulars, who were eating it up even more than usual, probably because of the "Birthday Girl" headband and sash she was wearing. She ended up with four drinks she didn't pay for and carried them back to the table where Emmy and the other girls were waiting.

I wanted to talk to Emmy just once, so I got behind the bar and started making something I never make: fucking lemon drop shots. That seemed like something a bunch of girls in a bar for a birthday would drink, right?

Whatever, I was doing it.

I finished the shots, put them on a tray, and made my way over to Emmy's table. This was it. This was all I was going to do. Bring her and her friends shots, and then I'd leave her alone for the rest of the night.

Emmy caught my eye when I was a few steps from the table. She smiled at me, and I nearly dropped the damn tray.

"Ladies," I said as a greeting. I felt like a fucking idiot. "I heard it was someone's birthday."

"Yeah, *that's* why you're bringing us free drinks," Teddy said sarcastically, but my eyes were on Emmy.

My eyes were always on Emmy.

"I can take these back," I said, throwing a quick glance at Teddy.

"Ignore her," Emmy said. "We'll take them."

I set the tray down in the middle of their table, and each of them took a shot glass off it.

"Brooks," Teddy started, "is this a fucking lemon drop?" At that, Emmy's smile grew.

"Yeah," I said sheepishly.

"You've been holding out on me for all these years?! I didn't even know you could make these here." The two women on the other side of the table giggled.

"This is a one-time thing. Don't get used to it."

"Thank you," Emmy said. She looked at Teddy. "Say thank you, birthday girl."

"Thank you, Brooksy. It is much appreciated."

The girls cheers-ed, hit the shot glasses on the table, and threw them back. I watched Emmy's throat as she swallowed.

God dammit. Everything she did gave me a hard-on.

They all set their glasses back on the tray, and I took it. "Happy Birthday, Teddy," I said and then winked at Emmy as I walked away.

The way she blushed brought me more pleasure than it should have.

I kept an eye on Emmy throughout the night. Not in a creepy way–just in a "I really like you and think you're the most beautiful woman alive" way.

After the shot I brought her, she didn't drink a lot, just nursed a mixed drink until her and that red dress made their way up to the bar. Hell if I was going to let anyone else get her order. I nearly knocked Joe over, trying to get to her.

I stood across the bar from her. "What can I get you, sugar?"

"Take a shot with me."

Her answer surprised me. She was looking at me with heat in her eyes, and I couldn't say no to her. I pulled two shot glasses from underneath the bar.

"Pick your poison."

"Tequila, please."

I turned around and grabbed a nicer bottle from the back bar, pouring a shot for each of us before sliding hers across the bar. "What are we drinking to?" I asked.

"New beginnings."

I tried not to read into that. We clinked our glasses together and took our shots down the hatch, keeping our eyes on each other the entire time.

Fuck.

It was a miracle I didn't try to take her on the bar right then. Joe could thank me for that later.

Emmy brought one of her hands up to her mouth to wipe away a drop of the liquor at the corner of her lips. I wished I'd done that.

I needed to touch her.

"How much do I owe you?" she asked.

"On the house."

"You sure?" she asked.

I leaned over the bar and used two fingers to gesture for her to come closer. She did, and I was finally in a position where I could talk to her and no one would hear.

"You can thank me by letting me tear that godforsaken dress off of you later." Even with the band playing and the patrons singing along, I could hear Emmy's sharp inhale.

I leaned away from her, returning to my upright position on the other side of the bar.

"Deal," she breathed before turning and starting back toward her friends. She bumped into a few people like she was in a daze and wasn't watching where she was going.

She had a hell of an effect on me, and I liked seeing that I had an effect on her, too. But then she bumped into a man I didn't recognize, which was rare, and he put his hand on her waist to steady her. Last time it was Kenny Wyatt, and now it was this fucker.

In my head, I gave him two seconds to take his hand off her before I took it off her for him. He did.

Good.

I rolled my shoulders back and down, trying to keep my jealousy in check, but the way he smiled at her had me seeing red, and not the good kind of red like Emmy's dress. I watched Emmy apologize for bumping into him and go back to her table.

He watched her.

I was going to have to keep an eye on that.

The next hour or so was a whirlwind. It really was wild here tonight. The band was focusing on nineties country, and there wasn't really anything that could hype up a bar like Alan Jackson.

Everyone in here was seriously drunk and seriously rowdy. Apparently, they all came to celebrate Teddy's birthday.

It was about halfway through "Good Time" that I noticed the man who'd put his hand on Emmy had made his way over to her table with a few of his friends. He was wearing denim on denim.

What an asshole.

They're just talking, Luke. Chill out.

Teddy and the other girls were very obviously flirting. I'd been on the other end of that and had worked here long enough to know what it looked like. Double Denim was talking to Emmy, but she kept looking over at Teddy and leaning away.

She wasn't interested. *Good.*

I walked to the end of the bar that was closest to her table, telling myself that's where I needed to be to wipe glasses down, which was bullshit, but I didn't

care. It was then that Double Denim made his move.
He put one of his hands on Emmy's knee that was
crossed over her other leg. She shrugged him away, but
he put his hand back.

Absolutely fucking not.

I made it over to their table in three seconds flat.
"Take your fucking hand off her." Double Denim's eyes
shot up to me. He looked surprised, but he didn't
move. "Now." My voice was unrecognizable.

"Hey, chill, man. We were just talking."

"It doesn't look like she wants to talk to you, *man*."
Double Denim looked at Emmy, who was eyeing me in
a way that was less than friendly.

I didn't care.

"We're alright, aren't we, honey?"

That was it. I stepped toward him so I could grab
him by the collar of his stupid denim shirt and brought
him face to face with me. He was a few inches shorter
than me, so I pulled him up on his tiptoes.

"Take your friends and get the hell out of my bar."

"You can't be serious, man."

"Dead fucking serious." I pushed him back, and
Joe, who had appeared from the bar, caught him
before he went to the ground. I guess I'd pushed him
harder than I thought. He started to lunge at me, but
Joe had a hold of him.

"Let's not make a scene, boys. Leave now, and your
last round's on the house," Joe said.

Double Denim shrugged Joe off of him. "Let's go.

This place is fucking stupid, and a bitch isn't worth this."

Before he could start walking away, I grabbed him by the shoulder and swung. Hard. My fist hit his face with a gnarly *crack*, and Double Denim was laid out flat on the ground for a few seconds.

He scrambled back up and came at me. I caught his fist in my hand—he threw a weak-ass punch—and twisted his arm behind his back. He was facing Emmy, but I made sure he wasn't close enough that he could touch her.

"Apologize," I spat.

"What the fuck, dude. What the hell is wrong with you?!"

"Apologize," I said again. Double Denim tried to turn back and look at me, but I tightened my grip on his arm and twisted. He looked back at Emmy, whose jaw was set and lips were pursed.

"I'm sorry," Double Denim ground out.

"Now get the fuck out of my bar." I pushed him into his friends, who all looked like they'd just shit themselves.

"Sorry, man. We'll get out of here." That was one of Double Denim's friends. Damn. I almost felt bad for punching the guy, considering how scared his friends looked, but no one talked to Emmy like that and got away with it.

The four of them made it through the door, and when it shut behind them, the whole bar erupted in a cheer. I guess when the bar owner punched someone, people figured that person deserved it.

I looked back at Emmy, who had her arms folded and was staring at me in the same less-than-friendly way. Instead of giving her a chance to yell at me in front of everyone, who had more or less gone back to what they were doing before the punch, I swooped her up off her chair and threw her over my shoulder like a sack of potatoes, taking extra care to hold her dress down so no one got a free show. Now it was Teddy who was cheering.

The birthday girl had a giant smile on her face. Knowing her, she probably somehow orchestrated this whole thing.

Emmy Ryder was mine, and I was going to prove that to her right fucking now.

"Brooks! Put me down now, you neanderthal. Are you kidding me?"

"No can do, sugar," I responded as I walked through the bar with her over my shoulder. She pounded her fists on my back. Cute.

"You are a fucking crazy person, you know that?"

"Only for you."

"Oh my god, put me down!" She continued to protest, but I ignored her. I didn't put her down until we made it into my office and the door was closed and locked behind us. I gently lowered Emmy to the ground, and as soon as her feet touched it, she pushed me.

"What the hell is wrong with you? You can't just go around hitting people when they talk to me."

"He put his hands on you, sugar. No one puts their hands on you."

"This is the real world, Brooks, not a fucking romance novel. I don't need you to rescue me from a creep in a bar. I can handle myself." Emmy stared me down. Her eyes were burning—just the way I liked them.

"Obviously, you can handle yourself."

"Then why did you swoop in and physically assault one of your *paying customers* like some sort of cowboy vigilante?"

I grabbed Emmy by the waist and pushed her up against the door to my office. I moved my mouth up the column of her throat, replacing my mouth with my hand once I made it to her lips. I gave her a quick kiss resting my forehead against hers.

"Because sugar. Seeing someone else touch you made me fucking crazy," I breathed.

Emmy's chest was heaving. The anger in her eyes had shifted to something else. "Y-you can't d-do that," she stuttered.

I brought the hand that wasn't on her throat to the hem of her dress before snaking it under and touching the soft skin of her thigh. "Why not?"

"B-because. H-hitting people is b-bad."

I chuckled and moved my hand further up her

dress to her panties. Or, at least, where they should have been.

Fuck.

"You wanna know what's bad? You bringing this bare pussy into my bar like a perfect little slut."

Emmy groaned. *Fuck.* She made me insane.

I teased her with my fingers. "You're dripping for me, sugar. How long have you been like this? Needy and desperate?" The sound of the band drowned out everything happening outside my office. It was just us now.

"S-since I saw you behind the bar."

"Yeah? Is that why you came to take a shot with me? To try and get me to pay attention to your needy cunt?"

"I was thirsty."

At that, I snagged the bottle of whiskey that was sitting on the table beside my office door and pulled the stopper out with my teeth.

"Thirsty? Are you still thirsty, sugar?" She nodded. "Open your mouth," I commanded.

She opened immediately, and my already hard cock jerked at the sight of her open mouth, ready to take anything I gave her.

I took a pull of the whiskey before setting the bottle on my desk, but I didn't swallow. I leaned into Emmy, my hand on her throat still keeping her pinned to my office door, and spit the whiskey in her mouth.

She swallowed.

I felt her throat work under my grip. *Fuck*. She was everything.

I brought my hand under her dress, and her eyes rolled back when I slid the tip of my finger between her folds. She started to move her hips, but I quickly pulled my fingers away. Her eyes shot open.

"What the hell?" she exclaimed.

"You're the one that was mad at me, sugar. I don't want you to do anything you'll regret," I said with a smile. I loved teasing her. I sucked her off my fingers, the taste of her mingling with the burn of the whiskey, before I released her throat and stepped back. My cock was painfully hard in my jeans.

"Are you kidding me?" Emmy gasped.

"No."

"Please?"

God, I loved hearing her beg for me. It was a reminder that she wanted me as much as I wanted her.

"You've also been drinking," I said, even though I knew she wasn't drunk–probably not even tipsy.

"I had two shots and half of a vodka soda, and no offense, but your lemon drop shots are weak."

I smirked at her. "Do you think insulting my bar skills is going to change my mind?"

"Depends on what you're into," she said coyly.

"Just you."

Emmy closed the distance between us, pressing her breasts against my chest. "If you won't touch me, then let me touch you."

Fuck. Emmy dragged her hand down my chest and over the hard bulge in my jeans.

I jumped. She giggled.

"You should really let me take care of this," she said sweetly. Shit. How did this happen? *Mayday, mayday.* I had lost control of the situation.

"I-I'm good." I was the one stuttering through my words now. Emmy rubbed her hand over my jeans, applying some pressure. She started to push me back toward my desk. I let her, until the back of my legs hit the edge of it. She went up on her toes and gave me a quick kiss before she—*shit*—lowered to her knees. I could see right down that red dress of hers. She started to unbuckle my belt.

"Can I?"

Did she really think I was going to say no? All words had temporarily left my brain as I looked down at the beautiful woman on her knees.

All I could do was nod.

"Tell me yes, Luke," she said. The tables had really fucking turned tonight, hadn't they?

"Yes, sugar. Let's see what you look like with my cock in your mouth."

Emmy managed to get my belt and pants undone in seconds. She leaned in and dragged her tongue up my length over the fabric of my briefs before pulling them down. My cock sprung free. The bastard basically tried to jump down her throat, but she didn't put me inside her mouth yet.

Instead, she grabbed my dick with one hand and leaned in, licking the pre-cum off the head slowly. I couldn't help the groan that came out of my mouth when her tongue made contact. She gave me a few more licks and pumped the base of my cock with her hand. Jesus Christ. I was going to come before she could get any further.

Chill out, Luke. Think of something else, anything else besides the girl who's about to put your dick in her mouth. I recited a list of unsexy things in my head. *Missed connection at the airport, broken refrigerator, cows giving birth.*

Okay. Okay. I could do this. I was sure of it...until Emmy put my dick in her mouth and took me as far back as she could.

"*Fuuuck*, Emmy. You're beautiful." I'd never really considered myself to be a vocal guy, but that was out the window with Emmy. I met resistance at the back of her throat, and she let out what sounded like a frustrated noise.

She adjusted her height, and I felt her tongue move. I slid deeper into her mouth, and she started to move her hand and her mouth on me.

"You love choking on my cock, don't you?" I said. My voice was husky, and my throat was tight. Emmy looked up at me through her thick eyelashes and nodded as much as she could.

I wanted the image of her on her knees with her red lips wrapped around my cock projected on my fucking headstone.

I fisted my hand in her hair, trying to remember to be gentle, but when I pushed my cock deeper down her throat, she moaned. She had slid her hand that wasn't working my length under her dress. She was touching herself.

"Sucking my cock turns you on, baby? You want me to fuck this mouth of yours?" Emmy took her hand off my length and put it on my ass, pulling me deeper.

I couldn't take it. I knotted both hands in her hair and thrust into her mouth. *Jesus Christ*, she was perfect. Both of us were moaning. Fuck, she felt so good, but I didn't want to come in her mouth. Not tonight.

"I need to come inside of you, sugar. Let me fill you up again." I was obsessed with marking Emmy as mine. She kept going, but I reached down and lifted her up to me, hauling her lips to mine harshly. Our kiss was rough, like each of us was seeing how much the other could take.

Emmy pulled back first. "I wasn't finished," she breathed.

I moved her in front of me so she was pinned between me and my desk, her back against my front.

"The only thing I want more right now than coming in your mouth is filling up your perfect cunt." I needed her to tell me it was okay before we got carried away. "Do you want me to fuck you on this desk, sugar? Can I?"

"Yes, Luke. Please."

Thank fucking hell. I pushed Emmy down so she was bent over my desk and lifted up the dress that had been teasing me all night. "This dress has been torturing me all night."

"I wore it just for you."

"Good. If you wore it for another man, I'd have to kill him." She laughed, but I wasn't kidding. I rubbed my hands over her ass, my thumbs spreading her pussy for me. She was wet and glistening. All for me. I started pushing my dick into her wet heat.

I saw stars.

I gripped her hips and worked my way in slowly, knowing this position would be intense for her. I knew I was big. When I was seated in her fully, I paused. Shit, I was going to come. *No.* Not before she got off.

Broken refrigerator. Broken refrigerator. Broken refrigerator.

Emmy pushed her ass against me. "Don't move," I rasped. "Just give me a minute." I squeezed my eyes shut.

"You good back there?" I could hear the smile in her voice. I fucking loved it. I loved it when she was happy like this.

"Yeah," I breathed. "I'm good." The danger had passed.

"Then please start moving before I lose my goddamn mind."

She didn't have to ask me twice. I pulled out slightly and then thrust back into her. Hard.

I did that again and again.

Emmy cried out. "Yes, Luke, just like that. Fuck me, please." She always asked so nicely. I thought about that guy putting his hand on her. My next thrust was harder. I could feel my desk moving across the floor, but I didn't give a damn. All that mattered was me and Emmy and the place where we were connected.

I pulled her back up to me so she was upright. I brought my fingers to her clit and started stroking as I fucked her. Her pussy started to tighten around my cock like a vice. She grabbed my hand that was on her hip and moved it up over her breasts and to her throat.

Fuck.

I gripped her throat lightly, applying the faintest amount of pressure on the sides. Emmy's head fell back against my shoulder.

"Yes, yes, yes," she breathed. "You're so deep like this, Luke."

"You were made for me," I told her. I thrust into her, harder still. "Tell me you're mine, Emmy." I needed to hear it.

"I'm yours."

"That's right, sugar. I'm the only one who gets to have you like this."

"I-I'm going to—" She never got to finish because both of us combusted at the same time. I spilled myself into her, my thrusts getting short and shallow.

Both of us were breathing heavily, and one of the straps of Emmy's dress had fallen off her shoulder. I slowly eased myself out of her and watched both of us drip down her thighs.

"Stay here," I said to her. I tucked my half-hard cock into my jeans and grabbed a few tissues before making my way back to Emmy. I gently wiped us off her thighs, bringing her dress back down over her ass.

She turned around, and I folded her into my arms. I held her there, placing kisses in her hair and on her temple. She sighed. She sounded...content. It made my heart soar.

I dragged my hands up and down her arms and brought one of her hands up to my mouth so I could kiss her palm before intertwining our fingers. I led her to the couch to the side of my desk. I sat down, bringing her with me. I set her on my lap, tucked her head under my chin, and continued to rub circles over her arms and back, happy as hell I was holding her again.

"Luke?" she said quietly.

"Yeah, sugar?"

"I'm in like with you."

"Are you sure that's not just all the dopamine we just made hitting your brain?" I asked jokingly, trying not to think too deeply about her confession.

She lifted her head and looked me in the eye. "No. I want you to know I like you. I don't know exactly when I'm going to be ready to tell my family, but I *will* tell them. I just need a little time, okay?

This woman had me wrapped around her finger,

and she didn't even know it. I brought my hand up to cup her face.

"Take all the time you need. I didn't mean to push you this morning," I said, and I meant it. Emmy was worth the wait. I'd been waiting thirty-two years for her without even knowing it, and she'd been right in front of me the whole time.

"You didn't. My processing time is just longer than the average human's." She tucked her head back under my chin.

Emmy Ryder might have been in like with me, but it was then that I knew I was falling in love with her.

20

EMMY

The next day, I had some errands to run in town with my dad. When I walked through the back door of the Big House, he was waiting for me in the kitchen.

Apparently, one of the hay balers was still acting up. We were already behind on baling, and because of that, Gus's forehead vein was about thirty seconds from bursting. Not Amos, though. The man was still as steady as ever.

He greeted me with a hug. I loved my dad's hugs. He didn't half-ass them. Every time he hugged us, he did it like it was the last time.

"Hey, Spud. Are you ready?"

"Morning. Yeah, let's roll." We walked out to his truck. My dad was a Ford man. Personally, I had my issues with the guy who created the forty-hour work week, but that was neither here nor there.

It was cooler this morning, a sure sign that fall was on its way. Willie Nelson was playing softly through the truck speakers. I looked out the front windshield. It was all green trees and a painted-blue sky. Within a month or two, the leaves on the trees would change, turning this green and blue landscape into fire.

"How are things going? Are you settling in okay?" my dad asked.

"Yeah, I am."

"It's been how long? A little over a month?" With that simple question, I now knew why we were going to town by ourselves. Yeah, my dad wanted to spend time with me, but he also wanted to know what my plans were.

"About that long, yes."

"I'm assuming you know what I'm going to ask next, Spud."

I let out a sigh. "I don't know, Dad."

"That's unusual for you." It was. I was always thinking about what was next. "What's going on?" I was honestly surprised it had taken him this long to ask, but to be fair, I hadn't really given him a chance. "You know when I came home, and you were here, I was so happy to see you, and I knew you were happy to be home, but the moment I saw you, I knew my baby girl was sad."

My dad rubbed at his chin with the hand that wasn't on the wheel. His eyes were on the road, and mine were on him. I took in his hair, which was so much more gray than I remembered, and his wrinkles were set more deeply. Worry was etched into them.

When I looked at my dad, who wasn't as young as he was in my head, the realization that time at Rebel Blue had kept moving even when I was gone hit me like a freight train.

I wondered what was worse for him; worrying about me when I wasn't here or worrying about me when I was right in front of him but out of reach.

Of course he knew I was going through something. He was my dad. As far as parents went, he was the only one I'd ever known. And instead of coming home and letting him in, letting him do what he did best—be a dad—I had shut myself in my cabin and put on a face around my family.

"It broke my heart, but I let you work through it alone because I know that's how you like to do things. Over the past few weeks, you haven't seemed so sad, so I figured you'd been able to work some things out in that messy head of yours. Have you?"

"Not really," I answered honestly. If anything, my head was more of a mess now that I was all tangled up in Luke Brooks, but my dad definitely didn't need to know that. "I don't think I want to go back to Denver, but I also don't really know what I'd do here long term. I can't run things like Gus, and I don't have a project like Wes."

My dad kept one hand draped over the steering

wheel while the other continued to rub at his short beard. "So, no racing?" he asked.

"No racing. I'm going to race in divisionals," I said, unsure when I had decided. Now, apparently. "And then I'm done. I'm already one of the older riders on the circuit."

My dad stayed quiet. I don't think it surprised him. It was annoying, but my dad and my brothers knew me well. I'm sure they figured I was done with racing the second I came home. Gus was the only one so far who had tried to get me to admit it, but even he didn't have it in him to keep pushing me.

"Do you still want to be around this life?" he finally asked. By "this life," he meant the ranch. "Or do you see yourself doing something else?"

It was a good question, and I didn't even have to think about my answer. "I want to be around the ranch." I saw a light flicker in my dad's emerald eyes.

I'd been thinking about it over the past few weeks, and I just couldn't see myself anywhere else but Meadowlark or Rebel Blue. For someone who worked so hard to get out of here, it was weird to feel like it was where I belonged.

"I could use a riding instructor," my dad said. His voice was kind of strained. The emotional kind.

"Dad, are you okay?"

"Yeah, Spud. More than okay. I'd be happy for you wherever you went, but I'm happy you want to be here." My dad had never tried to keep me in Meadowlark. When I told him about my plans, he went along with them and supported me wherever he could.

I wondered how hard it had been for him to watch me go.

"So, what do you say about being a riding instructor through the winter season? And I could use some help with horse training. Then we'll see where we're at."

"Luke teaches lessons."

"Luke, eh?" My dad raised one of his eyebrows at me. *Shit.* I never called Luke by his first name. He must've caught that. "He does, and he does a good job. But that boy is stretching himself pretty thin. I don't know how he does it all."

"Me neither," I said truthfully. He taught lessons on Saturdays, worked on the ranch most days, and literally owned his own business. I didn't know if I'd ever get over how different he was in reality than in my head.

"Plus, Ronald and his wife want to go to Yuma. Live out their golden years in warm weather. So if anything, you could take the teenagers and the adults. Luke could keep the kids if he wanted to, but something tells me he'd let you have them."

My heart picked up speed. "What makes you say that?" I tried to be nonchalant. It took a few beats for my dad to answer, and when he did, I wasn't quite sure what to think about it.

"Nothing goes on at Rebel Blue that I don't know about, Spud."

MY DAD and I rolled into downtown Meadowlark fifteen minutes later. After his comment about being the all-seeing eye at Rebel Blue, "Mama's Don't Let Your Babies Grow Up to Be Cowboys" started playing, and it was impossible for Amos and I not to sing along when it came to Waylon and Willie.

After that, my dad pulled out an aux cord. It would never not be funny to me that he had the nicest, most modern truck out of all of us. He handed it to me, and I quickly found my Highwaymen playlist. We sang our hearts out the rest of the way.

We pulled up to the tractor supply right as "Big River" came to an end. I'd only been to downtown Meadowlark a few times since I'd been home, all of them to see Teddy at the boutique, which was probably a five-minute walk from the tractor supply.

Inside the store, my dad went to the counter. He'd pick up his part, but he'd also shoot the shit with Don Wyatt, the owner, for at least twenty minutes, so I started browsing.

When something was literally called the tractor supply store, people would assume it only carried tractor supplies. Those people would be wrong.

The tractor supply sold almost everything, and both Teddy and I had been known to buy heaps of

Wranglers from here because they were cheaper than anywhere else.

While I was perusing, I saw a muscle tee and thought of Luke. This one was made that way, unlike his t-shirts that he just took a pair of scissors to and hoped for the best.

I snapped a quick picture and sent it to him.

> Emmy: How much did you have to pay Don to get him to stock these?

I SLID my phone into my back pocket and kept poking around and grabbing one of those dinosaur grabber things along the way to entertain me. A few minutes later, my phone buzzed with a reply from Luke.

> Luke: The ones intentionally made like that aren't for me.

> Emmy: Why? Not enough chance of a nip slip?

> Luke: What do you have against my nipples?

I SMILED AT MY PHONE. Considering I was the muscle tee's biggest hater, it was shocking they'd started to grow on me. Even though, in the back of my head, I knew it wasn't the muscle tee growing on me but the man wearing it.

And his arms. Good god, those arms.

"Emmy, hey." I heard a man call my name. I looked around until I saw Kenny. Of course he was here. I forgot his dad owned the goddamn tractor supply.

"Hey," I said. "Fancy seeing you here."

He smiled at me. That was good. Maybe he wasn't upset I wasn't answering his texts.

"Are you doing okay? I haven't heard from you since I saw you at the bar last month." Poor Kenny. He'd lost a race to a man he didn't even know was running.

"Oh yeah, I'm good. Just busy!"

"I'm sure. I didn't know you were staying in town this long," he said. He sounded hopeful, which made me feel like an asshole.

"Yeah, I'm enjoying being home."

"That's good." He paused for a second and ran a hand through his hair, a nervous habit he'd had for as long as I'd known him. "So, do you think you'd want to get dinner sometime?"

God, he was so nice, but I couldn't agree to dinner with him. Kenny was a good guy, but he didn't want to be just my friend, and I only wanted Luke.

"I'm sorry, I can't. I'm seeing someone," I said, in disbelief that I'd just told someone else that.

"Oh. Shit, I'm sorry. I didn't know."

"Don't apologize. Thank you for the offer." I gave Kenny the friendliest smile I could muster.

"Spud," my dad called from the other end of the store. "You ready to go?"

My savior.

"Yeah!" I responded. I put my dinosaur back and found my dad near the counter. "I'll see you around," I shouted back to Kenny. He just nodded.

Out the front store window, I could see the part my dad needed being loaded into the back of his truck by Don's guys.

"Hey, Emmy. Welcome home." Don nodded at me. "Kenny told me he'd seen you around."

"Thanks, Don. Good to see you," I said politely, hoping Don wouldn't push me on the Kenny thing. Before he had a chance to, my dad stepped in.

"Thanks, Don. Take care." He gave the counter a little tap before turning around and gesturing for me to follow. Once we were out of the store, he asked, "Want to grab a coffee before we head home?"

I nodded.

We walked across the street to The Bean. The inside was just as I remembered it. It was so cozy. Nothing matched. The tables, chairs, couches–they were all mismatched. Not in a chic Teddy way, but in a

chaotic flea market way. I didn't know if it made my
ADHD better or worse.

Teddy and I used to do homework here, but I never
got anything done. Now I knew why.

My dad walked up to the counter and ordered two
drip coffees, his black and mine with lots of cream, no
sugar. As far as I knew, he was the only other man in
my life who knew my coffee order.

We chose a table by the window to sit for a few.

"I'll take your deal, Dad," I said, unprompted.

"You'll teach?"

"Yeah, I'll do it. I don't want Luke's classes unless he
doesn't want them, but I'll take Ronald's."

"That's fine with me. You'll earn the starting wage
for the first season, and we'll reevaluate from there."

"Done."

My dad reached his hand over the table so we
could shake on it. We sat there for a while, looking out
the window and just existing. It was nice.

After a while, he looked at me and said, "You look
so much like your mom, Emmy." I knew my dad loved
my mom, and he missed her every day, but he didn't
talk about her unprovoked. I always had to ask. "You
know, she's the one who wanted to name you
Clementine."

I nodded. He'd told me that before.

"She used to sing the song to the boys when they were
fussy or couldn't sleep. It always worked. We thought we

were having another boy, but when you came out, I couldn't even get a word out before she named you. You rarely cried as a baby. I like to think it's because your name held part of your mom, even though she wasn't there."

That I didn't know.

"The older you get, the more of her I see in you. She was quiet, like you. She preferred to work things out in her own head, and she kept her cards close to her chest."

"Are those bad things?" I asked quietly.

"No. They made her fiercely independent and determined. I loved that about her. When I met her, I'd never met anyone like her. I love those things about you, too."

My dad never talked like this. "Why don't you talk about her more?"

It took him a second to answer. "When she's in my head, I can keep her safe."

My dad's eyes were sad. *Keep her safe.* Hearing him say that broke my heart. My dad was with her when she died. She got bucked off a horse and hit her head on a rock just right. It was a freak accident.

The parallel between my mother and me wasn't lost on me. I think that was part of the reason I didn't tell him what happened to me. "I'm sorry for not telling you more about her," my dad said.

"It's okay," I said. And it was. I loved my mom, and I wished I had known her, but I didn't miss her—not like

Gus or Wes did. It was hard to miss someone you never knew, but I still missed the idea of her.

Sometimes, it felt like there was a hole in my heart where she should be.

"Why are you talking about her now?" I asked, genuinely curious about what sparked this conversation.

"This place is the first place I saw her. It wasn't a coffee shop then, just a diner. When I looked up at you just now, it reminded me of that day. Her car broke down outside of town. She'd walked a few miles to get here. She planned on staying one night, but she never left." My dad was like a river, steady and strong. I could see how my mom got swept away in him.

"Is it hard? To love someone even though they're gone?" I felt like I needed to take advantage of this time with my dad when he was freely talking about my mom.

"No, loving Stella is the easiest thing I'll ever do, whether she's here or not." Who knew Amos Ryder was such a romantic? My heart grew heavy in my chest. I was afraid it would drop.

"Did she ever regret it? Staying here?" I asked, voicing my biggest fear to my father: that I would regret staying here. My dad looked at me thoughtfully, like he knew exactly what I was thinking.

"You know, I don't think she did. When she left her hometown, she was searching for something. I think she found it here."

"What was she looking for?"

"The things we're all searching for: love, support, purpose."

"And she found that in you?"

"And in the mountains. And in August. And in Weston. And in you." I felt tears prick in my eyes. Who was cutting onions in this fucking coffee shop? I'd never really cried for my mom, but today I cried for the man who'd lost her. Leave it to my dad to make me nice and misty-eyed in a public place.

He looked at me, and love was written all over his face when he said, "I hope you find that, too, Clementine. Whether it's in Meadowlark or somewhere else later down the line."

I understood my mom's decision to leave her hometown, but I also understood her decision to stay in this little town more than I would have a few months ago.

When I was younger, all I could think about was leaving. Every goal I'd ever had was somehow related to leaving Meadowlark: college, racing, everything.

But now, I wanted to stay.

I felt safe here.

Maybe I just needed to leave for a while to realize this place was special, that I was proud to be from here, and *because* I was from here, I had a different experience from any other person out there.

I used to think Meadowlark made me feel small, but in reality, I think I made myself feel that way by always chasing the next thing to mark it off my list. It

was hard to feel good enough when you never cele-
brated what you'd achieved.

But now, I was proud of myself and my accomplish-
ments. I was also content. And no, it had nothing to do
with Brooks. He was just a bonus.

There was something about Meadowlark.

"You know, Dad, I think I already have."

21

EMMY

I t had been over a week since Teddy's birthday, which ended with me having sex with my brother's best friend at a bar where half the town was on the other side of the wall.

Luckily, the crowd at The Devil's Boot that night was rougher and rowdier than usual, so no one noticed that Luke and I were gone for a while after he threw me over his shoulder and carried me to his office—except for Teddy, of course.

When I rejoined her at our table, her friends from the boutique, Madi and Emily, were starting to slur their words, so I wasn't too worried about them. Teddy, on the other hand, I was worried about. I felt bad that I'd left her birthday celebration, even if I *was* manhandled out of there.

But Teddy wasn't mad at all.

She was beaming.

The first thing she asked me was, "Where'd your lipstick go?" Followed by, "I can't believe you got railed in a public place. I haven't even done that."

Luke came out of his office a few minutes later and brushed my hand as he walked back to the bar. His bartender—I think his name was Joe—gave him a stern expression.

Luke, on the other hand, tried to smooth down his dark hair and looked like he was holding back a smile.

God, he was so *pretty*.

That was the thought I had then, and it was the thought I had now as he came into view. I was walking down to the stables to take Maple out for a ride.

This past week or so, I'd gotten a lot more comfortable in the saddle. I'd been able to take Maple to a gallop the other day, and she was loving it.

Every time I got on a horse, my stomach still did a little flip. I didn't know if my accident would ever leave me completely, but a few months ago, I thought I would never ride again.

This was so much better than that.

Riding was everything to me, and now that I could do it again, I could admit how much it had hurt when I thought I'd lost it forever.

I'd never felt pain like that before, and I never wanted to feel it again.

It was hard not to think about the improvement in my riding in relation to Brooks. Since I'd been home, the time I'd spent with him was my favorite time, especially over the past week. I spent a few nights at his house because if anyone asked, I could easily write that off as being with Teddy, and we didn't have to worry about my family wondering why his truck was around.

His house was a small two-bedroom bungalow in the hollow behind The Devil's Boot. He told me he'd spent the past few years fixing it up, and I could tell how much effort he'd put into it. I hadn't pegged Luke Brooks as a man who had more than one pillow, nice bedding, and a bed frame to boot. I told him as much, and he told me I needed to raise the bar.

He was full of surprises.

Just like the kitchen slow dance he surprised me with a few days ago.

We'd both had a long day, so when I went over there, I wasn't expecting anything. I just wanted to be with him.

But when I walked in, he had already made dinner for us, and Luke Brooks knew his way around the kitchen.

When we were cleaning up, the small speaker he had in the living room started to play a slow Randy Travis song. He threw the towel he was using to dry dishes over his shoulder and grabbed my hand, pulling me to him. He put one hand on my waist and used the other to intertwine our fingers.

We swayed together in the kitchen, and I could've stayed in that moment forever.

Later that night, we fell asleep on his couch watching my favorite, *Sweet Home Alabama*.

It was the small moments like those where I could see him clearly. Yes, he was absolutely a t-shirt mutilator, but he wasn't arrogant, irresponsible, or careless. He was thoughtful and protective.

For someone who'd spent their entire life begging for attention from others, he really knew how to make me feel like I was the only person on the planet.

The Luke I'd gotten to know since I'd come home was the kind of man I could fall in love with. I was starting to think he was the only man I could fall in love with.

And that was scary as hell.

I watched as he dragged a rake through the corral, which meant he had already cleaned it out. His gray t-shirt was starting to stick to him, and his skin was glistening in the late summer sun. He stopped for a second to grab the bottom of his t-shirt and brought the fabric up to wipe his face.

Goddamn.

I walked up to the fence of the corral and draped my arms over the top of it.

"Good morning," I said, announcing my presence. Luke brought his eyes to mine and started to walk toward me.

"Morning," he responded after placing a quick kiss on my temple.

"I missed you last night," I said honestly. He smirked at me, and I shoved his shoulder. "Shut up."

"Sorry. I had to wake up earlier than usual, and I figured you'd been losing enough sleep this week as is." The smirk on his face turned playful.

That was true.

It was weird...being with him. It was like I couldn't get enough. I liked sex but never had a particularly high sex drive until Luke. I was used to going long periods of time without sleeping with anyone. I never cared.

Obviously, the sex was great, but I think the thing that really did it for me was that Luke made me feel like he wanted me, and he didn't keep it a secret. He made me feel desired and even sultry, which was never a word I would've used to describe myself. I would use that word to describe Teddy, but not me.

I loved the way it felt.

"Why'd you have to wake up so early?"

"You'll see. Are you up for a ride?" He tucked a strand of hair behind my ear.

"Yes, but I need to do the stalls first, and I've got the boarding stables on my docket today."

"All done."

"That's physically impossible at this time in the morning."

Luke leaned over the rails and kissed me softly.

"It's all done," he said. I didn't even want to know what time he had to get here to make that happen. Did he even go to sleep? "We'll have to follow up on the boarding stables this afternoon, but everything that could be done this morning is done."

"Seriously?"

"Seriously. So"—he kissed me again between his words—"ready for that ride?"

I nodded eagerly and started walking toward the stable. Luke mirrored me on the other side of the fence until he made his way out of the corral. We walked to the main stable door together.

When we reached the doorway, I saw that both Friday and Maple were in the crossties–groomed, saddled, and ready to go.

"Wow, you really have been busy."

"They've only been here for a few minutes. I thought I had it timed perfectly to when you'd come down, but I didn't take into consideration how often you snooze your alarm."

I gave him another playful shove. "Shut up."

"How can you grow up on a ranch and still not be able to wake up with an alarm?"

"I stay up late. I like the quiet."

"I remember my quiet nights, but now I've got this woman ringing me dry and snoring afterward."

"I do not snore!"

"You do." He flicked my nose. "But it's cute. You sleep harder than anyone I've ever met."

I wish I could've denied that, but it was true. I was a hard sleeper. It took me a while to actually go to sleep, but once I finally got there, I could not be moved. The apocalypse could hit, and I wouldn't even have a chance to get away from the zombies because they'd get me in my sleep.

"Whatever," I mumbled. I walked up to Maple, and she nuzzled into my shoulder. I wrapped my arms around her neck. Maple was an affectionate horse, and I loved her so much. She'd only been mine for the duration of my professional career, but it felt like a lifetime. Between her and Moonshine, I was convinced I had the best horses at Rebel Blue.

Brooks and I walked our horses out of the stables and mounted.

"Do you feel okay?" he asked.

"Yeah, I do." And I did. My breathing was even, and my head felt level. "Where are we headed?"

"Small arena." The small arena was near the boarding stables. It was bigger than a corral but smaller than the full-size arena that sat near the old Big House. I used the small arena a lot growing up, but I hadn't been in there since I'd been back because it was on the ranch hands' maintenance schedule.

Brooks and I both urged our horses forward, and we started to make our way through the ranch. It was a good thing this place was massive because I didn't need any questions about what I was doing riding through with Brooks.

After a few minutes, Luke took Friday up to a trot, and I followed with Maple.

Riding through Rebel Blue Ranch was one of the best feelings in the world. The mountain landscape was made of greens, browns, and yellows. Against the backdrop of the blue sky, it created something that felt so otherworldly. There was no other way to describe it.

When Luke and I were about a thousand yards away from the small arena, he pushed Friday to a gallop.

I followed without thinking.

As Maple was getting up to speed, I stood slightly in the stirrups, feeling the air move around my body.

For the first time in a long time, riding felt like the most natural thing in the world. I felt the steady rhythm of Maple's hooves hitting the ground, her muscles working underneath mine, and my own hair whipping behind me.

Too soon, Friday and Luke started to slow, and I had to follow. We came to a stop outside the perimeter of the arena. We had approached this part of the ranch from the opposite side of when Wes brought me here a few weeks ago, so the old Big House was in the distance rather than front and center.

Unlike the big arena, this one wasn't covered, only fenced. Inside the fence, I could see three shapes. They looked like...barrels. They were in the shape of a triangle.

I dismounted Maple and tied her to one of the fence posts. Brooks was right behind me with Friday.

I looked over at Brooks. "What's going on?"

"It's a regulation barrel course, Emmy. Three barrels, triangle pattern, spaced accurately." He'd made a place for me to practice? "There are less than two weeks until divisionals come to Meadowlark, and if you want to go out, you're going to go out with a bang."

"You made this? For me?" He looked at me like making this was the most obvious thing in the world for him to do. I had this funny feeling in my chest. No one had ever done anything like this for me before. I couldn't believe it. "When did you do this?"

"Last night."

"And you got here early this morning?"

He nodded and rubbed the back of his neck with one of his hands. He looked like he was blushing.

It was hard to breathe, but not because I was panicking. It was because this man had quite literally taken my breath away.

"You need to practice," he said simply.

I looked at his makeshift course and imagined Maple and me speeding around the barrels in a cloverleaf pattern. I hadn't done it in months.

Looking out at the course, I started to get nervous. Really fucking nervous. I didn't know what I'd been thinking, deciding to ride in divisionals. I wouldn't be ready. There was no way in hell.

"Emmy, sugar, talk to me," Luke said, obviously catching on to the shift in my behavior. I couldn't hide anything from him anymore. I thought it would frustrate me, but honestly, I almost felt relieved that I couldn't just hide in my own head about this entire situation.

"I'm scared," I whispered.

"Honestly, I'd be more worried if you weren't. You experienced the thing that every rider dreads, but you still got back on the horse," he said.

I felt my hands start to shake, and Luke noticed immediately.

"Hey." He stepped toward me. "You can do this, Emmy. We're going to take it slow, but I know you can do this."

"How do you know?"

He cupped my face in his hands. "You're Clementine fuckin' Ryder." I laughed at that, and a single tear sneaked out of my eye. He caught it before it could fall, wiping it off my cheek. "Sugar, you deserve to go out on your own terms. Just because you got dusted doesn't mean you're done."

22

LUKE

mmy and I had fallen into a routine over the past week or so. We spent almost every night together, usually at my place, and in the morning, we would go to the barrel racing course at Rebel Blue. She would run the course for an hour or two. Sometimes I would stay with her the whole time and sometimes, I wouldn't, depending on what needed to happen on the ranch that day.

Watching Emmy ride was mesmerizing. When she was on Maple, she had absolute control. She was so focused and steady. There wasn't anything that could shake her.

I tried not to think about how bad her accident must have been if it had taken that sense of security away from her.

Pretty damn bad.

I hated thinking about how she was all alone in Denver for a month before deciding to come home.

We had created this bubble. Inside it, it was just the two of us getting to know one another. Even though I was grateful for all the time we were spending together, there was a part of me that was starting to feel guilty.

I didn't know how much longer I could do this without telling Gus. If he found out I'd been keeping this secret, he'd probably think it was because I was just dicking around with his sister. That's how it looked, especially when my track record with women wasn't great.

There was also a smaller part of me that worried Emmy wanted to keep us a secret because she didn't feel the same way I did.

But I couldn't think like that.

When I came back to the arena after taking care of some things at the stables, Emmy and Maple had finished up their session. Emmy was sitting on the dirt, and Maple had laid down next to her and had put her giant head in Emmy's lap.

Horses were basically just big dogs.

"How'd it go?" I asked as I approached.

"Okay. Still nothing under twenty seconds, but I feel good."

"Good," I said. I squatted down next to her so I could kiss the top of her head. "I've gotta get over to the bar, but I wanted to see you before I go."

"I'll ride back with you." Emmy got up slowly, making sure not to jostle Maple in a way that would startle her. We moved away from Maple to give her enough room to get up without risking her bumping one of us.

I pulled Emmy into my arms and held her there for a second, knowing I might not get the chance to do this when we made it back to the stables because someone could be there, and the thought of leaving her without touching her had me tied up in knots.

I pulled back to kiss her, soft and slow, just the way she liked it. Before things could heat up, my phone buzzed in my back pocket.

We were always getting interrupted.

It was probably Joe.

Emmy gave me one more peck on the lips before pulling back, knowing it was probably something to do with the bar. She tried to walk back toward Maple, but I held her to me with an arm draped around her shoulders. I wasn't ready to let her go just yet.

I answered my phone without looking at it. "Hello?"

"Luke, honey." It was a woman's voice, and it was shaky and sad. My body went rigid, and Emmy must've felt it because she looked up at me with concern written all over her face.

"Mom?" I asked. Emmy's eyes widened. I didn't talk to my mother. I had tried for a while, but I'd given up after too many disappointments.

"Yes, honey. It's me." My mom continued to talk on the other end, and it was like the world slowed. I hadn't heard from her in so long. I could barely recognize her voice. Had she always sounded this brittle?

After I hung up, Emmy gave me a squeeze. "Everything okay?" she asked. I didn't answer her for a minute, unsure of what my answer meant for me. "Luke?" She moved one of her hands up to my face. "Everything okay?"

I didn't look at her, just out into the distance of Rebel Blue.

"My mom's husband—" I started. "He was supposed to be home from his truck route a few days ago, but he never came back."

EMMY

After the phone call from Luke's mom, we got back to the stables as fast as we could to get Maple and Friday settled.

When we got them situated, Luke told me he'd call me later as he was walking away, but there was no way I was letting him go into that house, the house that made him feel like he wasn't worth anything, all alone.

That's how I ended up in Luke's truck, in the middle of the bench seat, with my head on his shoulder and our fingers intertwined.

He was tense. I'd never seen him like this. Ever. It

was unnerving to watch someone who was so even-keeled be wound so tight.

Luke and I had talked about his family when we started our riding lessons, which seemed like forever ago now. I knew he didn't give a shit about his stepdad or his brothers, but he still cared about his mom.

Lydia Hale lived in a trailer about twenty minutes from Rebel Blue. The closer we got, the tighter Luke held onto my hand. I didn't think he knew what to expect going into his old home.

I didn't even know the last time he was there. He completely stopped sleeping there when he was sixteen and moved all of his stuff out on his eighteenth birthday.

Luke rolled his truck to a stop in front of the house, and I lifted my head from his shoulder. It was lawn ornament central. He cut the engine but didn't make any move to get out of the truck.

"Emmy, you don't have to come in there with me."

I turned my face up to his and brushed his hair out of his face. "You've been there for me since I got home. I don't want you to have to do this alone."

"I didn't grow up like you did, Emmy," he said with a sigh.

"So?"

"So, I don't know what it's going to be like in there, or what *she's* going to be like. I don't want to put you in a situation that's going to make you uncomfortable."

When he looked at me, there was pain in his big brown eyes. It broke my heart.

"I'm not a princess, Luke. I can handle it. I'm here for you."

Luke sighed. "There's nothing I can say to make you stay here, is there?" I shook my head, and Luke kissed my forehead. "Alright then. Let's go."

We got out of the truck and walked to the front door, hand in hand.

When Luke knocked, it only took his mom a few seconds to answer. I hadn't seen Lydia since I was in high school, and she looked mostly the same but with more wrinkles. She was petite, with blonde hair that mainly had faded to gray and blue eyes. Her hair was cut short, right above her shoulders. She had a lit cigarette between her fingers, and her eyes were puffy from crying.

Luke didn't look anything like her. He looked just like Jimmy, probably making it even harder for him to survive in this house as a kid.

"Luke, baby, I'm so happy you're here." Lydia stepped out of the house and gave him an awkward one-armed hug.

"Hey, Mom." He didn't let go of my hand as she hugged him.

She pulled back and set her gaze on me. "Clementine Ryder? Is that you?" She looked me up and down, her eyes stopping at Luke's hand in mine.

"Yes, ma'am," I said.

Lydia pursed her lips. Was she upset that I was here with her son?

"Well, I wasn't expecting more company, but come in."

Yeah, she was definitely annoyed at me being here. Luke gave my hand a squeeze, which I returned as we walked into the house.

The front room was littered with beer bottles and Coke cans. The TV in the corner was playing old episodes of *The Newlywed Game*, and it smelled like smoke.

Lydia settled into a rocking chair next to the couch. There was another chair next to her that was empty. I assumed it belonged to John. Luke led me to the faded burgundy couch, and we sat down together. He still hadn't let go of my hand.

"Mom, tell me what happened. Where are JJ and Bill?"

Luke's brothers.

Lydia let out a shaky breath, the kind that told you someone could start crying again at any moment. From what Luke had told me about John, I didn't think there was much to miss, but I was trying not to be insensitive about her loss.

"I haven't heard from him in days." John was a truck driver, so it was normal for him to be gone for longer periods of time. If Lydia was worried, that must've meant something. "The trucking company hasn't been able to locate his truck. The last time they could find it, it was near the Nevada state line." Lydia took a drag of her cigarette. Her hand was shaking. "The boys are out, but I couldn't stand to be here alone. It's so quiet without John."

"I'm glad you called me," Luke said. "I didn't know you even had my number."

"I found it with John's things. It was on a note on his desk." Probably from the last time Luke called him and tried to get ahold of his mom.

"I'm sorry, Mom. I know John means a lot to you. I'm sure he's fine." Luke's voice didn't convey any emotion. He was probably trying to cover up the disdain he had for his stepdad.

"Mrs. Hale," I jumped in. "Is there anything we can do for you while we're here? Make you dinner or anything?"

Lydia took another drag of her cigarette and blew the smoke in my direction as she surveyed me.

"I don't need anything else from the Ryders," she said sharply. What was that supposed to mean? "Your lot already took my son away from me, and now I see you've got your claws in him."

Luke squeezed my hand again.

"Mom. You know I couldn't stay here," Luke said fiercely. "Don't hate the Ryders for giving me what you couldn't, and I'm not going to stay here if you talk to my girl that way."

My girl.

Something about that felt so significant. I'd been

people's girlfriend before, but I never really assigned any weight to the word. When Luke said I was his, though, it meant something.

He continued, "And considering it's been years since I've seen you, that'd be a damn shame."

Lydia contemplated his words for a minute, all while keeping her eyes on me. This woman really wasn't a fan of my family—or me, apparently.

"Fine," she said eventually.

After that, Luke relaxed a bit. I sat there while he and his mom talked. He told her about the bar and his house, about how he had fixed it up. The more they talked, the more Lydia brightened. I think she was proud of her son, and her anger with me might have been a projection of her own guilt.

Luke stood from the couch and went to the kitchen to grab his mom a soda. I followed, not wanting to be left alone with her. Punching an old woman in the face was not on my to-do list today.

"I'm sorry about that," he said as soon as we stepped onto the old vinyl floors of the kitchen.

"You have nothing to be sorry for. Are you sure we shouldn't try to get her to eat or something?" My dad fed us when we were sad. Or happy, for that matter. It was one of his ways of taking care of us, and I'd picked up on it.

"There's probably nothing here to make." Luke grabbed a Coke out of the fridge and set it on the counter before starting to rummage through the kitchen. Under the sink, he found a box of garbage bags and pulled it out. "But I am going to clean up a bit."

"I'll help you," I said. We went back out to the living room, and Luke gave Lydia her Coke and started picking up the bottles, cans, and trash throughout the room. We filled up three garbage bags, and Luke set them by the door for us to take out when we left.

While we were cleaning, Lydia disappeared into another room but re-emerged a little later.

She had a stack of photos in her hands, and she handed them to Luke. "I found these when I found your number. I thought you might like to have them." Luke took them from her, and we sat on the couch again.

The first photo was of him in a cowboy hat with one of those horses on a stick. He was adorable.

"How old were you here?" I asked him, taking the photo from his hands.

"I don't know. Probably five or six," he said.

Lydia nodded in her chair, indicating that was right. She had warmed up to me a bit probably because I'd cleaned her house.

"He always wanted to be a cowboy," she said.

We continued through the photos. There were pictures of fishing and playing outside, an excellent one of him wearing a cowboy hat, and a few Halloweens. There was even one of Jimmy holding him as a baby, but he moved past it too quickly for me to really look at it.

We got to a photo of a boy in a high chair eating a cake. A birthday cake, from what I could tell.

"Oh, I love this picture. You loved your birthday," Lydia said. "Thought it should be every day."

Luke stayed quiet, and I noticed his shoulders sagged a bit. He handed the photo back to Lydia. "That's not me, Mom. That's JJ."

As if on cue, the front door opened and a tall–but not as tall as Luke–blond man walked inside. He was wearing a dirty mechanic uniform. It was JJ. Even though I'd never met him, I knew who he was. He was the same age as Gus, and he worked at one of the auto shops in town. There were two—the one you wanted to take your car to and the one where JJ worked. He also had a side business that was less than legal.

The first words out of his mouth were, "What the fuck are you doing here?"

"JJ," Lydia said, "Luke came to check up on me."

Luke grabbed my hand, and we stood from the couch together. He positioned himself in front of me as we started walking toward the door.

"I've only been gone for a few hours, and you let this bastard back in your house?"

"Good to see you, too, JJ," Luke said with a sigh.

"Shut the hell up and get out of my dad's house," JJ barked.

Asshole.

"Look, man, I just came to check in on my mom. She called me, and she didn't want to be alone. Now that you're here, I'll go," Luke explained. "I'm sorry about your dad. I hope he turns up soon."

Luke started pulling me toward the door, but JJ blocked his path.

JJ wasn't built like Luke, and I was confident Luke could shut him up with one punch, but I didn't think he would. Not in front of his mom, at least.

It was funny. On Teddy's birthday, I was so mad at Luke for punching someone. Now, I wanted him to lay his brother out flat.

JJ's eyes were on me. "Emmy Ryder," he said coolly. God, why did every member of Luke's family seem to hate my guts? "What are you doing here with this loser?"

"Don't fucking talk to her," Luke said. There was venom in his voice now. I'd never heard that from him before. I wondered how much disdain for his family he kept underneath the surface.

"How does Gus Ryder feel about his right-hand man fucking his little sister?"

If Luke were a cartoon character, there would be smoke coming out of his nostrils right now. I didn't care about what JJ said to me—he was an idiot—but Luke did.

"I told you not to fucking talk to her." With one hand, Luke pushed JJ out of the way. Hard. JJ stumbled, and I knew if he came back at Luke, things would escalate. "Emmy, let's go." He started to lead me out of the house, but I turned back to JJ.

"You know, you should really stop being such an asshole," I said. "Mess with the wrong person, and someone might let it slip to the sheriff you've been dealing more than just weed out of your trailer."

JJ looked at me, stunned only for a second before he said, "I never want to see either of you at this house ever again. Get the fuck out."

Luke and I went out the front door, and before JJ could slam it shut, I looked back at Lydia. She had tears in her eyes.

Luke pulled me down the walkway, getting me to his truck as quickly as possible. Once we were there, he pressed me against the driver's side door and kissed me hard. There was something different about this kiss. It meant something.

I just didn't know what.

When he pulled back, he rested his forehead against mine. "What was that for?" I breathed.

"No one's ever stood up for me before," he said.

His words cracked my heart wide open. Luke Brooks, and his big heart, deserved so much more than the people in that house. He was kind, hardworking, and sincere. I wrapped my arms around him and held him to me. He buried his face in my shoulder, and we stayed like that for a while.

When we got in the truck, I took my place in the middle of the bench, and Luke draped his arm over my shoulder. Since we were on the town's back roads, we rolled the windows down and let the late summer air flow through the truck.

"Do you want to talk about what happened back there?" I asked.

Luke sighed. "I'm sorry about JJ," he said.

"You have nothing to apologize for. You deserve better than them, Luke. You're more than just Lydia and Jimmy's mistake." I looked up at him, but he kept his eyes on the road.

He was quiet for a long time until we pulled into the gravel drive in front of his house. When he cut the engine, he laid his head on the steering wheel and let out another sigh. I rubbed my hand over his back.

"That sucked," he finally said. "Is it bad if I hope that John just stays gone?"

"No," I responded.

Luke lifted his head from the steering wheel and looked at me. It didn't feel like I was looking at Luke, the thirty-two-year-old man. It felt like I was looking at Brooks, the fifteen-year-old boy who would've done anything for a family.

I saw him so clearly at that moment. I brought my hand up and brushed some of his rogue dark hair out of his face before kissing him softly.

When I pulled back, he said, "Thank you for coming with me, Emmy."

"I'd go anywhere with you," I responded.

I meant it.

23

EMMY

You know, I'd never really understood the expression "they were shaking in their boots" until now because I was quite literally shaking in my boots.

I didn't normally get nervous before races, but that was before. This was now, and my stomach felt like it was two seconds away from dropping all the way down to my ankles.

It felt like I'd blinked, and divisionals were here.

I'd been practicing with Maple—walking, trotting, and loping a few days each week, taking care not to overwork her. Sometimes Luke came with me, and sometimes he didn't. I didn't get nervous while I was practicing anymore. I finally believed I was safe.

While I was practicing, it was easy to remember why I loved barrel racing. It was the only rodeo sport where horsemanship wasn't judged—it was all about the time—but you still had to be a damn good rider to pull off a successful barrel race. I liked that being a good rider was so integral to the sport it didn't even need to be judged. It was one of the things that drew me to the barrels in the first place.

Being here in an arena surrounded by competitors and people I knew was different than practicing. People I loved were here. My dad, my brothers, Luke, Teddy, Hank—even Cam and her fiancé had come so Riley could be here. It was like my safety net had been pulled from under me. I didn't know if there was anything I could have done to better prepare for it.

I did my normal pre-race routine, but the shaking didn't stop. I didn't think I was in danger of a full panic attack, but this was definitely at least panic-lite.

Teddy had to pin my number onto my shirt because my hands were quivering so badly.

"Emmy. What's up? I've never seen you like this before a race." There was no reason to lie to her now. I'd been lying to her for so long, and I couldn't do it anymore. I didn't want to.

"This is my first race since I got thrown from a horse in June. That's why I came home. That's why I was so mopey and closed off, and that's why I can't get my shaking under control right now." The words fell from my lips before I could think them all the way through.

Teddy blinked slowly. I thought she was going to reprimand me for not telling her about everything. I should have. She was my best friend. I should have told her. I should have told everyone.

Instead, she said, "I'm sorry that you've been carrying that by yourself."

I didn't know how to respond because I really hadn't been carrying it by myself.

Luke had helped me.

"Teddy. I need you to do something for me."

"Anything, babe."

"Can you get Luke?"

TEDDY RETURNED a few minutes later with Luke in tow. He was wearing his normal jeans and boots, but instead of a t-shirt, he'd opted for a cowboy button-down along with a black cowboy hat.

My cowboy.

He walked into the riders' area, and worry was written all over his face. When I saw him, my shaking didn't stop, but it wasn't as intense. His eyes found mine, and he made a beeline for me, Teddy following behind him.

When he got to me, he immediately cupped my face in his hands. "What's wrong, sugar? Are you having another panic attack?"

I shook my head. I wasn't. "I just needed you."

"I'm here." He wrapped me up in his arms, and I melted into him. He stroked my hair and rubbed his hands over my back and my arms. We stayed there for a while, and it was like with every pass of his hands over me, the shaking got less and less until it stopped.

He must've felt it, too, because he pulled back and put his hands on my shoulders.

"What's going on inside that beautiful head of yours?" His voice was the soft one. I think he only used that one with me.

"Do you think I can do this?" I asked.

"Yes," he responded immediately. "But it doesn't really matter if I know you can do it. It only matters if you know it, too."

Of course, he would choose this moment to get all inspirational.

It did make me feel better, though. *He* made me feel better.

"Wow, I'm really looking forward to your TED talk," I said sarcastically.

Luke flicked my nose. "Smart-ass. But if your sarcasm is in check, then I'm guessing you're feeling a little better?"

"Yeah, I am." I folded myself into him again. I could stay here forever. I wanted to stay with him forever. "Thank you."

The event coordinator came into the contestant area to give us our ten-minute warning.

"Sugar"—Luke kissed my forehead—"I am so proud of you."

"I haven't even raced yet," I said against his chest.

He pulled back so he could look down at me. "You

don't need to race for me to be proud of you. You could call this all off right now and walk out of here, and I would still be proud of you."

"You would?"

"Yes." He kissed my forehead again. His forehead kisses made me feel like I was floating. Something about them felt so intimate. He pulled back again and tucked his finger under my chin, forcing me to look at him. "So, are we walking out of here?"

I wanted this.

I wanted to ride.

And I wanted to win.

"No."

"That's my girl." Luke smiled big enough that I could see the wrinkles around his big brown eyes. They were the last thing I saw before he kissed me.

You know in the action movies, when the hero and heroine kiss right before the battle, and all of the sudden they're ready to take on the aliens or the mutated monster or whatever?

I understood that now.

LUKE

The coordinator called for the barrel racers, and it took everything in me to let Emmy out of my arms. I wanted so many more moments like this with her.

She grabbed her cowboy hat off a table next to us.

"Thank you," she said. Then, she turned and started walking toward the racer's entrance.

And damn, did her ass look good in those jeans.

I watched her until I couldn't see her red shirt anymore. When I tore my eyes away from where I saw her last, Teddy was staring at me. I couldn't place the look on her face, but I didn't think it was bad. Hopefully.

I had honestly forgotten she was standing there with us, that she had just seen us together in a way no one else even knew existed.

"What?" I asked her.

She shook her head slightly like she was in a daze.

"You're in love with her," she said. It wasn't a question.

"Yeah, I am." I didn't have any reason to lie to Teddy. If she didn't punch me in the face the day she came into my office to interrogate me, I was pretty sure she wouldn't now.

"Does she know?"

"Not yet."

"You should tell her."

"I will."

"She loves you, too, you know."

The thought of that terrified me, but it also made me feel like the luckiest man alive. I didn't really know how to be in love, but I knew I wanted to be with Emmy in every way I could. I wanted the kitchen slow dances, nights out with shots, rides through the mountains, hot sex, afternoon naps, and two-lane highways with the windows down.

I wanted it all.

"How do you know that?"

"She asked for you." Teddy shrugged. "Emmy never asks for anything. She just puts her head down and deals with things in the only way she knows how, by kicking shit around in her own brain. But she asked for you."

24

LUKE

Teddy and I walked back to the stands where Emmy's cheering section had settled in.

When Teddy came to get me, I was waiting in line to grab everyone some beers, but now here I was, back and beer-less. Maybe they wouldn't notice.

"Where are our beers, man?" Wes asked.

Damn.

"The line was long as hell." Which was true. I just didn't stand in it that long..

"So?" Wes responded.

"I don't like you that much," I said. Wes flipped me the bird.

Camille and Riley weren't here when I left, but they were here now, and so was Camille's fiancé. I couldn't remember that guy's name for the life of me, so I just tried never to put myself in a situation where I'd have to say it.

I sat in the space Gus had saved for me, between him and Amos. Amos gave me a shoulder squeeze when I sat down.

"Thanks for coming, Luke," Amos said. "I'm sure Emmy is happy you're here."

I didn't know why he would say that. Did he know something?

"U-uh, yeah," I stammered out. "Maybe."

Smooth.

Amos just gave me a lopsided smile. It made me uneasy as hell.

Before I could read too much into it, the announcer's voice blared through the speakers, announcing that barrel racing was about to begin. Everyone in Emmy's corner snapped to attention. According to the program, she was going last.

"You know," Amos started, "the last time Emmy raced in Meadowlark was before she went to college. I've seen her race hundreds of times since then, but there's something about seeing her race in her hometown."

Amos sounded...choked up? The man wasn't afraid of feelings or emotions or anything like that. He told his boys he loved them, he hugged everyone, and let Riley paint his nails, but I don't think I'd ever seen him get misty.

The first and second racers came and went, averaging around sixteen seconds. The fastest Emmy had done the course at Rebel Blue was sixteen point five, so she was pretty evenly matched here.

Two racers in the lineup knocked over a barrel, so they got a five-second penalty added to their time. I knew Emmy could beat them.

Barrel racing moved fast, so it didn't take long to get to Emmy. The rider before her came to the starting line. When the gun went off, she went right. She was fast. Her horse was kicking up dirt and hauling ass, but she looked unsteady—she even hit a barrel. She still came in as the fastest so far at fifteen point seven seconds. The barrel she hit didn't get knocked over, so there was no penalty on her time.

"And last but certainly not least," the announcer started speaking. I saw Emmy's red shirt in the arena. She and Maple were making their way up to the starting line. My leg started bouncing up and down. "We have four-time champion and record-breaking racer, racing in her hometown for the first time in nine years, Clementine Ryderrr." The announcer extended the last "r" in Ryder, and everyone who was there for Emmy stood up and went wild. Most of the people in the stands stood, too.

Meadowlark showed up for their sweetheart.

Emmy was at the starting line, looking fucking beautiful in her brown cowboy hat, red button-down, and Wranglers. She was stroking Maple's neck. Both of them looked calm.

Good.

A few seconds later, the gun sounded, and Emmy was off.

And she went left.

Why the hell did she go left? All of us must've thought the same thing, because I heard Gus say my question out loud.

In barrel racing, the most efficient way to make the clover-leaf pattern that was required was to go to the right barrel, then the left, and then the center. But Emmy went left, and she rounded the first barrel tighter than I'd ever seen her do it. Dirt from the arena was flying everywhere, but Emmy was in complete control.

Even from here, I could see she was focused.

She headed for the right barrel, maintaining her speed, but rounded it a little wider than the first barrel. At this point, she was basically tied with the rider before her.

That's my girl.

There was only one barrel left, and Emmy was beelining for it. She didn't slow, and she didn't go wide. Holy shit. Her control was out of this world. She made it around the barrel and as soon as she could, pushed Maple harder on the straight away.

All of us were yelling something along the lines of "Go, go, go," and Emmy was fucking *going*.

I held my breath as she crossed the finish line, only starting to slow Maple at that point.

Fourteen point eight seconds. My heart stopped

dead in my chest, and the crowd erupted as the clock stopped. Their cheers were all directed at Emmy.

"Folks! Clementine Ryder remains a force to be reckoned with, sliding easily into first place and breaking her own record of fourteen point nine. What a race!" the announcer said over the speaker.

We all cheered. Amos hugged us all, Gus slapped me on the back, and even Teddy got a high five from him.

Emmy and Maple came back out to the arena, taking their victory lap. Emmy was beaming. Her smile was like a wild flame, and I could feel its warmth from here. She spotted all of us in the crowd and tipped her hat.

Amos, Gus, Wes, Teddy, and I all started to leave our spots, not bothering to stick around for any of the other events. Camille, her fiancé, and Riley stayed with Hank. Teddy quickly checked in with them, making sure they were okay to help him down the stadium stairs, and told them where his wheelchair was.

All of us were here for one reason and one reason only, and that reason was Emmy, so we went to her.

I let Teddy lead the pack, not wanting to be front and center when I offered her my congratulations, no matter how much I wanted to be.

Damn, I was so proud of her.

When we made it down to the entry area, I spotted Emmy in her red shirt. My eyes had found their way to her before my brain could catch up.

"Emmy!" Teddy called out, and Emmy looked over and started running toward us.

Wait, no.

Not toward us.

Toward *me*.

EMMY

I did it. I *fucking* did it.

After the accident, the panic, the anxiety, and the spiral that brought me home, I did it. I raced my last race in a way I could be proud of, and I *was* proud.

I took Maple to a holding paddock and showered her in hugs and kisses before starting toward the entry area, hoping my family and Luke would be waiting for me.

I looked around, but I couldn't see them.

"Emmy!" I heard Teddy's voice and turned toward it. There they were. My family, my best friend, and the man I could finally admit I was completely and totally in love with.

Before I knew what my feet were doing, they were running toward him.

I threw myself into his arms, both of our hats falling to the dirt.

Luke let out a chuckle as my body collided with his, but he still caught me. He spun me around a few times before bringing us to a stop.

"You were a wonder out there," he said. The way he

was looking at me lodged my heart firmly in my throat. Instead of answering him, I kissed him while he held me in his arms, and I didn't hold back.

My feet still off the ground, he kept ahold of me with one arm and snaked the other one into my hair. I didn't care that my family and nearly all of Meadowlark were watching. Luke wasn't my secret.

He was just mine.

We kissed for a second, completely immersed in this moment, before I pulled back. I smiled at him. His big brown eyes searched my face. He looked dazed like he couldn't believe what just happened. I couldn't quite believe it, either—the race *or* the kiss.

"Emmy, I—"

Luke didn't get to finish his sentence because at the same time, Gus said, "What the *fuck*?"

Luke lowered me to the ground but didn't let go of me completely. He was tense like he was ready to jump in front of a bullet.

I looked over at where everyone was standing. Teddy was smiling. My dad had this weird smirk on his face, and poor Wes just looked confused as hell.

Gus looked like he wanted to light Luke on fire.

"What the fuck?" he repeated.

"Look, man, I can explain—" Luke said.

"Gus—" I started.

"Shut up, Emmy."

I shrunk back, and felt Luke hold me a little tighter before letting go and stepping in front of me.

"I know you're mad, but you don't get to talk to her that way," Luke said firmly. "If you want to be mad at someone, you can be mad at me."

"Oh, I am. Are you fucking kidding me, Brooks? My *sister*? That's who you chose to mess around with?"

"August, calm down," our dad said. His gravelly voice was stern. He didn't use that voice often, but when he did, it normally set us all straight.

Not this time.

Gus stalked toward Luke and me. Wes tried to stop him, but he shrugged him off. Luke acted fast, pushing me behind him, but not fast enough to dodge the punch Gus threw at him.

Gus's fist met Luke's face with a crack, and Luke's head snapped back. He didn't fall to the ground, but he did stumble, taking care not to knock me over.

This man was still looking out for me even after he just got decked by my brother.

"What the hell, Gus!" I screeched. Gus was shaking out his hand like the punch hurt him.

He started toward Luke again, but I stepped in front of him. Wes had made it over to us and was grabbing onto Gus's shoulder, holding tighter this time.

"I can't believe you. I knew you were a screw-up, but I didn't know you were a liar, too," Gus spat.

His words seemed to affect Luke more than his punch.

"Gus, calm down," Wes chimed in. "Let's just take a lap, okay?"

"Take a lap? You want me to take a lap when we just saw this asshole with his tongue down our sister's throat?" Gus's voice was venomous. Luke kept me firmly behind him, protecting me from Gus's vitriol. A small circle of people were gathered around us, and I knew this would feed the Meadowlark gossip monster for weeks to come.

"Gus, get over yourself." That was Teddy. She stepped between Gus and Luke and me, shielding me from the wreckage, just like she said she would. "Walk away before your daughter gets down here and sees you acting like a raging lunatic who just punched her uncle in the face."

The mention of Riley did it for Gus. He didn't calm down, but he didn't look like he was going to throw another punch. He stared down at Teddy, then at Luke and me.

"Walk away, son," my dad said.

"I can't believe all of you are just okay with this," Gus said bitterly, but he turned to walk away, and Wes followed. Wes would take care of him.

My dad walked over to Luke and me, and put his hand on Luke's shoulder. "You okay, kid?" he asked him.

"Yeah, I'm fine. Amos, I'm sorry—"

My dad held up his hand, signaling for Luke to stop. "None of that." He turned to me. "Clementine, why don't you go home with Teddy? Maybe give Gus a few days to cool off. I'll take care of Luke."

"But—" I started to speak, but my dad shot me a look that told me this was non-negotiable. Teddy made her way over to me and grabbed my hand, pulling me away from Luke, which was exactly what I didn't want to do.

"Teddy, I can't leave him."

"Yes, you can. It's only temporary. Half the town is waiting for Gus to show up and hit him again, and your dad will take care of him. Let's get out of here."

25

LUKE

I looked in the mirror. Gus had given me a hell of a shiner, but I couldn't blame him. The outer edges of it were starting to yellow, but it still looked pretty gnarly.

It had been a few days since divisionals, and I still hadn't seen Emmy. I wanted to give Gus some more time to cool down, but I had no intention of giving Emmy up. Ever.

Even though I hadn't seen her, we talked every day. She was mine.

I needed Gus to get to a point where I could talk to him without him throwing another punch. Emmy didn't like it, but I had a feeling it would take a lot longer for Gus to speak to me if he kept seeing me with his little sister.

Teddy was staying with Emmy at her cabin, which made me feel better. I had been effectively barred from

Rebel Blue for the time being. Emmy was pissed at Gus, and Gus was pissed at me.

I felt like shit.

When Emmy left with Teddy after everything went down, Amos went to one of the concession stands and got me an ice pack for my eye. He didn't ask me when it started or what the hell was wrong with me, which was what I was expecting. Instead, he walked with me back to my truck and said, "He'll get over it."

"I don't know if he will," I responded.

"I do. Emmy came home broken, and it doesn't take a rocket scientist to figure out who helped her put herself back together.

"Thank you," he continued, "for taking care of my baby girl."

"She can take care of herself," I said.

"I know she can, but you made sure she didn't have to do it alone."

I wasn't really expecting a ringing endorsement from any of the Ryders, but Amos actually seemed happy about Emmy and me. That was enough to get me through a few days without her, even though I missed her like crazy.

It was weird thinking about how I'd known Emmy for nearly my entire life, but we had just been living our lives semi-adjacent to each other. Now, I couldn't imagine my life without her. I was so caught up in her.

I loved her. Deeply.

And I hadn't even gotten to tell her yet.

My phone buzzed on the bathroom counter. It was Emmy. She had sent me a picture of her phone screen. She was listening to Brooks & Dunn.

> Emmy: Good morning.

> Emmy: I miss you.

> Luke: At least you've got another Brooks to keep you company.

> Luke: I miss you too, sugar.

My doorbell rang then, which was weird—no one ever came out to my house. Most people didn't even know it was here. If someone needed me, they looked at The Devil's Boot or Rebel Blue first. I walked out of my bathroom, giving my black eye one more good prod before making my way to the front door and swinging it open.

It was Gus. He looked disheveled like he hadn't been sleeping. His beard, which was normally trimmed neatly and close to his skin, was longer than I'd ever seen it.

"Can I come in?" he asked.

I leaned against the door frame and folded my arms over my chest. "I don't know," I said. "Are you here to blacken my other eye?"

Gus looked at his feet. "No. I'm here to talk about Emmy."

That wasn't what I was expecting. I moved out of the doorway, giving him the go-ahead to come in. I hated that it felt awkward between us.

"Do you want a cup of coffee?" I asked. It was early, around seven, or else I would've offered him a beer. I might need one to get through this conversation.

"Yeah, that would be great."

I went to the kitchen, where my coffee pot had stopped brewing the pot I'd put on when I woke up this morning. I poured a cup for each of us, and we sat at the kitchen table.

This was so fucking weird. In nearly two decades of friendship, there had never been an awkward moment between Gus and me. There hadn't even been a fight that lasted longer than a few hours. We sat in silence for a few beats. Gus was the first one to speak.

"I'm sorry I punched you," he said. Apologies from Gus Ryder were a rare thing. "But you know that's my first instinct when I see someone kissing my sister."

"I'm sorry you had to find out that way," I said, and I was, but I wouldn't apologize for kissing his sister. No matter what, Emmy was mine.

We were silent again.

"I'm sorry. For what I said to you at divisionals. I didn't mean it." I didn't know what to say to him. Gus's words had fucking stung, even though I'd tried to let them roll off of me. Gus looked down at his coffee cup before he said, "You're one of the best people I know."

"You know where to hit a man where it hurts," I said.

"I really am sorry."

"So am I." I sighed. I hated that this was all so fucked up, and I knew it was my fault for falling in love with Emmy, but I could never regret that. I would never regret crossing the line with her. We'd crossed the line together, and it was the best thing that ever happened to me.

"How long has it been going on?" Gus asked.

"It started a few weeks after Emmy came home," I answered honestly. Gus pursed his lips. I could tell he wanted to get angry but was holding back.

Thank god. I didn't want to take another punch or another verbal assault.

"And you never thought maybe you should tell me that you were into my little sister?"

"Of course I did, and I was going to as soon as Emmy was ready, but can you honestly say you would've reacted any differently?"

Gus blinked slowly. "Wait." He shook his head in disbelief. "Did you say you were going to tell me as soon as Emmy was ready?" I nodded. "So you weren't the one who was keeping it a secret?"

"No, Emmy wanted to wait before we told anyone."

"You weren't the one who wanted to hide it?"

"No. As soon as I realized what was going on between us, I wanted to tell you." That was true. I just didn't know how to do it.

"So, what is going on between you two?"

I took a deep breath, hoping what I said next wouldn't earn me another punch, but Gus needed to hear the truth.

"I'm in love with her. Like, really fucking in love with her." Gus's eyes widened. He was my best friend. We talked. He knew I'd never loved anyone the way I thought I was supposed to, that I didn't even know if I knew how to, but that was before Emmy.

She was everything.

"Does she love you back?" he asked after a second.

"I don't know. I haven't told her yet," I admitted.

"You haven't told her?"

"Well, I was about to, but then some asshole punched me in the face. It kind of ruined the moment, you know?"

Gus gave me a sheepish grin and rubbed the back of his neck. "Listen, it's fucking weird that you're with my sister, but she's been mopey as hell since divisionals. She refuses to talk to me, and she has been doing all of her work on the ranch solo. I hate it when she isolates herself like this."

That was Emmy's go-to when she was upset.

"And I'm pissed that you lied to me, especially about the one person on the planet who should have been off-limits to you, but I didn't think I had to tell you that. I'm not going to lie to you and say I'm okay with this because I'm not."

Ouch.

"But, I think..." He sighed. "I could be. Someday." I looked at him, waiting for him to continue. "Emmy is on heifer watch on the south side of the ranch this morning." I must've looked confused because he went on, "I'm telling you so you could find her if you needed to, to tell her that you love her or whatever."

Was he being serious?

I wasn't about to look a forgiveness horse in the mouth. He didn't have to tell me twice. I stood from the kitchen and grabbed my keys from the hook by the front door. I came back and outstretched my hand to Gus, hoping he would take it.

He did, and we shook hands.

As I ran out the front door, he called after me, "Just so you know, if you break my sister's heart, a black eye is going to be the least of your worries."

26

EMMY

I looked out over Rebel Blue and saw patches of yellow and red among the green trees. Fall was on its way. I was on the south side of the ranch this morning, making sure no heifers made their way through the fence. They'd been doing it more than usual this year, and we hadn't been able to mend every hole in the fence quite yet.

So here I was.

Alone.

Maple and I walked along the fence. The silent morning made it easy to get lost in my thoughts. They were racing again, just like they had been when I came back to Meadowlark.

It was early, but I hadn't really been sleeping that well, so getting out of bed wasn't much of a chore, which was saying something.

I slept a lot better when I was wrapped up in my boa constrictor cowboy.

I was still so fucking pissed at Gus. He'd been trying to talk to me over the past couple of days, but my guard dog, Teddy, wouldn't let him in my cabin. I knew if I talked to him, I would say something I'd regret.

Teddy had been staying with me for a few days, allowing me to mope but also giving me a chance to talk through everything going on—the fact that I won divisionals, what I was going to do next, and obviously, Luke.

"I still can't believe Luke took a punch for you. He's normally the guy that does the punching," she had said while we were lying in my bed the morning after the race. "He's down bad for you, Emmy. You should've seen him in the stands at the race. He couldn't take his eyes off you. How everyone didn't know the man was hat over boots for you before the whole kissing incident is beyond me.

"I'm sorry your big moment got overshadowed by Gus being a complete and total dickbag," she continued.

"He really was terrible. I can't believe the things he said to Luke," I responded. Luke had flinched more at Gus's words than he had at his punch. Luke could take a punch, but he couldn't take his best friend hating him.

"He was so fucking awful," Teddy said. "I know they'll work it out, though. They would miss each other too much if they didn't."

"I hope you're right. Thank you for stepping in when all of it happened. You're the one that made him calm down, or at least just walk away."

Teddy had known exactly what to say to Gus that day.

"I told you I'd handle him," she said. "Have you talked to Wes? He seemed pretty calm about the whole thing."

"Yeah, he is. He's protective, but not in the same way Gus is. Wes can tell when people are unhappy, and I was so unhappy when I got home. I think he's just relieved to see I'm doing okay," I said. "Plus, he knew something was up when I opened the door in a familiar men's t-shirt the morning after family dinner and when Brooks wasn't in the stables even though his truck was on the ranch."

Teddy laughed out loud at that. "God, you two really are the worst at keeping a secret."

"I know. I think my dad knew, too. It was like everyone was just waiting for us to slip up so we could all go back to normal."

My dad had come down to my cabin after the whole punching situation to tell me that Luke was okay. Before he left, he gave me an Amos Ryder hug and said, "I like it. You and Luke,"

"I mean, once I got over the initial shock of it, I think you and Luke make sense. And then when I watched him calm you down before the race"—Teddy fanned herself before continuing—"I was like, damn, these two are red hot."

"Shut up," I laughed.

"It's true. I've never seen you just melt like that. And I've never seen Brooks's face look anything other than careless. I think both of you bring out each other's soft side."

"What does that even mean?"

"Some love stories burn hot and fast, but you two are more low and slow," she said. "It's a strong and steady kind of love." She was right. More than anything, Luke made me feel safe. "Gus will come around," Teddy concluded.

I really hoped so.

I saw Gus this morning at the Big House and gave him the cold shoulder, which probably just pissed him off more. I didn't care. I loved my brother–enough that I hadn't seen Luke in a few days because I wanted to give Gus some time to come to terms with the fact that his best friend and his little sister were together.

In the grand scheme of things, a few days without Luke was nothing compared to the lifetime I planned on spending with him, but I still hated being away from him.

I knew Luke wanted to talk to Gus, to at least try

and clear the air, but at this point, I was really sick of not being able to see him.

I loved him.

And I hadn't even had a chance to tell him.

Luke was so unexpected, especially for a woman who'd spent her life checking off things on her to-do list. Nowhere on there did it say "Fall in love with Luke Brooks," but I did it anyway.

It also didn't say, "Come back to Meadowlark," but I did that, too. At first, I didn't come back to Meadowlark —I just ran away from Denver.

Now, I planned on staying.

And I planned on staying with Luke.

As soon as Gus stopped being an overgrown man-child about it.

I swept my gaze over Rebel Blue with Luke on my mind. I missed him so much it was like I could almost hear him calling my name.

I sighed.

But then I heard it again. Maple's ears twitched, so she must have heard something, too. That meant it wasn't all in my head.

I pulled on her reins so I could guide her in a circle to find out where the voice was coming from. Due north, I saw a horse and its rider galloping toward Maple and me.

I would know that rider anywhere.

Luke.

He was riding through the ranch, pushing Friday as

fast as he could go in the dewy morning. As he approached, I quickly dismounted Maple and looped her reins over the fence post we were by.

Luke jumped off of Friday, literally, when they were about fifteen feet from us. He somehow landed on his feet. Friday came to a stop near Maple. I noticed he wasn't even tacked up. Luke had ridden through the ranch's roughest trails bareback.

All to make it to me.

I looked at him. His chest was heaving, and his eyes were bright. He didn't have a hat on, so his hair was messy from riding. He looked like a man possessed.

In a good way. The best way.

It had only been a few days, but I felt like I hadn't seen him in months. I couldn't go another second without touching him.

We both moved toward each other simultaneously, running to one another until our bodies collided.

He held me tight—like he was afraid I could disappear.

"Hey there, sugar," he said in my ear.

"Hi," I breathed. "What are you doing here?"

"I have something to tell you."

I had something to tell him, too, but I'd let him go first. He pulled back and cupped my face in his strong hands. I held onto his wrists. His big brown eyes searched my face. He seemed nervous.

"I love you, Clementine Ryder," he said earnestly.

My breath caught in my throat. "I'm so fucking in love with you."

Tears started to well behind my eyes as he spoke.

"You and your fucking skirt you wore to my bar a few months ago have turned my life completely upside down, and I never want it to be any other way."

A tear snaked its way out of the corner of my eye. Luke caught it.

Just like he'd caught me countless times over the past few months.

"Don't cry, sugar. You know I hate it when you cry."

"These are happy tears," I said. He kissed me then, soft and slow. The feeling of his lips on mine was one of those things I'd never get used to. It just felt so *right* —like, what were my lips even for if not kissing the hell out of this man? Our mouths moved together, and we were caught up in each other. His grip on my waist made me heat up from the inside out.

"You're it for me, Emmy," he said against my mouth. Now I wasn't just drunk off his kiss, but off his words, too.

Kissing Luke made my head all fuzzy. In a good way. "I have something to tell you," I said between kisses.

"Later," he growled and kept kissing me, snaking one of his hands lower on my back. I put my hands on his chest and pulled away. He looked at me hungrily, like a few days without me had driven him insane.

That made two of us.

But I had to get this out. "I love you, too, Luke Brooks. You're it for me, too."

Luke gave me one of my favorite smiles, the one that brought out the crinkles around his eyes, and I fell into his arms once again.

Home sweet home.

EPILOGUE

LUKE

I looked over at Emmy, who was still dead asleep next to me. I'd never met someone who slept so *hard*. I didn't think a bomb would wake her. Her legs were entwined with mine, her mouth was wide open, and her hair was a tangled mess. She was snoring a little. She looked damn good in one of my old t-shirts.

This woman was the love of my life.

I moved a piece of hair that was covering part of her face, and she leaned into my touch. I planted a soft kiss on her temple, and she continued to stir and wrap herself around me.

And she thought I was the boa constrictor.

"Good morning," she said with a yawn.

"Morning, sugar. Sleep okay?"

"Mmmhmm. What time is it?"

"A little after six." Emmy groaned at that. Mornings were not her thing. "You've gotta get to the ranch, sugar."

It was the first day of indoor riding lessons at Rebel Blue. Emmy had taken over all the classes. I had given mine to her gladly. Gus still asked me to help out at the stables during the week, but not teaching lessons freed up a lot of my time. That meant I could focus on the bar.

Things between Gus and me weren't perfect, but they were getting there. He had stopped visibly flinching every time I touched Emmy in his presence, which I took as a win.

"Is there coffee?" Emmy asked. She had buried her face in my chest.

"Always," I said, placing another kiss in her hair. I loved waking up to her. She usually spent at least a few nights a week at my place, and they were my favorite.

Emmy started to kiss her way up my chest and to my neck, and my dick immediately came to attention. *This woman.*

"Emmy." There was a warning in my voice. Emmy just giggled, and I felt her breath against my skin. When it came to my girl, I couldn't help myself. I slipped my hands under the t-shirt she was wearing and started dragging my hands up and down her body as she brought her mouth to mine.

I rolled us so I was on top of her. "You can't be late

on your first day," I said against her mouth. Even as I said it, my fingers were already moving her panties to the side and slipping inside of her because I didn't actually care if she was late.

"You better be quick, then." Her voice was breathy.

I pulled back and gave her a pointed look.

"Is that a challenge?" I said as I sunk two of my fingers inside of her. She arched her back and gave me a small moan. "Answer me, sugar. Are you challenging me to make you come?"

"Yes," she breathed. "Please." I pumped my fingers in and out of her and used my thumb to circle and press down on her clit. When I brought my mouth to her nipple and bit down gently, she gasped.

"You're already wet. I bet you were having dirty dreams about me," I teased before licking my way up her neck. Emmy started to grind herself against my hand with abandon.

That meant she was close. I knew her body inside and out. I continued to tease her clit and applied pressure as she continued to move her body against my hand. I knew she needed it, along with the friction.

Her body started to tense, and I knew she was careening toward the edge. I pushed myself up so I could look at her. Watching her come was more beautiful than a Wyoming sunset. Her mouth was open, and her eyes were rolling back into her head. Normally, I'd make her look at me.

But not today.

Today, I just wanted to watch her come apart.

And she did.

I stroked her through her orgasm, and my cock was aching for her. As she came down, I haphazardly pulled her underwear down her legs and threw them across the room. I positioned myself at her entrance before thrusting inside of her. Both of us moaned, and I lowered to my forearms so I could kiss her again before rolling us so she was on top of me.

Her head fell back, and I could feel her long hair skimming my thighs as she moved on me.

What a fucking view.

"Ride me, sugar."

I MADE a quick breakfast while Emmy was in the shower—eggs and toast. I was a whole wheat type of guy, but sourdough was Emmy's favorite. While I was cooking, my phone buzzed. It was a text from my mom.

John came home a few days after we'd visited. Apparently, he went off-route and couldn't find a safe place to turn around. I'm sure the fact that his truck's tracker turned back on outside a strip of casinos in Reno had nothing to do with him going off the grid for a few days.

My mom and I still didn't really have a relationship, but now that she had my number, we talked a little bit more. I wasn't sure how to feel about it, but I couldn't deny it was nice to feel like she cared.

When Emmy walked into the kitchen after her shower, my heart sped up.

She was so fucking beautiful in her tight jeans and a long-sleeved white t-shirt. I loved her messy hair, but I also loved it when she pulled it away from her face like she did today.

"It smells so good in here," she said as she grabbed the pill holder I got for her off the counter. She'd been trying to be better at taking her ADHD medication consistently, and I'd figured she wouldn't forget if she didn't have to worry about bringing it with her every time she stayed the night.

She went to a cabinet and pulled two mugs out— one for each of us—and filled them. I was by the fridge, so I took out the half-and-half and pushed it across the counter to her. I didn't like cream in my coffee, but I'd started buying it for Emmy.

She set the cups of coffee on the table, and I followed with our breakfast. We sat across from each other. When Emmy started to eat, I dug around in my pocket until I found the small piece of metal I was looking for.

I set it on the table and slid it toward her.

She paused mid-bite, and my heart was hammering in my chest. Was this a mistake?

"Is that what I think it is?" she asked as she set her fork down. She looked at the key on the table and then back to me. I just nodded, unable to get any words out.

Her gaze shifted back to the key and stayed there

for a while. *Shit*. I really fucked this up, didn't I? Of course she didn't want a key to my house. That was fucking crazy.

My thoughts continued to spiral until Emmy looked back at me and smiled. That smile stopped my heart dead in its tracks.

She picked the key up off the counter and stood from her chair, then rounded the table and positioned herself on my lap.

"We can start slow," I said quickly. For a man who couldn't speak less than a minute ago, I sure was fucking vomiting words now. "N-no pressure or anything. Like I said, we can start slow. I cleared out a drawer for you in our room and the bathro—" I didn't get to finish because Emmy kissed me then.

"Shut up, Luke," she said when she pulled back. Our foreheads were pressed together.

"Is...is that a yes?" I asked. My voice was a low whisper. I was afraid anything more than that would scare her off, but Emmy nodded. I took one of her hands in mine and brought it up to my lips, so I could place a kiss on her palm.

"I love you," she said. It didn't matter how many times she told me. Those words still warmed me all the way through, just like they had the first time.

Emmy coming back to Meadowlark was the best thing that ever happened to me. When she came back home, I never expected to become her friend, let alone fall for her. We'd spent most of our lives in each other's periphery, but now she was front and center.

I thought back to the first night I saw her at The Devil's Boot. I didn't know it then, but my girl was struggling. Back then, she was the shell of the woman who I now loved more than anything. All she'd needed was a little fire.

"I love you, too, Clementine Ryder."

ACKNOWLEDGMENTS

To my parents, who have supported every decision I've ever made, even the stupid ones, I love you. You two are the reason that I adore love stories, the reason I can write them, and the reason I believe in happily ever afters. That being said, please, don't ever read this book. I'll give you the cliffs notes.

To Stella: My angel pup. You've been my writing buddy through college papers, sad amateur poetry, a graduate school thesis, all of the unfinished books that lurk in the depths of my Google Drive, and now *Done and Dusted*. I love you always, even when you push my laptop off the couch.

To my Lexie gal: This book wouldn't even exist without you. Thank you for listening to every idea I've ever had and supporting each one. Your faith in me could move mountains, and for me, it has. Meadowlark was built for you and Mav.

To Sydney: You keep me on track in all things, and this book is no exception. Thank you for being there every step of the way. You tame the chaos goblin in me in the way that only a friend can.

To my brothers: Mom would get mad at me if you

guys weren't in here, so thanks for not having any hot friends for me to fall in love with, I guess. Still, I think you guys are pretty alright.

To my seventh grade English teacher and the writing club at Sunset Junior High: thank you for being the first people who read my stories. This story doesn't have any dragons, but it wouldn't be here without the stories that did.

To my Beta Readers, Amanda & Candace: you saw this book in its purest form and didn't run away screaming. Thank you for helping me mold and shape *Done and Dusted* into something worth reading. I can't overstate how much the both of you mean to me. I'm so incredibly grateful for you. Thank you!

Emma & Kayla: Because of you two, I never feel alone. Thank you.

Angie: Thank you for your unconditional support of my dream.

To my Editor, Tayler: You are an absolute star. You were my teammate in the truest sense of the word while I was writing this book. Working with you is a delight and an honor. Thank you for everything.

To my incredibly talented cover artist, Austin: You made me the cover of my dreams. I never thought the inspiration I pulled from vintage rodeo posters in my hometown would turn into the most perfect book cover. I can't wait to see what you do with the rest of this series.

To my ARC Readers: Thank you for taking a

chance on my debut and being excited enough to read it first. Your energy helped me power through the last few weeks before release. You are seriously the best!

To everyone who supported *Done and Dusted* before it's release: Thank you. I wish I could hug every single one of you. Your support and kind words meant everything to me. This book has brought me to so many kind people, and I'm so grateful.

To the person who is reading this right now: Thank you for picking up a copy of *Done & Dusted*. I hope that Emmy and Luke's story brought you some joy, made you smile, and maybe even made you laugh. Thank you for being a part of my dream.

And finally, to me. You did it. I hope you never stop telling stories. I'm so proud of you.

Done and Dusted

Lyla Sage

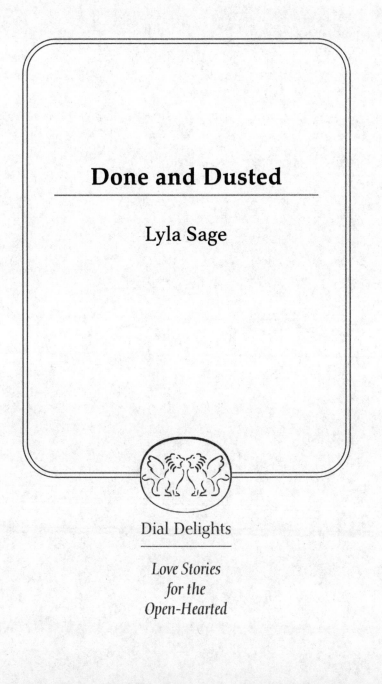

Dial Delights

*Love Stories
for the
Open-Hearted*

A Q&A with Lyla Sage

What was the inspiration for *Done and Dusted*?

In so many ways, *Done and Dusted* feels like a love letter to the people and places that helped build me. I drew inspiration from the small town I grew up in, from my friends and family, and from the Rocky Mountains that I love. The first scene that I wrote in *Done and Dusted* was Luke and Emmy at the springs, and that backdrop was inspired by a real place that I love. When I first started writing that scene, Luke didn't have a name, and Emmy wasn't yet a fully developed character, but I already felt like I knew them. Looking back, I think that's because the setting was already so familiar to me. There are so many pieces of me and the people who I love in *Done and Dusted,* and that's something I'm so proud of!

You say you drew inspiration for Luke from *Friday Night Lights:* Did you have any other inspirations when creating the other characters from *Done and Dusted*?

I always joke that Luke is Tim Riggins if he grew up, washed his hair, and got a savings account. Luke was the first character that I fully conceived, so we started off strong. There is one character that had a lot of real-life inspiration: Amos Ryder. Not only do I love to tell stories, but I love to listen to them, and Amos's character came from a wonderful guy who has become a dear friend and has been sharing his stories with me for years now. He's this very rad tattoo artist who I met while I was in college. He is strong, steady, and fiercely loving, like Amos. Amos and Stella's love story has many nods to this man and his wife, who let me come to their house nearly every Saturday while I was in college and drink their coffee while I thumbed through their record collection.

Emmy and Teddy have a good amount of real-life inspiration, too. I can write a friendship like theirs because of the really wonderful friends that I have, and for that, I am so grateful.

Have you been a lifelong reader? What books and authors contributed to your love of reading?

Yes! If I got in trouble growing up, my punishment was getting my books taken away—which was a fitting punishment because the reason I usually got in trouble was because I would get caught reading my book under my desk at school when I was supposed to be doing something else—like math. I hate math.

My favorite author of all time is Rick Riordan, who wrote the Percy Jackson and the Olympians series. My mom bought the first book for me at a Scholastic book fair, and I inhaled it. His books still resonate with me, and

I re-read them often. As an adult, the fact that his stories are centered around neurodivergent kids whose struggles become their superpowers tugs at my heart.

Some of my favorite books are *Love Is a Mix Tape* by Rob Sheffield, *Ninth House* by Leigh Bardugo, *Eldest* by Christopher Paolini (I will never not love dragons), *Getaway Girl* by Tessa Bailey, *Writers & Lovers* by Lily King, and, of course, *Beach Read* by Emily Henry. More recently, I've fallen in love with Helen Hoang, Ashley Poston, Riley Sager, and Abby Jimenez. To me, these authors are absolute masters of their craft, and I can't wait to read everything they write for the rest of forever.

I started reading romance (it all started with Sarah Dessen) earlier than I probably should have, but once I found the genre, there was no going back. I was enamored. There is something special to me about love stories—about two people who overcome odds, who love each other because of who they are, not despite it—that feels like magic. Happily ever afters and the journeys that lead to them are my favorite type of adventure. For me, love stories never get old.

Also, as a woman in her late twenties, I feel like I need to mention *Twilight*. Team Edward forever.

Why do you love small-town romances?

Because they're so GOOD. Seriously, I don't know if I've ever come across a small-town romance that I didn't love. I think what I love most about small-town romances is that the small town gets to be a character in the story. At least that's how it feels to me—that this setting is a living, breathing thing with its own personality and motivations. I think they also create such an excellent backdrop for family ties, whether it's the family we're born with or the family we find, which is one of my favorite things to explore as a writer.

What do you love most about the cowboy romance? How did you go about making your book stand out in this genre?

I mean, there's just something about a cowboy, am I right? In my opinion, not all small-town romances need cowboys, but all cowboy romances need to take place in a small town. I'm from the West, so when I think of a cowboy, I think of someone who represents strength, authenticity, and heart, so that frame of reference makes cowboy romances special to me.

Even though Luke Brooks is wonderful, I don't think it's the cowboy who makes *Done and Dusted* special—I think it's the cowgirl. Emmy is the standout character for me in this story, and I think it's her, her relationship with her family, her general badassery, and her journey that makes the story.

Why was it important to you to include ADHD representation in your story?

I don't know if I ever consciously decided to include a character with ADHD in the book. When I started writing Emmy, it just came through naturally, and I decided to run with it immediately. Her ADHD was part of her from the beginning. As a reader, I understand the joy that comes with reading about a character who you can relate to, and the more I wrote, the more I wanted Emmy to be that character. Since releasing *Done and Dusted,* I've received so many lovely messages from readers telling me that Emmy's experience and inner monologue were so deeply relatable, and that truly means the world to me.

Emmy and I don't have a lot in common, but I loved being inside her head. She was a delight for me to write, and I'm so proud of her.

What have you learned about yourself while writing the book?

The most important thing was that I really could write a book. I love to write, and I always have, but writing *Done and Dusted* required me to overcome a massive amount of self-doubt and imposter syndrome. It's the scariest thing I've ever done. It's also the bravest thing I've ever done. Because of *Done and Dusted,* I learned that I am brave, and that's priceless to me.

What do you hope readers feel after reading this book?

Joy. Pure and unbridled joy. I set out to write a book that made readers happy. When people read *Done and Dusted,* I want them to get the same feeling they get when they're driving with the windows down and their favorite song playing on the radio.

Writing *Done and Dusted* was truly the most joyous

experience of my life, and I hope that reading it is joyous, too.

What does the future look like in the Rebel Blue Ranch series?

I am thrilled to be continuing the Rebel Blue Ranch stories. In every Rebel Blue Ranch book, you can expect Wild West vibes, family shenanigans, and heartfelt love stories that are so sweet you might get cavities. There are four books planned, and the story that's coming up next belongs to Weston Ryder, my favorite middle child, and Ada Hard, a newcomer to Rebel Blue. I love their story, and I can't wait for you to read it!

And yes, Gus and Teddy are getting a book, too. I promise!

Keep reading for

an exclusive sneak peek

at the first chapter from *Swift and Saddled*,

the next book in the Rebel Blue Ranch series!

1

ADA

I've come in contact with a lot of liars, but none quite so big as Google. I'm not trying to discredit the search engine, but I am trying to bring attention to its most annoying inaccuracies. In this case, telling me that the dive bar I was sitting in—only because it was the only establishment in the small town of Meadowlark, Wyoming, that was open past 10:00 PM—served food.

It did not.

Google's stupid bar graph busy meter also said that the Devil's Boot—not sure if that's actually the name of the bar, considering that there's not a sign anywhere that indicates that—wasn't busy.

It was.

Not insanely busy, but busy enough to at least get the "moderately busy" distinction on Google.

There was also a very boisterous cabal of old men at the bar—Google couldn't have told me that. But if there were any pictures of this place on its business page, I probably could've deduced that for myself.

And avoided the Devil's Boot altogether.

Stupid Google.

This place was exactly what I thought of when I pictured a small-town dive bar. There was old-school country playing on a jukebox, an excessive amount of neon signs, and there were spots on the floor that my Doc Martens stuck to when I walked.

I'm not a snob. I've got nothing against a good dive bar. I just didn't think I'd end up sitting in one. Not today.

When I left San Francisco yesterday and started making my way to Wyoming, a dive bar would've been the last place I wanted to be the night before I started the biggest job of my career.

But I was hungry, and the small, but still weirdly quaint, motel I was staying in tonight didn't have the best Wi-Fi. So I left in search of sustenance and internet access, but I only found one of those things. What kind of dive bar doesn't have any food but has good Wi-Fi?

The kind with a very tall and very hot bartender that took pity on me when I asked about food and fished out a snack-size bag of Doritos from behind the bar and gave them to me with my whiskey and Diet Coke. I didn't ask how old they were—I didn't want to know, but I had a pretty good idea, considering they were almost soft.

They tasted like the bag had been open for a while, but somehow, it was still sealed when I got it.

After that, I settled for a high-top table in the corner. On the wall behind it, there was a neon sign of a cowboy riding a beer bottle like a bull. When I saw the sign, it tugged at the corners of my mouth, and I liked that feeling.

Honestly, I didn't know if eating the Doritos that could

probably qualify for a senior citizens discount was better than eating nothing, but here I was, eating them.

I dusted the nacho cheese dust from my fingers so it wouldn't dirty my iPad screen. I had pulled up the email threads between Weston Ryder and me, double-checking the time I was supposed to be at Rebel Blue Ranch tomorrow morning, and making sure I had the map downloaded to my phone, just in case.

That was me, Ada Hart, nothing if not prepared.

I didn't know much about Rebel Blue—just what Teddy had told me over the past few months. I knew Teddy from my first year of college. We went to the same school in Colorado—at least for my first year. After that, I ended up transferring at the end of my first year to be closer to home.

Going home was now a decision that I deeply regretted because it led to what would forever be known as "the incident" to me but was also known as my wedding to others.

I shook any thought about *that* and *him* out of my head.

After I left Denver, I stayed in touch with Teddy—mostly on socials—and I was grateful for that now. She was the one who referred me to Weston, who I think was the owner of Rebel Blue, but I didn't know for sure. When you Google it—again, stupid Google—you only get the information that it's a cattle ranch and that it's nearly 8,000 acres.

I guess I could've asked Teddy, but I didn't want to bug her. She'd done enough for me.

I didn't know how to conceptualize 8,000 acres. *Fucking massive* is what I was thinking to myself when I heard one of the old men at the bar giving the bartender a hard time.

"What kind of bar runs out of ice?" he said incredulously.

"The kind that has a bunch of sad old men who drink whiskey like water," the bartender fired back. I looked up at them. The bartender had a small smile on his face, so he couldn't be too upset with the jabs. "Gus is bringing some, so make that drink last for the next ten minutes." He pointed at the glass in front of the man, and the man scoffed at him.

I felt my phone vibrate on the table and flipped it around.

Teddy: Hey! Did you make it okay?
Me: Yeah—just doing some prep before tomorrow.
Teddy: EXCELLENT.
Teddy: This is going to be so fun.
Teddy: I'll stop by this week.
Teddy: Can't wait for you to shine!

I saw that I also had a text from my business partner, Evan—he was the contractor—and my mom, who was no doubt telling me that I was wasting my time in Wyoming.

Maybe I was, but for some reason, I really didn't think so.

I slid my phone back onto the table and flipped it face-side down. I needed to focus. Over the past four months, I'd exchanged hundreds of emails with Weston. We discussed his vision, and we decided on timelines, crews, and costs. People always thought that tearing down walls was step one, but it was actually step three hundred. I was going over steps one through two hundred and ninety-nine when a giant ball of white fluff showed up at my feet.

"Waylon! Goddamnit," I heard the bartender yell. I assumed Waylon was the dog sitting at my feet and staring up at me with his tongue hanging out and a crazed look in his eyes.

What an angel.

I leaned down and gave him a scratch on his very soft and furry head. Huh, less than a few hours in Meadowlark, and this place was pulling smiles out of me at a record-setting rate.

"Seriously?" I heard the bartender whine. "Who the hell brings his dog to a bar?" I looked up just as a man walked in the door of the bar.

Damn. What the hell were they putting in the water in Meadowlark, Wyoming?

From here, I could see that he wasn't as tall as the bartender, but close. His open flannel shirt covered a white T-shirt that clung to his chest. My eyes glided over him until I hit his worn-out cowboy boots.

Maybe it was because I'd been surrounded by tech bros in Patagonia vests for too long, but this man was doing something for me.

I bet he had rough hands. Working hands. For a split second, I imagine what they would feel like if he dragged them across my body.

Nope. No. Definitely not.

Do *not* go there.

We were not about to have fantasies about the mystery cowboy in the dusky dive bar—no matter how good-looking he was.

I was here to *work*.

I got snapped back to reality by my new furry friend licking my hands—probably tasting the elderly Dorito dust.

No matter how hard I tried, I couldn't help but listen to the exchange between the bartender and the cowboy. Eavesdropping was one of my favorite hobbies. "What kind of bar runs out of ice?" the cowboy volleyed back at the bartender. The group of old men whooped in agreement.

"Where's your brother?" The bartender asked.

"Busy." The cowboy shrugged his shoulders.

"Where's my ice?"

"Truck."

"You couldn't bring it in?"

"I figured you could do that part." The bartender shook his head but came out from behind the bar and walked out the door anyway. It was obvious that there was some sort of bond between these two. I didn't think they were brothers—they didn't look alike—but there was something.

Not brothers, but definitely bros.

"Get your dog," the bartender said on his way out. "Please."

The cowboy's eyes started scanning the bar—probably looking for his dog—but landed right on me. Me, whose hand was currently getting a thorough licking and who was unashamedly and unabashedly staring at the cowboy.

His eyes landed on mine.

I should've looked away, but I didn't.

I couldn't tell what color his eyes were from here, but I wanted to.

We stared at each other for way longer than was socially acceptable, and he flashed me a small smile that hinted at a dimple on either side of his face.

Not the fucking dimples.

Those should be illegal.

Or at least require some sort of warning before flashing them at people.

Warning: dimples may appear and cause panty-dropping.

It looked like he was about to start coming toward me, but our weird and intense stare-off was interrupted by the bartender putting an ice cube down the back of the cowboy's shirt.

He made a distinctly unmanly noise that made me laugh. Everyone's hot and badass until there's an ice cube down your shirt.

"Brooks! What the hell!" he exclaimed and did this little shimmy thing as he tried to get it out. It was cute.

Really cute.

The bartender—Brooks—just laughed as he made his way back behind the bar, the bag of ice in one hand, and said, "Get your dog, and I'll let you stay for a drink."

The cowboy adjusted his shirt and ran a hand through his sandy brown hair. "Fine."

He took a step toward me, catching me in his unrelenting eye contact again. Why was he approaching me?

A warm tongue licked my hand again.

Oh. The dog. Right.

I looked down, breaking his stare. I had to. I couldn't be held responsible for what might happen if we maintained eye contact for much longer. There was something about it—the confidence it communicated—that felt electric.

"Sorry about him." His voice was close to me now. My fluffy companion wagged his tail as his owner's footsteps neared. "He's got a thing for beautiful women." My eyes snapped up, and yet another smile was pulled from me, but this one was directed at the man who was now less than two steps away from me.

"Has that line ever worked for you?" I said with a shocked laugh. It felt foreign—not quite comfortable. Like when you talk for the first time after waking up.

"You tell me," he said. His eyes were bright. And green. *So* fucking green.

"Not bad," I responded, "but I feel like the delivery could be improved."

There was another flash of dimples. "How so?"

"You've got to mean it," I said.

His expression changed. He looked confused. "Of course I meant it." *Huh.* He was so convincing. Maybe if I'd had better experiences with men, I would've believed him.

"Hey!" Brooks's voice cut through our conversation, and the cowboy looked back at him. "Bottle or draft?"

Instead of answering, the cowboy looked at my table—the iPad must've made it obvious I was working on something, because instead of trying to sit or insert himself, he looked at his dog and said: "Let's let the beautiful woman work, Waylon." Waylon obeyed and went to his owner, whose eyes were back on me. "I'll be at the bar when you're done—if you want company."

Wait. He wasn't going to pressure me. Try and make his way into my space? He was just going to . . . let me work?

Damn. I guess men were built differently in Meadowlark.

The cowboy gave me one last dimpled smile before turning back for the bar. My new friend, Waylon, followed him.

I watched him walk away, and it was an effort for me to tear my gaze away from him.

Trying to get back on task, I shook my head a little—like I was trying to shake off every thought about the handsome stranger.

I didn't know why, but it felt good to be noticed by him—to be the object of his stare. Right after my divorce, my self-esteem was at an all-time low. Even now, over a year later, it wasn't great.

But I couldn't deny that I liked someone looking at me like I was the only person in the room.

My ex-husband had never looked at me like that.

Now that was a train of thought I was not dealing with today. I pushed it down and went back to my iPad, and I noticed a new email from the owner of Rebel Blue.

Ada,

I hope your drive was okay and everything went smoothly. Excited to meet you and get started tomorrow.

Best,
WR

Sent from Mobile

ABOUT THE AUTHOR

Lyla is a hopelessly romantic twenty-something who lives in the Wild West with her loyal companion— a sweet, old, blind rescue pitbull. She writes romance that feels like her favorite things: sunshine and big blue skies. When she's not writing, she's reading, usually about cowboys or hometown heroes, but she's been known to dabble with mob bosses, monsters, and billionaires, too. You can usually find her under her heated blanket, at her favorite local bookstore, or in the mountains. To stay up to date on Lyla's upcoming projects, connect with her on social media @authorlylasage, sign up for her newsletter, or go to www.lylasageauthor.com.

*The Dial Press, an imprint of Random House,
publishes books driven by the heart.*

Follow us on Instagram:
@THEDIALPRESS

Discover other Dial Press books and
sign up for our e-newsletter:

thedialpress.com